Jake Trickle was a journeyman printer who loved reading, kept to himself and moved restlessly from small town to small town. Then in August 1949 he stepped off the bus in Williamstown, Illinois, and life opened like a flower in spring.

He learned to love, to care about a community and to spot a problem in the local political system. But he also learned that "road oil and romance don't mix," through a series of discoveries tumbling one after another that changed lives all over Williamstown—including his.

This insightful look at mid-century life in central Illinois will provide a walk down memory lane that touches your heart while it broadens your feeling for people and politics. Jim Nowlan knows what he is writing about, and it shows. Your view of small town America will never be quite the same, but you will be richer in understanding people everywhere.

The Itinerant

A HEARTLAND STORY

The Itinerant

A HEARTLAND STORY

James D. Nowlan

Conversation Press, Inc.
Winnetka, Illinois

My thanks go to the Toulon, Illinois, Public Library, where I have been a reader all my life and where I first met several of the people who inspired me to create the characters in this story.

The Itinerant: A Heartland Story is a work of fiction which, while set in a real place at a real time, is neither biographical nor historical. The actions and behavior of the people depicted are purely the product of the author's imagination, and should not be attributed to any real persons, living or dead.

ISBN 0-9634395-6-1

Contents

The Itinerant

A HEARTLAND STORY

May 15, 2000

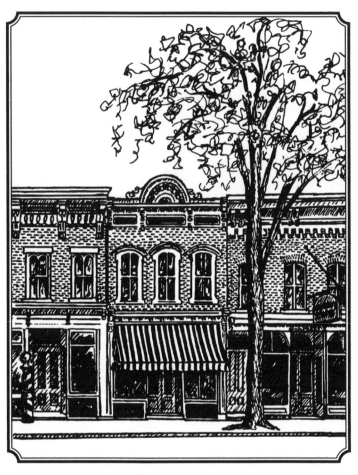

Main Street, Williamstown

Billtown

The 11 A.M. Blackhawk Lines bus pulled up on Main Street in front of the Standard Oil station. The driver unlatched the baggage bin and jerked out one tan suitcase, while Jake Trickle grabbed a box of books secured by heavy twine.

"Can I put these somewhere for a couple of hours?" Jake asked Marion Burcham, the proprietor. Marion was cleaning the windshield of a red '47 Frazer, whose paint was already beginning to oxidize to a dull finish. He took a deliberate measure of Jake. Angular, six-foot, Marion figured. Gray, penetrating eyes that said quiet, reserved. "He's on foot," Marion thought, "so sure, why not."

"Put 'em in the back room, next to the toilet."

"Appreciate it. . . .what kind of town is this?" Jake was squinting in the late August sun, a well-worn gray felt fedora shading his forehead. He looked up and down the long main drag of two-story red brick business buildings. "Depends," said Burcham, not sure whether to be honest or play the booster. "A few asses, but good folks for the most part. We're doin' pretty well, what with cash and goods pumped into the economy after the war, and hungry people around the world getting our corn. Guess that's true of most places, though. Why do you ask?"

"I'm a printer. Heard that the local paper could use one. What time's the next westbound bus leave?"

"Bus for Davenport comes through at five-twenty this afternoon."

Enough time to look around before visiting the paper. The highway sign had said 4,000 pop., and the Greek Revival courthouse, with imposing beveled Ionian columns, made it clear this was the county seat. Jake set off down Main. He loved to walk, even though his left leg was a bit shorter than the right, a birth defect, he had been told. This kept him out of the war, to his everlasting dismay, almost shame. He tried to enlist at four different stations, but the docs saw it immediately. A built-up heel made his limp slight and walking country roads not a problem.

Williamstown, or Billtown, as locals called it, was the market town set smack dab in the middle of its namesake, Williams County. Or was it the other way around? Anyway, Williams County was a perfect square, twenty-four miles on a side. That is, sixteen townships, each six miles square stacked in rows of four on the tabletop prairie just west of the Illinois River in central Illinois.

When the U.S. Congress set up the Land Ordinance in 1785 for what would become the Northwest Territory, the lawmakers decreed that it should be surveyed for easy, precise land buying, in what came to be called congressional townships. So the checkerboard that now unfolds below from a window seat in the United flight out of Chicago's O'Hare Field was the brilliant brainchild of our forefathers, looking ahead with supreme confidence.

Each township comprises thirty-six square miles; each square mile is called a section, and has six hundred and forty acres. Years ago a quarter section of one hundred and sixty acres represented about all the land a farm family could till, but now the big farmers are taking on a whole section. Township and county roads crisscross the land every mile on section lines, for up to seventy-two miles of road in every township, making it easy for farmers to get their crops out and to market.

The land around Billtown looks boring to passersby, but it's black gold to those who live there. The coal-black Sable, Tama and Ipava topsoils reach down for one, two or three feet. Nothing better in the world for corn, now beans and hogs.

Billtown was out of the cookie cutter of farm market towns, like Watseka and Princeton to the east, and Aledo to the west, dotting the rich flatlands of Illinois, hugging the Illinois Central or Rock Island rail lines. The Kroger and A&P chains each had a standard twenty-six-foot-wide red-brick storefront. They competed with Dutch Arganbright and Jim Rashid, who operated local groceries. Butcher shop, bakery, pool hall, the typical medley of thirty or more stores. Next to the imitation stone cement-block City Hall stood the icehouse, which stored blocks sawed in winter from the nearby Spoon River to keep iceboxes cold. But demand was down. Central Illinois was entering the era of gleaming white Frigidaire and GE appliances.

Two taverns on the main street. "Good, not a dry town," Jake thought. Two mugs of cold Pabst (What'll You Have?) or Edelweiss (It tastes so nice!) were a reasonable reward after a hot day fighting a balky Linotype. And a Carnegie Library. The Starke Township Library was more imposing than most, which suggested turn-of-the-century civic pride and maybe a strong education ethic. Jake's two basic needs were in place.

Jake had noon dinner in Humphrey's Cafe—hot beef sandwich and mashed potatoes, smothered in brown gravy, with creamy cole slaw and apple sauce on the side in small dishes, and choice of berry pies. All for thirty-five cents. Margy Humphrey served meals at the counter, along with a tart remark and a smile for everyone. Jake got only the smile, while the regulars looked him up and down. In the kitchen a lanky Bill Humphrey presided over the steam table and grill, a Lucky Strike dangling precariously from his lower lip, right over the vegetable soup kettle.

So far, so good. Now down to the paper. *"The Republican.* Every Wednesday since 1856" declared the painted brick on the alley side of the building. "So," Jake thought, "the owner should be somewhat at ease on a Thursday afternoon."

Jim Dunlap owned and edited *The Republican*. Stout, bespectacled, round face, kindly soft blue eyes, he looked every bit a local prominence. He was rocking slowly in his slat-backed desk chair, proofreading what looked like wide galleys for a legal brief for the appellate court. For lesser jobs, social editor Eileen Benedict would do the proofreading.

No need to ask who the proprietor was. "Sir, I was told over at the *Bureau County Republican* that you might be looking for a printer. If so, I might be interested." Dunlap came to the waist-high oak counter, wooden library card catalog drawers at one end for subscriber records, an ornate steel cash register at the other.

"We could use a printer and Linotype operator combination. Our last one got into the sauce too regularly, and he left town in a pout when I chewed him out once too often. What can you do?"

"Just about everything. I grew up an orphan, apprenticed out at twelve to a printer in Indiana. For eighteen years I've been running Linotypes and presses, making up forms for weddings and catalogs, you name it. And, I can fix things."

This last made music in the ears of a small-town newspaper owner, and Jake knew it. Lots of journeymen could operate Linotype machines, but few had the mechanical skills to keep the cantankerous machines—which injected molten lead against brass type molds to form lines of type—up and running.

"Sound too good to be true. You don't look like you have a problem with the bottle. Most itinerants do, though, probably because they're loners."

"I've been alone all my life. Guess I've gotten used to it. Just restless, I guess. Was at the Watseka *Times-Republic* for three years, then spent almost that at the Pontiac *News-Leader*. Now I've moved on again. No hard feelings, so far as I know. Give John Bailley, the Pontiac publisher, a call.

"Don't know what I'm looking for," Jake added, surprised at his garrulousness, "but when I find it, I'll know it. Seem to keep moving west little by little, like Horace

Greeley said. I stick to myself, so guess it doesn't much matter where I am."

"You sound like you've done some reading," the publisher wondered out loud.

"Had to drop out of high school at fifteen to work full time for my printer. Developed a love of words, though, and for typefaces and the artistry of good printing."

"I can offer a buck-and-a-quarter an hour. You can start tomorrow on a trial basis for two weeks."

"I'm worth more than that. You'll see. How about a buck-and-a-half, and time-and-a-half after fifty hours? I can put in lots of hours, if you need them."

"You've got a deal, but only after the two-week trial."

They shook on it, and Jake inquired about rooming houses. "Maude Jackson's is a block from here across from the funeral home. Reasonable, clean, but no meals."

Maude was frail, stooped, tired. "I have one room available, upstairs at the back. Has two windows, north and west. Good for ventilation. You share a bath with three other men. Dollar a day, a week in advance. I change sheets and towels once a week. Take a look."

Jake found a single bed, four-drawer dresser with mirror, small closet, straight-back chair, seat and back cushioned. A rack for a towel to dry, and a floor lamp between the chair and bed. The bed had a firm mattress, almost unyielding, but to be preferred over the opposite, the norm in rooming houses. The dark green flowered wallpaper curled a bit above the door frame, but the room and Maude's house seemed clean and picked up. Not bad, especially with the windows. Most rooms had only one window, which allowed summer heat in but not out.

"What about the other roomers? Noisy? Any problems?"

"Not the present crew, but you'll have to negotiate with them on using the bath."

Jake paid her the seven dollars, and retrieved his suitcase and books. The brown plastic, shoe-box-size Philco radio went on the dresser. He used the wire hangers for three shirts to be worn after work and put two hangers together to support a brown gabardine suit, which he hadn't worn since he went grudgingly to the Pontiac paper's Christmas party a year-and-a-half ago. Jake needed three hangers for a heavy, navy winter coat that would be called a car coat today.

In the top drawer went a zippered, leatherette folder that contained his savings account book from the Pontiac State Bank; fifty dollars in fives; and a high school freshman photo of himself, in sepia and cream tones. In the other drawers went the necessities of work, plus a long-sleeved, buttoned caramel wool sweater and a single tie. That was about it.

Jake pulled off his shoes, lay on the bed, hands knitted behind his head. "What the hell am I doing here?" he mused, more stoic than sad or pleased. "Have I gotten used to being lonely? Wonder what it's like not being alone in a rooming house?"

🔀

Friday morning at eight sharp Jake was at the paper. He walked into the back shop after nodding a 'mornin' to Jim Dunlap, who was rocking slowly in his chair while preparing manila jacket folders that laid out the specifications for commercial printing "jobs," as they are called.

Jake surveyed the room. Three Mergenthaler Linotype machines sat at the heart of the shop, side by side. Seven-foot-high typesetting monsters with black steel arms that flailed the air, and innards that whirred, coughed and burped out hot lines of type. Models 5 and 8 set straight matter, the news columns. The "14" had "magazines" with four different type faces and sizes. This machine set headlines and the guts of the grocery ads that were the bread-and-butter of a profitable community newspaper. At the back of the shop stood a flat-bed newspaper printing press shouldering a great steel cylinder—a slow lumbering hulk decades past its prime.

Jake took a deep, satisfying draught of the acrid essence of printing shops. "The same the world around," he imagined. Printing ink ethers. Paper dust from man-high stacks of newsprint. Gasoline-soaked rags for cleaning type forms. Hints of smoke from gas-fired pots that melted lead. This was Jake's home.

Three men had slipped in behind Jake. Harry Campbell was the chief Linotype operator. Short, with thick glasses, his head pulled forward from squinting for too many years at the copy above the Linotype keyboard. Harry went directly to the Model 14 and pulled on his green plastic visor. Frankie Biba and Dave Gelvin were the journeymen printers, and Gelvin also sat at a Linotype Monday through Wednesday. Frankie and Dave, both sallow from lives spent indoors, pulled on their grey striped printer's aprons.

"Fellas, this is Jake Trickle. He starts today as printer, floor man and fill-in on the Linotype," intoned Jim Dunlap, who had waited for the back shop crew to arrive. "Says he can do most anything, even a bit of a machinist. Introduce yourselves and make him welcome."

Within a week the men had become a quiet, functioning team, except when the two high-school-age printer's devils were there to create, well, deviltry. Thursday and Friday were for job work—invoices, fair catalogs, letterheads, sale posters. Saturday the printer's devils tore up last week's newspaper pages and melted the lead in a pot furnace. They ladled the brilliant liquid into long ingots called pigs, which were hung into small pots on the Linotype machines, to be transformed into type for next week's *Republican*.

Monday the Linotypes ground and clanked and spit out "slugs" of type from eight till six or later, depending on the size of the week's paper. Tuesday, heads were set for news stories; Jim and the three women reporters in the front office were back and forth all day, putting copy on small low tables next to Harry and Dave at their typesetting machines. On Tuesday, Jim and Frankie began making up the seven-column pages for the first runs of the paper. Astride the fifty-year-old flatbed newspaper press, a great cylinder rolled a bedsheet of off-white newsprint paper over the four inked pages on the bed and out to a waiting table. Twelve hundred an hour until thirty-eight hundred had been printed.

By Tuesday evening the first run was flipped and run through to be printed on the blank side. A folding machine was attached to the press, its myriad cloth belts and metal folding blades looking like the route from purgatory to hell. On this run the sheet went through four folds and came out—if everything was working—as the eight-page Section II of the Williams County *Republican*.

Wednesday was newspaper day. The back shop was clanking and whirring from 6:30 A.M. on. Another eight pages had to be set in type, made up and pounded to a smooth printing surface on great marble make-up tables. Proofs were taken, the proofs read, corrected, printed, addressed on a foot-driven stamping machine and carried to the post office in hand-tied bundles. Townsfolk were waiting, maybe after a green river soda at McClenahan's Drug Store, for postmaster Bud Doden and clerk Jeff McClellan to stuff the paper into their mail boxes.

If all went well, the front and back office crews could wash their blackened hands by 5 P.M. with punishing, pumice-loaded Lava Soap, cleaning nails with a tight-bristled brush that hinted at how hideous wartime fingernail torture could be.

Then came the first opportunity of the week for a moment of self-satisfied banter. "The wedding picture of the Carlsons makes her look taller than him," smiled Eileen Benedict, the always-inquiring social reporter, "but that's what they gave us."

"And what's wrong with that?" bristled Harry Campbell, as he emerged from the back shop, not needing to mention that his wife towered over him, like Brünnhilde over a dwarf.

Jake liked the chatter but didn't participate. As he stepped outside on Main Street the late summer sun bounced off the baking sidewalk and hit him full force. Not a time to go back to his stifling room. Jake took refuge instead at the public library. In 1905 steel magnate Andrew Carnegie had agreed to provide $5,000 to help build a community library, so long as townsfolk matched the amount and made provisions to sustain the library.

The dignified rectangular burgundy brick, tile-roofed building featured twelve-foot ceilings in the two main rooms, inset bookshelves all around, screened windows above. If the tile roof had extended a foot more on all sides, the architect would have mimicked the Prairie Style of Frank Lloyd Wright. The library wasn't cool in August, but with the ceiling fans churning, and the towering oaks and maples blocking the afternoon rays, it was tolerable.

Jake nodded a silent howdy to the male librarian, the first Jake had encountered. Jake sauntered to the new books display. He picked out Sandburg's recent *Remembrance Rock* and sat down at one of the straight-backed, wood chairs. The hard seats were scalloped slightly in lieu of cushioning. Jake liked Sandburg's salty *Chicago Poems*, and the magisterial six-volume Lincoln biography, so he paged slowly through the first and last pages of this weighty new book.

By seven Jake's head was heavy, lids drooping, seat aching. He went to the librarian's desk at the divide of the two reading rooms. The imposing walnut desk and librarian's swivel chair were on a raised platform above the hardwood flooring. Jake looked straight into the librarian's gaze. "I'm Jake Trickle, sir, new in town. Work at the local newspaper. Like to read. Wonder if I could get a library card."

That's how Jake met Ernie Robson, librarian, photographer, town eccentric. Ernie was in his forties, had reading glasses perched out a ways on a long prominent nose, and thick, bristly salt-and-pepper hair in a crew cut, so he wouldn't have to bother with it.

Ernie issued a shy smile as well as a card for Jake to fill out.

Card in hand, Jake checked out Sandburg and headed for Peachie's Diner, a turned-out-to-pasture railroad car converted to cafe. A counter ran the length of the car to a small grill. Just enough room for a six-footer to stand straight but you felt obliged to bend over anyway. A slant-roof, jerry-built addition to the backside of the car provided seven small booths and a Wurlitzer jukebox, three plays for a nickel.

Jake took a counter seat. He flipped through the jukebox offerings, presented in notebook fashion inside a plastic cylinder clamped to the back of the counter, leaving little room to eat. Two other fellows were at the seven-seat counter. They nodded, without speaking. A female school teacher, Jake guessed, sat alone in one of the booths, visible through the tight archway Peachie or the waitress navigated to deliver orders. "Whaddaya want, son," Peachie called out from the grill. "Hamburger steak, American fries, baked beans and an iced-tea," Jake shouted back.

After supper Jake walked down the three blocks of Main Street businesses, through a modest square block city park and up the seven blocks to the north end of town and back down to Harry's Place, one of two taverns on the main drag. Sandburg still in hand, Jake took a seat at the bar, looked at himself in the mirror of the back bar, saw a rectangular face, high cheekbones, sallow skin that didn't see the out-of-doors until late in the afternoon, dark hair and gray eyes that gave away little. "Not bad," he thought, "but who would care?" He chanced a quick smile at himself.

Jake ordered a frosted mug of Pabst Blue Ribbon from the tap. PBR was an Illinois favorite, brewed in Peoria Heights, forty miles to the south.

Jake surveyed the long barroom through the massive oval mirror on the back bar. "The back bar must be fifty feet long," Jake thought. The mirror was held in place by mahogany pillars and a high-back counter cluttered with jars of pickled pigs feet, hardboiled eggs, whole dill pickles and salted nuts. As he sipped from the heavy mug, Jake watched a couple of local straight-ball champions move deliberately around one of the two Brunswick pool tables situated between the bar and an east wall of booths. Sweet smoke from the pipe of the older player hung in the air, caught in golden silhouette by the two lamps that hung down low over the emerald felt of the table.

If Jake were a talker, he would have complimented the proprietor on his handsome establishment. That proprietor was Harry Wilson, who thought Jake was admiring his bar, so he responded. "The company built this bar in 1898, one of three showplace bars. The others were in Chicago and Milwaukee. Old man Pabst wanted one in a small town and was friends with the owner at the time, so the story goes. They put a helluva lot of mahogany, cherry and leather into the place. I try to keep it just the way it was then."

Jake nodded his appreciation toward Harry, who looked like he might have been part of the original package as well, garters holding his white shirt sleeves in place, an unlighted cigar clamped in his jaw, apparently since noon. Out of the side of his mouth, Harry asked Jake if he wanted another fifteen-cent mug of Pabst. "Yeah, thanks, if you've got another frosted mug."

"Comin' up." After the two beers, it was about nine. Jake walked off Main Street and three blocks to the rooming house along streets of handsome, eclectic-style, frame homes, several with wraparound porches. The creaks and squeaks of porch swings blended with the chirping of the crickets. Jake could tell people were watching him. He even heard a "Good evening, young man," from one porch. He looked toward the house. A light from a living room outlined a man and woman, swinging slowly to make their own breeze.

"And good evening to you both. Nice night for a walk."

"Sure is."

In the still of the evening the corner windows in his room were of little help. To stir the air, Jake turned on a rotating, eight-inch fan he purchased for $4.95 at Miller's Hardware. He read from Sandburg's sentimental attempt to tell the story of America in family saga form. After an hour, Jake turned out the light, still wondering why he was in Billtown but finding it tolerable so far.

Two weeks later Jake returned *Remembrance Rock*. Ernie, the librarian, felt he was coming to know Jake, who was at the library most evenings. He liked his quiet style and serious interest in books. "How'd you like the book?" Ernie asked. "I prefer the young firebrand Sandburg to the mellower old man. This one's a bit too sentimental, even corny, for me."

Ernie nodded in understanding, then excused himself to quiet down two grade-schoolers who were getting rowdy with the hand-held stereopticon viewers that brought World War I photos into three dimensions.

Jake had been in his routine a month or so when he arrived at the library and was startled to see in the high librarian's chair, not Ernie Robson, but a striking young woman who reminded him immediately of Barbara Ann Scott, the blond Canadian skating star. "Good evening," she offered with a quick smile. Her attention then focused back on the book before her.

Jake went to the new book rack, then to the magazines, where he picked up the new *Life* and sat down. Jake couldn't keep his eyes off the new librarian, but he wouldn't dream of starting a conversation. Probably about thirty, near his own age, Jake guessed. The librarian greeted schoolchildren and their mothers by name as they came in but didn't initiate any small talk. Jake noticed her move to help a teen find a reference book. She wore the longer, rather tight skirts that had just come into vogue. She was tall, like the skater, and in equally good shape, or so the profile suggested. Reserved, self-confident. "Damn, she's appealing," he thought.

Over his glass of Falstaff (The Finest Product of the Brewer's Art!) at Harry's Place, Jake could think of nothing but the librarian. What was she reading? Would she be at the library again? How could he find out?

The next evening Ernie Robson was back at his stand, and Jake was clearly pleased to see him. After a while, Jake came to the desk and stood for a few moments as

Ernie checked out *Gone with the Wind* for Mrs. Eagleston. When they were alone, Jake inquired, "Excuse me, sir, but could you tell me who the attractive blonde was who served as librarian last night?"

"Yes, that was Kay Townsend. She fills in for me on evenings when I have a photography appointment."

"Oh," Jake acknowledged, "she seems very nice."

Ernie understood Jake's interest; he had felt the same way for years. "She is. Kay teaches English at the high school. Sticks to herself and her books. Kay's a widow."

"A widow, at her age!"

"Kay married her college sweetheart from the University of Illinois. Right after their honeymoon, he was sent off to the Navy in June of '42. He never made it—killed in a car wreck en route to officers' school. Kay came back to live with her father and teach." Ernie was surprised at his talkativeness, yet seeing Kay frequently, when she spelled him, he thought about her often.

"She's also your boss's daughter."

"She is? Well, thanks. Sorry to have bothered you," Jake said, not knowing how to pursue the inquiry further and needing to think about this last bit of information.

🕃

"Where's Silas?" thundered Lloyd Ryan, the pugnacious banty rooster lawyer who was ringleader of the 9:45 A.M. coffee klatch at the Shackateria.

"Hell-fire, Ryan, ol' Si hasn't blessed us with his presence in months. You know that," responded Bert Churchill, honorable mayor of Billtown and owner of Churchill's Auto Repair Shop. Everybody who wanted to think of himself as a peer of Lloyd Ryan called him Ryan. Everyone else in town called him Mr. Ryan.

Ryan sat down lightly, like a prizefighter ready to spring up at the bell for round one. "Norma. NORMA! I'm waiting here for some of your miserable coffee."

"Keep your pants on, Ryan. I've got customers up front here who act like gentlemen." Norma Rice, proprietress, shouted over her left shoulder to the back of her establishment. Norma didn't take any guff from Ryan, and he loved it.

Nine business and professional men crowded around the shiny blue formica tabletop, rendered in swirls to look like Grecian marble. The big round table was trimmed in chrome to give the overall appearance of Century of Progress modernity, right here in Billtown.

Norma sauntered back toward the Ryan table, not wanting to appear to be hurrying. With her free hand she tried to plump up her frizzy strawberry-blond hair. Norma had been around the track a couple of times, as they say; but everybody liked her and even accepted her as part of the community, if not the Establishment.

She went round the table to refill the thick ceramic mugs with more of her coffee, which was indeed miserable, but not her fault. The town water was heavily laced with natural fluoride, sulphur, iron, salt, and who knows what else. The result: salty, smelly water and few cavities. Instead of the five dentists a town its size might support, there were only two–Doc McClenahan at the Ryan table being one of them.

"Ol' Si" was Silas McDermott, gentleman farmer, long-time Starke Township Supervisor, leader of the county board and incoming president of the Illinois Association of County Officials. Si had driven a tractor in his day, but with a mile-square section of land and one-hundred-and-twenty-head of purebred Black Angus cattle, Si could apparently afford his two tenant-farmer families. They kept the home place humming while he enjoyed his politics and cattle sales. Si had even taken to raising Shetland ponies, a miniature breed popular with the children of wealthy folks who had places on the outskirts of Peoria and Chicago. Si enjoyed driving his six-pony hitch of Shetlands in local parades and even at the State Fair.

"Heard that Si and Margaret joined a country club in Peoria, and that he's taken up golf." This revelation from

Harold Kidd, popular owner of Kidd's Funeral Home. Word was that Harold was so good-natured you left his funerals chuckling.

"No self-respecting farmer belongs to a goddam sissified country club, let alone plays golf," declared Marion Burcham, the Standard Oil man, who had stored Jake's suitcase on his arrival.

"Hate to see a good man like Si get too big for his britches," mused Doc Williamson, the town's senior physician.

"Hell, you belong to Midland Country Club, Doc," boomed "Dutch" Arganbright, owner and meat cutter at Arganbright's Supermarket, a new term for grocery store.

"Yeah, but I need an outlet after a day in a stuffy office poking around disgusting, corpulent bodies like those arrayed around this table," retorted Doc, pulling on a Lucky Strike, pleased with his response.

"Well, what are we going to do about Silas?" grumbled Charlie DeBord of DeBord's Hardware. "He should be right here with us, solving the world's problems, the way he used to be. We need a farmer in our midst. Otherwise, we don't know how bad things are."

"When's Si up for election again, Ryan?" wondered Harold Kidd, a gleam in his eye.

"Township elections are first Tuesday, this coming April. Why do you ask? You don't want to run against him, do you, Harold? I can see the newspaper ad now—'As your supervisor, I will never let you down, but when it's your time, come to Kidd's Funeral Home, and I will.' " Ryan let out a guffaw at his humor, and the others joined in.

"Hell no. But maybe if we organized a little write-in campaign against him, to show that not everybody's happy with his uppity ways, he'll get the message. They did this against a lazy coroner friend of mine over in Iroquois County a few years back. He got the message. Now they say you can't take a nap in church for fear he'll perform an autopsy on you. So all of us—including Si—can have a good laugh about this little prank, right here at Table # 1 at the back of Norma's Shackateria."

"Who's gonna put his name up for write-in? Nobody at this table, I'm sure." Earl Turner, president of the State Bank of Willliamstown, always looked for the flaws in an idea. Earl's hair was beginning to go gray, pomaded back slightly at the sides, crew cut on top. You'd never see that on a big city banker, but Earl was right at home with the farmers who made up his primary customers.

"We can write in anyone's name," continued Harold. Looking around the restaurant, he saw many prospective customers in the booths along the wall. He clearly didn't want to alienate them. Then he saw a lone figure at the counter, hunched over some cereal and a huge book. "What about that fellow at the counter? Who's he?"

"A printer at the newspaper. Been here a few months. I met him when he got off the bus," said Marion. "Seems decent. Sticks to himself. Trickle, Jake Trickle."

"Then he's our candidate," declared Ryan, looking around to make sure nobody else in the restaurant had heard him. "Somebody nobody's ever heard of. How's that for sending a message to Si. Harold, that's a helluva'n idea. First good one you've had since you decided to use embalming fluid in place of motor oil.

"Now let's keep this cockamamie idea under our hats till we get closer to the election. Can't let word get around. So nobody says nothin', right?" Ryan's gaze went around the table, yielding a formal nod from each man, like a blood oath at the lodge hall above the bowling alley.

Norma came around with more coffee. Ryan ordered a round of vanilla-frosted, sink-to-the-floor-of-the-stomach cake donuts, contending that his associates were too cheap to buy their own.

⌗

After a few months, Jake had fit into the weekly rhythm of Billtown. Main Street merchants nodded as he walked to Humphrey's or the Shackateria for his meals. Harry Campbell extolled Jake's skills as a mechanic and tireless back shop worker at the newspaper. The pool sharks at

Wilson's once invited him into a game, but he said "no" with a smile, allowing that his game wasn't in their league. Just a quiet fellow with a book in hand who did his job and stuck to himself.

Jake and Ernie began to talk about books. "Have you read Faulkner's *Light in August*, Ernie?"

"No, I just can't get into Faulkner, hard as I try; but I recall that Kay Townsend checked that out this past summer. You might ask her," Ernie suggested. They both smiled sheepishly, silently empathizing as to the challenge that represented for them. Jake went back to his reading, never quite finding a comfortable position in the straight-back chairs.

One evening in mid-November, as Jake headed out at eight for his mug of beer at Harry Wilson's, Ernie asked, "You have any plans for Thanksgiving? Just a week away."

"No, thought I'd set some type at the paper."

"Then why not come out to my place in the early afternoon. Won't be fancy, but you can try my cherry preserves and pickled beets, and I'll open a bottle of my rhubarb wine, all made on the premises."

"Well, thanks, I'd like that."

Ernie lived in a cabin on the edge of Williamstown. Some in town called it a shack, but it served his purposes and limited resources. A Franklin stove sat out from the center of the east wall of the one large room. Opposite was a claw-footed, two-burner stove. Plank and brick storage shelves held his stewed tomatoes, relishes, beets, cherry preserves, blackberry jams and homemade wines.

Ernie made the bathroom light-tight, to double as a darkroom, where he developed children's portraits, as well as photos taken now and then for Jim Dunlap at the newspaper. Outside, stacked to the east of his cabin, was enough cherry, white oak and pine to get him through the winter to come.

In Jake's honor Ernie folded the Army cot he used for a bed, set it aside and put up the card table in front of the Franklin stove. The rhubarb wine was raw but drinkable in an icy cold state. They downed the whole bottle and enjoyed the simple fare, mostly a small baked chicken with sweet potatoes from the garden. Jake had brought a box of Russell Stover chocolates for dessert.

Afterward Ernie proposed a walk along Indian Creek, back of the cabin. The day was crisp and sunny. Ernie offered Jake a walking stick to poke under the oak leaves. "Never know when an arrowhead from a Sauk or Fox campsite might work its way up."

They walked in silence for the most part. "What brought you to Billtown?"

"Guess I'm interviewing towns, trying to find a place where I fit and the town fits me. I never had a family or a community I belonged to, for that matter. Could be my fault for not trying to join in; yet the towns I've been in don't exactly embrace outsiders with open arms. I'm not a churchy type, so that's out. They wouldn't take me in the war, because one of my legs is a tad shorter than the other, so the veterans groups are out.

"Billtown seems about like the other towns I've tried. The merchants and farm owners are the belongers to a closed club; and the working folks raise their families as best they can in hopes their children might make it into the Rotary one day, if that's what they want."

"But with your skills, you could take off for anyplace and find work. Why not go to California?"

"I've thought about it, but though I'm an outsider, I think deep down, crazy as it sounds coming from me, I want to belong to the Rotary, to belong to something, somewhere. As likely in the Midwest as anywhere, there's a community where people care about one another first and their own place in the community second. That's what I'm looking for."

"But in California you could be part of building that community from the bottom up."

"Maybe you're right. But for some reason, I'm drawn to small town America, warts and all. Who knows, maybe my father was a prominent and satisfied Main Street merchant somewhere who fathered me illegitimately. With that blood in me, maybe I'm looking for the perfect small town, which we know doesn't exist."

"I guess I'm a poor one to talk this way, because I prefer it on the outside, and the petty jealousies and jostling for place in town mean nothing along the creek bottoms where I find my company. But with all that said, a fellow has to work to make a small town a better place. A town'll never be perfect, not even close, but there must be some satisfaction in trying to make it better. That's probably why Rotarians and the Lions look like they feel so good about themselves."

A hundred feet above, a red-tail hawk soared upward on a shaft of sun-warmed air, its beady eyes capable of counting the few dandruff flecks on Ernie's dark shirt but more interested in rodents and rabbits.

"Yeah, you're one to talk about going to California, Ernie. You go off to war in your forties, see England, even Paris. Then, with nothing much to return to, you come back to a cabin on the outskirts of a small, featureless town on the flatlands."

"Guess it's a lack of gumption," Ernie said, somewhat at a loss. "The absurd and hideous war among supposedly intelligent beings maybe drove me back to the quiet and logic of my natural world."

"Yeah, but what's more scary and cruel than this creek bottom, where the rabbits freeze in fear that they'll become finger food for that red-tail hawk?"

"At least there's a logic, an equilibrium, a balance in the natural world. Maybe a biologist or sociologist, perched on the lip of the fishbowl of life, could peer down at this last war and declare that us bastards were just seeking a new equilibrium. But he wasn't swimming around in that fishbowl. So if you must, chalk my lifestyle up to a search for calm and beauty in an ugly world. Not all that different from what you're looking for."

They walked back to the cabin, their breath pushing out little cumulus clouds, gobbled up by the late afternoon sun. The vertical shafts of air were subsiding. One, then the other looked up. The hawk was pedaling his wings every now and then to make up for the loss of lift.

Starke Township Public Library

Jake and Kay

Thursdays had become a big deal, Jake thought to himself. The paper was out for the week. Thursday at work was relaxed. Catch-up time, to tinker again with the distributor on the Model 14 Linotype, where the thin "i" mats sometimes failed to fall quickly enough into their magazine channel, jamming the whole works.

More important, Kay Townsend had become the regular librarian on Thursdays, as Ernie was taking family portrait photos on Thursday evenings for a month at the Williamstown Bank, part of a bank goodwill promotion.

So after work on Thursdays Jake took a bath, shaved and put on one of his three dressy shirts, an Arrow brand solid powder blue, straight collar. Over that went his cardigan sweater. Jake arrived at the library about six. He always had a book to return as he reached the librarian's desk at the top of the stairs. By seven-thirty or eight, Jake had another book to be checked out.

Kay had come to know Jake through his reading habits, though they hadn't discussed his selections. Jake went in for the great storytellers—Hemingway, Faulkner, Conrad, Ferber, Hammett, Sandburg's six-volume biography of Lincoln. But he was also reading the trashy new novels about Mike Hammer by a Mickey Spillane and sometimes the westerns of Louis L'Amour.

Several times each evening Kay stole a glance toward Jake. He was so serious, she thought. And lonely. Kay mused that maybe the printer tried to live among the characters in the stories he read. "Don't we all?" she sighed.

"What's this fellow like, Jim?" Kay asked her father at dinner one evening.

"Jake works hard, almost relentlessly, as if his work is all he has to hang onto. He treats the commercial printing like works of art. Last week he suggested changing the typeface for the cover on a legal brief of Lloyd Ryan's, headed for the Appellate Court. Instead of the traditional Cheltenham, with its softly rounded letters, Jake recommended a Goudy. 'Those serif feet of the typeface look like they've been chiseled by an old Roman. The face would add dignity, authority to the brief,' he said.

"I showed the proofs to crusty old Ryan. He was delighted, thought the cover reflected the class he deserved.

"Jake wants to open up, I think. But for some reason he can't. All of us get along fine with him at work, even kid around about how well the Bradley Braves are doing this year, but then he drifts off after work to his own private world."

⌛

Jim Dunlap was a big fish in a small pond. When he was born in 1890, there were too many brothers on the quarter section his family had bought in 1853 when they moved from Ohio. So Jim was apprenticed at fifteen to the printer-publisher in town. Fifteen years later Jim purchased a half interest in the paper. Just before the Depression, he bought out his older partner.

Somehow Jim saw the paper and his small staff through those terrible years. Since hard currency was hard to come by then, Jim held an "egg day" twice a year, when cash-strapped farmers could renew their subscriptions with eggs and butter and hams and the like. Jim then divvied up the produce among his workers as part of their wages, and nobody squawked.

Though Irish, Jim's family became Protestant in the 1860s, for lack of a priest to say the Mass. When in 1918 big, handsome Jim married the proper Nellie Dewey, she brought a quarter section of land with her. They became equally proper Congregationalists of the business and professional class.

Carrying the plumpness that reflected modest success and an agreeable personality, Jim took to community leadership easily: worshipful master of the Masonic Lodge, president of the local Civic Club and of the new Lions Club that he organized, and service on the board of the state press association of community newspapers, as well as chairman of the county Republican Party. Jim became somewhat worldly through required trips to Peoria, Springfield and Chicago, the way up-and-coming business folks without formal education did in the first half of the century.

The trips were an outlet not only from the numbing regularity of small-town life but also from the loneliness of a widower. Nellie, his wife of one year, died bearing Kay. Jim reared Kay with the everyday help of Minnie White, who lived with her husband Archie just down the back alley from the Dunlap's. Minnie had not been able to have children of her own. But from 6 A.M. every day until supper dishes were done (staying overnight when Jim was out of town), Minnie directed the Dunlap household.

Jim and Nellie Dunlap had a wonderful, if brief, life together. Nellie was a vivacious young lady with a gifted soprano voice and Jim a fine Irish tenor. The two courted for a year before marriage and were invited to a steady stream of socials, where piano and accompanist just always happened to be on hand. Jim and Nellie were pleased to oblige, favoring the guests with a medley of popular romantic ditties from the operettas of Victor Herbert and Rudolph Friml.

Ernie Robson told Jake how he could still hear the lilting, "Ah, sweet mystery of life, I've found you," from the second floor "opera house" above McClenahan's Drug Store, which the folks took him to for some reason. "I swear they were as good as Nelson Eddy and Jeanette MacDonald."

After Nellie died, Jim never sang again in public, though Kay could coax him, only now and then, into singing softly as she sat in his lap. At the newspaper office Jim would sometimes rock slowly back and forth, staring blankly over his Smith-Corona typewriter or through the plate glass windows, silent for an hour or more before his reverie was broken. Nobody bothered him during those moments. Among the staff those were simply Jim's "spells of the melancholies."

Kay grew up happy, loving Jim, Minnie and the community around her. Yet even as a child Kay felt an ache whenever she caught her young father looking wistfully out the window, and she sensed that she could never fill the loss caused by her birth.

From five each afternoon till supper at six-thirty Jim and Kay played at whatever went with her age. Jim was a dutiful, appreciative guest for tea parties; he helped organize Kool-Aid sales for the sidewalk, put on jointly with the Heaton girls down the street. And he sat at the Steinway upright to encourage Kay in her unenthusiastic piano practice.

After supper Kay often sat on Jim's lap, and he would read to her from *The Saturday Evening Post*. Jim especially enjoyed the old articles by George Fitch, a fellow newspaperman from Peoria who created every man's small college in his "Old Siwash" stories, based on his years at nearby Knox College. The sounds rushed over Kay, while Jim absorbed bits and pieces of a bigger world.

Without fail Jim also read to Kay at bedtime. And later young Kay would read to Jim as well. They shared the roles in Louisa May Alcott's *Little Women*, laughing uproariously when Jim's baritone made an incongruity of it all. The Dunlap house on Miller Street, wraparound side porch shaded by two great tulip trees, filled with books, was a loving place, yet incomplete.

Kay, the Heaton girls and their friends led the cheers for the Williams County Warriors and won the good parts in the farcical junior and senior plays. They flirted with the boys on moonlit evenings on the steps of the library until Hattie Robson turned the lights off at nine and shooed them home just as the town curfew bell was ringing from the water tower. A big evening for the seniors included a double date for a movie at the local Show-Bill theater, followed by huge pork tenderloin sandwiches, twice the diameter of the buns, washed down with chocolate milkshakes. Norman Rockwell couldn't have framed it better than it seemed to Kay in 1938, while much of the world suffered through the Great Depression.

Only Kay and three others in her graduating class of sixty went on to college. Money for tuition was hard to come by. As Republican county chairman, Jim arranged a General Assembly scholarship at the University of Illinois for Kay. Tuition and fees for four years, gratis, thanks to Senator Fred Rennick of the neighboring county, whose four-county district included Williams.

Separated for the first time from the cocoon that Jim and the community had spun around their favorite Junior Miss, Kay cried her eyes out at night for the entire first semester in Champaign-Urbana. She tried to shield her homesickness from her more sophisticated sorority sisters at the Chi Omega house, some of whom had even been to the East Coast. By the January winter term Kay gritted her teeth, decided she was too old to be homesick and threw herself into campus life. Beers at Prehn's improbable Moorish casbah tavern with the upperclassmen from Sigma Chi and Phi Delta Theta, and picnics in the spring at Turkey Run over the line in Indiana.

Kay and Paul Townsend met in an American Lit class. He, an electrical engineering student from Oak Park, filling out a humanities requirement. She, an English major in love with the spare gritty style of Hemingway and the haunting images of Faulkner. Paul was tall, slender, blonde, maybe descended from the Viking-Angle combination that settled the northeast of England. A typical UI double-E major, smart as a whip, eyes dancing with ideas of all the possibilities of electrons. But hopeless at spelling. "Soap" came out "sope," and "soup" was "supe."

His surface shyness was a disarming put-on, and his self-effacing smile pled with Kay for some help in getting through the course. "I know what I want to say about tough guy Hemingway, but I have a deuce of a time getting it down on paper. My slide rule is helpless in this class. You help me, please, over a beer and an Italian beef at Prehn's. In return, I'll tell you of a future when you and I will be watching our favorite radio programs over a screen in our living room." He smiled at his audacity. So did Kay.

The war stole everyone's time, including that for a big wedding in Billtown. Instead, Kay and Paul married on campus immediately after their graduation in June 1942. Jim Dunlap, the Heaton girls and a few others went down for the wedding. Jim nursed his loss by drinking Crown Royal on the rocks, one after another. But he never let on and was the life of the reception. The young couple drove to the venerable Drake Hotel in Chicago for their honeymoon. Three days later Paul departed alone by car for Naval OCS training in Florida, where Kay was to join him. Instead, he was killed in Kentucky by a drunk driver in a head-on collision.

Kay returned to Williamstown, took a job in the two-person English department at the high school and salved her hurt. Over the years a muted normalcy came back to Kay's life but not much color to her cheeks nor sparkle to her eyes. Kay directed the junior and senior class plays, which were big community events. Instead of a long farce, she met the audience halfway with two one-act plays, a serious piece by, say, Thornton Wilder, followed by a light comedy. The kinetic energy the students brought to play practice did, for that moment anyway, bring out Kay's natural vivaciousness, and she exulted when that rare student asked to know more about the playwright and the why of the characters.

⌛

This Thursday Jake had pulled Ross Lockridge's *Raintree County* off the new book rack. As he handed the book to Kay, who had become the permanent Thursday evening librarian, he opened the cover to the card envelope pasted inside. Kay pulled the card and began to write his name before stamping a date on it. As a printer who stared at type forms all day, Jake was better at reading upside-down-and-backward than most were at rightside-up reading. He saw that Kay Townsend had also checked out *Raintree County*.

Kay handed Jake the book. "I think you'll enjoy this. Please tell me what you think of it." Jake looked up quickly, his intense gray eyes shining, face crinkling into a big smile. He nodded, said "Thanks" and hurried out. After a quick supper at Humphrey's, Jake settled in at Wilson's on his regular stool, two-thirds of the way down the bar. Without asking, Harry brought him a frosted schooner of Falstaff.

Elated by Kay's invitation to discuss a book with her, Jake flipped quickly through the thousand-plus pages of

Lockridge's one-and-only magnum opus, published a year earlier. Jake knew this because he had read in last week's *Life* that the author had committed suicide at age 39, just months after release of his first novel.

A gulp of the frosty Falstaff, carbonated and hopped to bite, braced Jake, already high on the anticipation and trepidation of discussing a novel with the untouchably attractive, poised Kay Townsend. Jake read well past midnight, first in his chair, then in bed, determined to finish and understand the 1,066 pages of *Raintree County* by the following Thursday.

Over wheat cakes and Aunt Jemima syrup at Humphrey's the next morning, Jake kept his head in the book, looking up only once to smile at Margy. As Jake paid his ticket, he added, "Sure a nice looking new hairdo you have, Margy. "

"My heavens! Jake told me how nice my hair looks," Margy reported in the kitchen to Bill, who stood back from some sunny-side-up eggs to pull a Pall Mall off his lower lip. "If he gets too talkative, kick him out." Bill and Margy laughed.

⏳

"Ernie, do you know anything about the book *Raintree County*?" Jake asked on Saturday afternoon, when he had walked out to the cabin.

"Recall a review in *Time*. Said it was a sweeping attempt at stating the Great American Myth, as seen through flashbacks during a single day in 1892 in small-town Indiana. Something like that. Plus, a great new talent in Lockridge. You want some more apple wine? I have another bottle to get rid of."

"Save me. I think you ought to scour your sink with that stuff. It's stronger than Ajax, the foaming cleanser, 'soaks the dirt right down the drain.'" Jake was half singing the jingle he had been hearing on evening radio.

Back at the Shackateria, Ryan had revived the idea of the write-in campaign. God, how he hated for people to get uppity, not that he wasn't a bit arrogant himself. "Dammit, I just get a kick out of recounting to people how I have won my cases," Ryan thought to himself. "Best damned courtroom lawyer in the territory," said State Supreme Court Justice Max Johnson himself, when he spoke in Billtown last year at the annual Civic Club Banquet. Ryan recalled this with more than a dollop of pride.

But clearly Silas McDermott had no call to be uppity, Ryan thought. "Inherited his land. Hasn't added to it. Besides, we miss him at coffee, which is where he's supposed to be, dammit."

"So here's what we do, fellows. The election is April 5, a month away to the day. I talked with Tom Velon, the Bureau County clerk—don't want our Tommy Jackson in on this, as he's one of Si's guys. Here's how you cast a valid write-in vote: Below Si's name on the ballot, for the post of Town Supervisor, draw a box just like that in front of Si's name and write in the name of Jake Trickle beside the box. Then—and don't forget this—put an X inside the box you've drawn. Velon says a lot of people forget to do that. That's all there is to it.

"Bert, the next City Council meeting is what, a week from now?"

"Yeah, Ryan, next Monday."

"After adjournment, tell the other councilmen what we're up to and why. Don't tell Sam Ackerman, since he's Si's buddy. You see, fellas, we have to keep this under our hats till the last moment, otherwise Si'll hear about it beforehand. Fortunately, I read in the paper that he and Margaret took the Panama Limited to New Orleans last week to go over to Biloxi. Won't be back till the night before the election. Of course, we'd be the last to hear that, since Si dropped us," Ryan jabbed.

"Dutch, you tell the boys out at the Grove. Get Hayden Heaton and Bob Nolan in on it. They love practical jokes.

And ask Al and Ole to mention it to several of the regulars but otherwise to keep it under their hats."

The Grove was Catalpa Grove Tavern, a cottage road-house where those Main Street businessmen who were into highballs would go after work. The dark walls were festooned with lighted, moving or blinking signs promoting Canadian Club, Seagram's new Golden Spike vodka, and Atlas Prager, Gipp's and Blatz beers. A hand-written sign said, "No foul language, please." And there wasn't much. The place was roaring by five-thirty each afternoon; dead as a doornail by seven. Al Hill and Ole Olson ran the place, so it was known as Al & Ole's. Al was young, smiling, quiet. Ole was barrel-chested and loud. Ole loved to stir up an argument, then tone it down before tempers got out of hand—the perfect bartender.

"Charlie, is the Legion meeting before the election?"

"No, but we have an officers' meeting, so I can mention it there."

"Doc, you threaten some of your patients with enemas unless they write in Jake Trickle."

"Hell, I haven't given an enema in years, Ryan, too messy. But I guess my patients won't know that. Wilco."

Charlie DeBord offered to run the practical joke by some of the Masons after lodge meeting in two weeks; Ryan said he'd take the Civic Club executive committee, and Harold (You stab 'em, we slab 'em) Kidd would cover the Lions Club.

"Looks like we've got the town covered, fellas. Norma—NORMA!—another round of those sinkers with the vanilla frosting."

There was no way Jake could finish the 1,066 fine-print pages of *Raintree County* in that one week. Monday and Tuesday Jake and Harry Campbell had to work until eight to set, make up and print a special farm supplement to *The Republican*. The supplement was chock full of national ads from Allis Chalmers, John Deere and International Harvester. And from the new hybrid seed companies like DeKalb and Pioneer, which trumpeted yields from their revolutionary seeds of as much as ninety bushels of corn per acre!

Jake was exhausted when he got back to his room and the book. And he had trouble sorting out the convoluted historical flashbacks that brought the reader through the great transitions of America's 19th Century—the Old South, the War Between the States, the great new American City and the robust small towns of the Midwest, exemplified by Waycross, Indiana, (not a real place, but real all the same.)

Finished or not, Jake had to talk with Kay about the book.

Thursday Jake put on his good cardigan sweater and was at the library by five-thirty. He sat at his table, reading for a third time the chapter where Johnny Shawnessy, the handsome teacher, courts and loves beautiful Esther Root on a mystical island in Raintree County.

Kay was on and off her perch at the librarian's desk, first helping a high schooler with sources for an assignment, then firmly scolding the twelve-year-olds who were having too much fun with the Mathew Brady Civil War stereopticon pictures. She was the perfect librarian, thought Jake—neat, professional, prettier than a Wallace Nutting postcard picture of the blue Atlantic coast.

By eight Jake, who had been screwing up his courage since he arrived, found himself walking to the librarian's desk. "Excuse me, Mrs. Townsend, but I have some questions about *Raintree County*, if ever you have time."

"Of course I do, Mr. Trickle. Could we wait until nearer closing time, when most of the youngsters will be out of my hair?"

"Sure, great. Just let me know."

At a quarter to nine, Carol Sensenbrenner and Mollie Smith took two books each to Kay for check out and lingered to chat. Having caught the fleeting exchange between Jake and Kay earlier, they delighted in torturing Jake, stealing his precious moments with Kay.

By eight fifty-five the library was almost empty. Kay flicked the lights to admonish all that the local Carnegie was closing. Then she came over to Jake. "I'm sorry. I meant to get over sooner. We can take a few minutes at least with Ross Lockridge."

"But my questions are as big as his book," Jake sighed. "What is he trying to say? And why would he commit suicide just months after finishing his first—and highly successful—novel?"

Suddenly he blurted out, "Would you join me, please, for a hamburger at Peachie's Diner? He's open till ten."

"Uh, well . . . sure. A hamburger sounds great. I didn't have time to eat after school because of play practice."

Jake had no car, and Kay had walked; so after helping Kay with her long, deep-brown, cloth coat, the two set off into the crisp early March evening. Jake exhaled clouds of frosty breath all the four blocks to Peachie's. They talked little. Kay asked how Jake liked Williamstown. Jake said it was just fine, that he enjoyed the staff at *The Republican*, and thought her father was a good boss, fair and willing to get his hands dirty in the backshop when necessary.

At Peachie's they took one of the booths in the ramshackle add-on room. Four high school senior girls gossiped in a back booth. Startled to see their teacher with a man, they waved and shouted in unison, "Hi, Mrs. Townsend." Kay smiled and nodded in their direction. She took her coat off, Jake not thinking to help.

Audrey, the waitress, another student of Kay's, came to the booth from the grill, where Peachie presided, grease-splattered white tee-shirt stretched over a prominent stomach, testimony to too many of his own hamburgers and chocolate malts.

Kay ordered a hamburger and a Coke. Jake, a cheeseburger, fries and Coke. Audrey headed for the grill, shouting the order to Peachie as she went.

"Well, what do you think of *Raintree County*, Jake? And may I call you Jake? Please call me Kay."

"Sure. The book's incredible. I've never read anything like it. I wish I were like Johnny Shawnessy, so literate, handsome, observant and confident. Yet always searching. Wonderful," Jake finished, pleased with himself and beginning to think he might even relax a bit.

"My favorite is 'the perfesser,' " offered Kay. "Cynical yet good. Tired of all the bombast and posturing of people, the perfesser still sees a lot that he likes. He wants Johnny Shawnessy to be as good and pure as he can, yet not be blinded and fooled by the manipulators around him on all sides.

"To be honest, I haven't read the whole book yet," Kay admitted. "Maybe you'll finish it and tell me what you think then." She wondered if anyone else in Williamstown other than this quiet printer had even heard of *Raintree County*.

"I will!" declared Jake, seizing the opportunity.

He walked Kay the two blocks down Miller Street to the Dunlap family home, a turn-of-the-century eclectic style, with turret alcove rising to the third floor and a wrap-around porch. Not the biggest home in town but solid, bespeaking prosperity.

"Thanks for joining me. This is the best time I've had since I came to town." A good line, yet he couldn't figure out how to follow up, so he said simply, "Good night," and walked back to Main Street, *Raintree County* in hand, a kick in his step.

Jake decided a mug of beer was in order to treat himself for screwing up the courage to invite Kay to Peachie's, a first for Jake. Then back to his room to read more about Johnny and the perfesser. "Let me have a Falstaff, Harry, since I feel a bit like that jovial character out of Henry the Third or Fourth, or whatever it is." Harry looked blankly at his regular, shifted his unlit, half-smoked White Owl cigar from the far left side to the opposite with a deft roll of the tongue and served up Jake's frosty beer.

X

Jake realized some changes were in order if he was going to try to see Kay Townsend again, and he was. "Ernie, I really need your help in shopping for new clothes," implored Jake. They were sitting in front of Ernie's Franklin stove, warm as toast on the front side, almost chilly on the backsides. A cruel wind was slipping through the cracks in the cabin. Sharp as it was, the rhubarb wine, vintage of the past June, warmed their innards.

"You're asking the halt to lead the blind," Ernie responded, as he surveyed their woebegone attire. They smiled.

"I need more and better clothes—and a car."

"A car! Do you have a driver's license?"

"No, but I need a car to take the driver's test. You drive. Teach me. Look, I can't just walk Kay Townsend to Peachie's for hamburgers after the library closes."

"Can you afford all this lavish spending?"

"Yeah, I'm in good shape. I'm up to a dollar-fifty an hour now, more with overtime, which I always chalk up. I pay seven dollars a week for my room, twenty bucks or so a week on meals and beer. Don't have much else to spend on. So I put money in my savings account every week, as much as $35 some weeks. Have been for ten years."

"Gad, you're loaded."

"No, but at least now I know why I've been saving.

"Kay and I talk about Faulkner—she understands and appreciates him and his characters better than I do—and Edna Ferber, whose stories we both love. Kay likes the strong women in Ferber's novels. I simply like the sweep of a story like *Cimarron*. We wrestle with Sinclair Lewis and whether he had the number on the Billtowns of the world. Kay thinks Lewis is right about the vanities and narrow thinking along our main streets, but she is more forgiving, and also sees the good in people like her father and his friends.

"I grew up on the tough side of the tracks, working for a man interested only in my labor at the printing business. He had no affection gland. Maybe that's why I like the Jim Dunlaps of the world for trying to make their anthills better places, even if they are oblivious to the cold shoulder they often turn to outsiders, newcomers and poor folks.

"And *Raintree County*—Kay and I could spend a lifetime, I swear, on analyzing the characters in that book, their good and bad points. I've never been happier, even though Kay and I have only been to Peachie's three times now. I want to take Kay to movies, and not just to the Show-Bill here in town, to restaurants and to dances. Can you teach me how to dance?"

"Whoa, you'll get no help from me on that. Never had occasion to dance nor the nerve to ask a girl if she might be interested. Always figured my huge Gallic honker discouraged any interest in me from the other sex."

"Well, let's take the bus to Kewanee. I set the type for that Kirley's Men's Store ads. Looks like a classy place but not out of line, though who am I to know. I never bought a suit in my life other than a cheap gabardine I got for a holiday party I was almost forced to attend awhile back. Kirley's has a sale on. I can get Arrow dress shirts for $2.88 and a Palm Beach suit for $27.50, and they're having a sale on Botany 500 suits, which must be good, 'cause they're down from $55 to $40. That still seems pricey, but again, who am I to know?"

They took the late-morning Blackhawk Lines to Kewanee, twenty miles away. Kewanee was an old industrial town of 20,000, enough bigger than Billtown to have a real men's store. Jake was acting like a kid. Ernie mused to himself that love—at least some affection—requited must be quite a tonic.

Kirley's had been in business since the 1880s, and the family prided itself on having clothes just like you'd buy on State Street in Chicago. Mark and Frank Kirley, brothers, greeted the two shoppers. The haberdashers were both tall and handsome, dressed in top-of-the-line suits, Ernie figured—great ads for their store.

Jake addressed Frank. "Sir, I need your help in being outfitted so that I can take a new lady friend to nice restaurants. I've never owned a good suit in my life, so I'm at your mercy. But Jim Dunlap, my boss, said he knew you fellows and you'd treat me right."

Ernie and Jake walked out of Kirley's having bought Jake a Palm Beach summer-weight suit in khaki, a two-button year-round blue blazer, a grey-herringbone wool suit by Botany and charcoal wool slacks that would work with the herringbone jacket; plus shirts, a couple of ties, even French cufflinks for the shirts, a navy windbreaker, two V-neck sweaters, one burgundy and another forest green, plus black and brown leather belts and a handsome, navy, all-wool top coat by Hart Shaffner & Marx; and finally a pair of Florsheim burgundy wing-tipped dress shoes, which would go with both suits, and a pair of penny loafers. Jake was ready.

The bill was almost $300, a staggering amount, Ernie thought. Jake said he'd pay by State Bank of Williamstown check. "Feel free to call the bank to make sure that I'm good for the money."

"If you're a friend of Jim Dunlap's, that's good enough for us."

☒

The car came next. Billtown had four new car dealers. Harold Settles sold Fords; Shube Fell, Dodges; Bob Young handled the new post-war Kaisers and Frazers; and Andy Ashmore sold Chevies, Pontiacs and Buicks. You had to go to Kewanee or Peoria for Cadillac, Chrysler and Packards, which were just too showy for most Billtown folks. It was okay if your successful relatives drove one into town to visit, but clearly a local was getting uppity if he even talked out loud at Humphrey's of his admiration for the fancy cars.

The big issue for Jake was whether to buy pre-war-used (much less expensive) or a newer model. "I want a decent, clean, reliable car that Kay will find comfortable. That's it. I'm no spendthrift, but I don't want her to feel out of place when we pull into Maple Shade for rock lobster tails on a Saturday night."

"All I know is Henrietta Silliman's '47 Buick, which I take it is more of a car than you want." Ernie drove Henrietta, the town matriarch and longtime high school principal, to Cape Cod each summer. He returned home by bus, then went back in late August to drive her home. Nobody messed with Henrietta. If she wanted a Cadillac, which she wouldn't because she was too tight, nobody would say a word. She got her Master's in English from Columbia University in '03. She taught everybody in town, and everyone treated her with great respect. Scared to do otherwise. Toughest bird in western Illinois but always a lady. Never married. Word was, nobody ever had the nerve to invite her out.

"But at least I've got a driver's license, so we can take anything that tickles your fancy-bone out for a whirl."

It didn't take Jake long to settle on what he wanted—a '38 or '39 Ford Coupe. "Those models will be classics fifty years from now. They have a liquid, teardrop design, swallowtail trunk, front fenders melt down to the running boards. The key is to find one in decent running order, after a decade. Fortunately, what with gas rationing during the war, mileage was held down some."

Prices ran from $295 to $425. The car dealers couldn't make outrageous claims. Locals knew the lineage of most every car—who had owned it when, how they drove it, how they took care of it. If the car came from out of town, all bets were off, of course, and extreme caution set in.

Jake and Ernie kicked a lot of tires one brisk Saturday, and by four o'clock Jake and Harold Settles were talking seriously about a '38 coupe. You didn't dicker much then over price. Instead, you bargained on a better pair of front tires, or some slip-on seat covers to fit over the worn seats, maybe new rubber floor mats. Jake and Harold were talking $400, which Ernie thought was steep, but who was he to know? Harold was a slight, nervous sort, in perpetual motion, hopping around the car, rubbing his chin, nodding, muttering to himself. Jake and Ernie stood to one side and contemplated the decision, serious even for Jake's big but hard-earned savings account.

Ernie took the car for the test drive. Jake was co-pilot, watching Ernie's every move as he confidently palmed the black gear shift knob, screwed onto a metal stick mounted on the floor. Jake tried to mimic Ernie's feet—push in the clutch, shift, depress foot-feed pedal and at same time let up on the clutch. "You're making me nervous, Jake! Engine sounds fine. Car shifts easily."

They went out on state route 91 north of town and slowly took the Ford up to 50, then 55, 60, 65. At 65, which you never drove unless you were a crazy man, the car shimmied a bit. "Front tires, probably," Ernie said. Jake nodded, all business.

When they returned, Harold offered up the car's pedigree and ownership, appreciating that neither of them were into the cafe intelligence network. "Max Hatfield bought it new. He drove his girl friend Joyce in it till he went off to war, when he sold it to old Gary Whittaker, the bachelor farmer, who you know, Ernie. Gary just traded it in on a new Mercury I got him from a dealer over in Peoria, as I don't handle Mercurys yet. Max probably catted around a bit in the car like any young buck would, but he also took great care of it. Whittaker never drove it over forty-five. I'd lay money on that. Twenty-five thousand miles on it. Quite a few, but good miles. You're getting one helluva good car, fella, and you can check out what I say with any of the regulars at the Shackateria or Humphrey's.

"If you have any problems during the first two weeks, bring it in, and I'll make it good," said Settles in a particularly expansive mood, he thought, trying to make the sale before day's end.

"Okay, Mr. Settles, you've got a deal, so long as Ernie can teach me how to drive it." Jake laughed.

▓

The car opened up endless possibilities for Jake—and Kay, of course. A Bradley basketball game, maybe. And rock lobster tail with drawn butter (a delicacy Jake had seen in the ads but never tried) at Maple Shade, the stylish old manse of a restaurant on old Route 88 north of Peoria. Then to the Madison or Palace theaters in Peoria for first-run movies. Possibly even dancing to Freddie Stevens or Blue Barron at the Inglaterra Ballroom in Peoria, or at the new Hub Ballroom out in the country at Edelstein ("Always a breeze at the Hub").

"Now I am getting carried away," thought Jake. "I've never danced in my life. Who'm I kidding, anyway?"

The Republican

The Election

Each of the sixteen townships in Williams County elects one supervisor, regardless of population, and he—they're all fellows; always have been—is responsible for meeting the needs of the town's residents. Henrietta Silliman could maybe get elected if she tried, but she's too smart to be interested. Local politics is a man's world, primarily a farmer's world, as nearly all the supervisors are farmers. Kind of a Jeffersonian thing. The farmers are stewards of their flocks—both the stupid animals and us less stupid animals—and, most important, protectors of their property tax bills.

Each township has at least one voting precinct. Billtown is located in Starke Township, named like so many of them after a Revolutionary War hero who was granted a section of land after his service. As the most populous township in the county, Starke had four precincts of about 500-800 registered voters each. The two precincts within Billtown proper were too big at more than 800 voters per, but County Clerk Tommy Jackson never got around to dividing them.

The supervisor doles out "poor relief" for families down on their luck. The relief comes in the form of coal for heat and so much credit at a favored store for groceries. In some townships you have to be way down on your luck to cadge any help out of the supervisor, who can make Scrooge look like a generous soul. In other locales a more charitable supervisor prevails. Pretty much the luck of where you live. It's said that some poor folk do some shopping around for more generous townships.

The township roads are a more important responsibility, most would agree. There can be up to 72 miles of road in each township. The roads intersect at the corners of every mile square section of land. A township highway commissioner is also elected, and the post is sought after. The supervisor and the three elected township trustees approve the budget of the road commissioner.

Townships can also assume other responsibilities, such as the Starke Township Public Library in Billtown.

The supervisor is automatically a member of the county board, which is a big deal post for local politicians. County roads, the sheriff and jail and courts, the county nursing home, county hospital, superintendent of schools— all are within the purview of the county board. Many of the supervisors are also active on the Williams County Republican Central Committee and the Farm Bureau, serve as church deacons, and masters of fraternal groups like the Masons and Odd Fellows. So you do more than county board business when you gather for the monthly Thursday all-day session of the board, which meets in the vaulted ceiling court room on the second floor of the antebellum Greek revival courthouse. And you feel good about yourself and your place in the world.

All sixteen Williams County supervisor posts are up for election every four years, in the spring of the year following a presidential election, such as April 5, 1949. Supervisors run on local party labels, with the People's Party being popular in Williams County. It doesn't mean anything because all but one supervisor is a card-carrying Republican. There is an enclave of Irish popery up in Penn

Township, and the supervisor there is a People's Party Democrat. Actually, dapper Bill McNulty comes in real handy when Republicans are out of power at the state and national levels, because Bill has good links to state-level Democrats. When it comes to core values, Bill McNulty is really a Republican conservative through and through, so Republicans never run anyone against him. Bill even served a term as county board chairman, elected by his Republican peers.

There is no primary election for supervisors. The local township People's Party holds a nominating meeting, in the supervisor's home usually, where nominations to the ballot are made. There is little electioneering since there is rarely competition. After being re-elected, the supervisor puts a two-column-by-four-inch ad in *The Republican*, thanking those who voted him back into office. After a supervisor passes on, and most die with their supervisor boots on, the People's Party nominee might be contested by the previously moribund Citizens' Party, which puts up a challenger. In such cases, there are ads in *The Republican* before the April election, in which candidate Russell Smith asks for the voters support, nothing more. No promises; no glorifying one's military service. Just, "I'd appreciate your vote on election day. Russell Smith." Candidate Sam Johnson of the revived Citizens' Party does the same.

The actual electioneering takes place after church, on the steps leading back down to the secular world, where comments are passed around about Russell deserving the post because he's been so active in church and Farm Bureau. Who's this upstart Johnson, anyway? His folks have only been in the area two generations. Solemn nods, and "Thanks for a thoughtful sermon, Reverend." Women listen for cues, as they are expected to vote like their husbands.

And so it goes at the Farm Bureau, the restaurants and school board meetings. The word gets out. Jim Dunlap never editorializes at *The Republican* for or against local candidates. You learn how Jim is leaning on important local races, of course. Not through the paper but at the Masonic Lodge oyster supper or at Rotary over bread pudding.

There weren't any contests on the printed ballot in Starke Township in the spring of 1949. A threat by disgruntled farmers to put up a road commissioner candidate against Rusty Smith, who had always been a bit slow about spring grading work, fizzled when the putative challenger got cold feet, and when Rusty promised to hustle a bit more.

Election day arrived. "Si's going to be madder than hell at first, but he'll get the message," Ryan told his fellow conspirators. "Ol' Si will come charging in here to read us the Riot Act, and we'll have a big cake with Welcome Home on it—hear that, Norma—and we'll all have a rip of a time over coffee. He won't be able to stay mad because he loves a good practical joke."

The farmers in precincts 1 and 2, surrounding the town proper, were outside the hearing of the practical joke. Some went to vote as usual out of habit. Wives were let off, as there wasn't any reason to vote. In town the Main Street business folks and those others privileged to be in the know smiled as they remembered how to write in Jake Trickle's name. "Remember," all had been admonished, "you must put an X in the box after you've drawn it."

Jake was in the dark about all this. Unwittingly, he had even aided the jokesters. "Put a couple more slugs of space between each line," Jim Dunlap had scrawled on the job printing ticket, which contained a sample from the last township ballot printing job. Dunlap smiled to himself that the extra space would make it easier to write in Jake's name.

The polls closed at six o'clock Tuesday evening, and the four sets of precinct judges started counting the ballots. When a precinct finished its counting, an election judge called in to the paper. With a grease pencil, Jim Dunlap scrawled the results onto huge sheets of newsprint and then hung them in the front window so cars driving by on Main Street could see the results. He also did this to announce deaths of prominent citizens and for other breaking news.

Precinct 1 called in 53 votes for McDermott, and Precinct 2 reported a tally of 74 for the only candidate on the ballot. At the Precinct 3 polling place in the city fire station, counting went slowly. When they finished, chief election judge Ruth Whittaker called in to Jim Dunlap that McDermott got 75 votes and Jake Trickle 157. Dunlap immediately called Ryan, who was out at the Catalpa Grove, having a highball. "Jeesus-H-Kee-riiist!" Ryan exclaimed. "Does everybody have to get in on the joke? Can McDermott lose, Jim?"

"Haven't heard from Precinct 4, which is at Sam Wrigley's garage. I'll call Sam."

"Sam, what you hear about the vote out in your garage?" Jim asked.

"They've just wrapped up, Jim, and Si only got 42 votes, while the other guy got 127 good votes, with 19 being tossed out because they lacked the box, or the X, or both."

Jim did his addition, then called the Grove. "Ole, get me Ryan."

"Ryan, your joke worked better than you would have wanted. Trickle got 284 valid write-in votes to McDermott's 244."

A pause. "Don't worry, Jim, we'll disqualify this Trickle somehow. He's probably not registered to vote. Say, don't put the results up in your window just yet, Jim."

"Okay, Ryan, but word'll get around pretty quick from the polling places."

"Ole! Do me a favor. Get Tommy Jackson on the phone, if you can."

"Sure, Ryan, anything for a guy who sets 'em up regularly," Ole said, loud enough for fellas down the eight-stool bar to hear.

"All right, you bloodsucker, set 'em up for everybody," Ryan barked back. Ole's partner Al was already laying out the glasses along the bar.

"Tommy, you're the election expert. A candidate for office has to be registered to vote, doesn't he?"

"Not technically, Ryan, just has to be a resident of the jurisdiction."

"For how long, Tommy?"

"Just 60 days."

"Shit-fire."

Beads of perspiration popped out on Ryan's forehead. "This guy Trickle would never want to serve on the county board. Probably didn't even know what it did. But I've got to get him to reject the idea," Ryan realized, "otherwise the joke'll be on me. And the joke's never on me," he thought, belligerently.

At the paper Jake was astride the raised platform of the old Babcock flatbed press, oblivious to the world, hypnotized by the rhythmic rumble of the five-foot diameter printing cylinder. His right thumb and third finger worked automatically, becoming a part of the machine. They grabbed a corner of the top sheet, flicked it, sending a layer of air under the great sheet, floating the creamy newsprint down to the guides. At that moment clamps on the great cylinder grabbed the newsprint at the top of the cycle, pulled it over the hump and down to meet four pages of raised lead type, inked and ready for the thrust.

A black electric motor, hung from the reinforced wood ceiling like a hornet's nest, strained to drive grizzled leather belts down from the ceiling to pull the cylinder and flatbed of type, now married, through the cycle. Metal blades on the folder poked and trimmed the broad sheet, once, twice, thrice, four times, finally pushing out a neatly folded section. All this effort to let the world know—*The Republican* was sent to subscribers in forty-two states— that "Mrs. Olive Plant hosted the African Violet Club Monday for its monthly meeting. Dorothy Ham from the U of I Home Extension Service provided the program on 'All that's gold is not marigold—new varieties of brilliant flowers.'"

Jake was daydreaming about his first real date with Kay, set for Saturday, when he would drive her to the Madison Theatre in downtown Peoria to see tough guy George Raft and Nina Foch in "Johnny Allegro." "Should they go to supper before or after," wondered Jake, "and should he wear his blazer and slacks, or put on his new suit?"

Ernie had been teaching Jake how to drive his new-to-him coupe. The two had gone to Kewanee a couple of times to test Jake in downtown traffic, which he handled with no difficulty. Ernie worried, though, about Jake getting stuck at a traffic light in Peoria heading up the steep Main Street hill. At times like that Ernie always felt like he needed three feet, one each for the clutch, brake and foot-feed. But Jake wasn't worried for a moment.

"Jake . . . Jake!" shouted Jim Dunlap over the rumble from the concrete floor. Jake shook himself from his reverie. "When you finish that stack, come out front. I want to talk to you."

Jim liked Jake. Couldn't figure him out completely, but Jake was a topnotch, all-around printer, typesetter and machinist, just like he promised. And now Jake had begun to date Jim's precious daughter. "Jake wasn't bad looking," Jim thought, in fact he had the appeal of a serious, no-nonsense guy.

"First section's printed. I'm going to call it a day," said Jake, as he sat down next to his boss, who was rocking back and forth, proofreading Arganbright's full-page grocery ad. It was about eight-thirty in the evening.

"Jake, what do you know about the township elections held today?"

"Nothing, other than what I set for last week's paper. Guy named Silas McDermott unopposed for re-election to fifth four-year term here in this township. Longtime chairman of the county board's finance committee, I think your story said."

"And do you know Lloyd Ryan?"

"No, but I hear from my friend Ernie Robson that he's a locally prominent lawyer who's rather taken with himself and his courtroom skills."

"And a practical joker," Jim added. "Anyway, Ryan wanted to send Silas a message about getting too big for his britches and no longer having time for Ryan's daily coffee klatch at the Shackateria."

"So?" Jake responded, wondering why he was being brought into local affairs, when Jake only wanted a mug of beer after a thirteen-hour day.

"Well, anyway, Ryan organized a quiet write-in campaign against Si, and it appears the write-in won, which wasn't what Ryan had in mind."

"Hah, sounds like it serves 'em both right! Who was the write-in?'

"That's just it, Jake. It was you."

"Me! Who you kidding? I haven't even registered to vote yet, and I'm sure as hell not a glad-handing local politician. Nobody even knows who I am, which is, I guess, the way we all like it."

"Well, Ryan apparently saw you at the counter in the Shack one day and hit upon you as the perfect candidate—new to town and unknown."

"Well, why the hell didn't this Ryan have the courtesy to tell me about his little prank? Would seem like the Christian thing to do, if anybody in town ever thinks along those lines," a tart, bemused tone rising in Jake's voice. "What have I ever done to this guy, anyway?"

"Absolutely nothing, and you're right. Ryan—and the rest of us, for that matter—aren't always so sensitive to others as we ought to be."

"You mean you knew about this and didn't tell me?"

"When Ryan and his coffee crew get something going, I guess others in town just go along. Ryan's respected by most of us, and he intimidates the rest.

"Remember when I asked you to space out the ballot job? That was my contribution, so folks would have more room to write your name in. Nobody meant you any harm. The joke was to be on ol' Si. All Ryan did was take your name."

"That's about all I have, my name, and I don't even know where that came from. But I've gotten used to it, and think I stand up for it pretty well, even if I'm not part of any coffee table group or your Masonic Lodge.

"Jim, you know I respect you as a boss, and while this isn't the time to say it, you probably also know that I think your daughter Kay walks on water. But this little trick is pretty shabby; and that applies to everyone who knew about it and lacked the decency to tell a fella they were going to use his name in a public joke."

Big Jim Dunlap wasn't used to getting dressed down, especially by an employee. He stopped rocking, straightened up a bit from his slouch, fleshy face turned up a couple of shades of pink. "Now, Jake, don't get your dander up!"

"Why in hell not? How would you like it if people you didn't know used you as the lead figure in their little joke? Or do the proper folks get a pass when the jokes are played?"

"I don't think that's fair. Look at Si McDermott. Ryan and his buddies are decent folks. They—we—didn't mean any harm to you."

"Then why didn't you use one of your own as the write-in candidate? "

Jim knew the answer but also knew he didn't have an answer for Jake. "Okay, I guess the question now is what are you going to do about it?"

"First, I'll give this Ryan a piece of my mind. Where is he now, would you guess?"

Jim didn't answer. "I mean about being township supervisor and county board member?"

"Hell, I'm not even registered to vote!"

"I don't think you have to be. But I figure you'd want to refuse the office, wouldn't you, Jake, seein' as how you don't know the community well yet?" Jim was recovering his dignity and hoped this gentle nudge to Jake would put the joke behind everybody.

"Yeah, I suppose so. I'm so damned mad I wouldn't want anything to do with the likes of this Ryan and his buddies. By the way, where did you say I'd find Ryan?"

"I didn't. I don't know."

"Yes, you do, you're still stringing me along."

"Well, you've got me again. He's probably out at Catalpa Grove. Usually is after supper. But leave it alone tonight. Go have that beer you deserve. Nobody meant anything by it. I don't do this often, but I apologize for not letting you know about it. Looking back, it was a dumb idea and unfair to a mind-your-own-business fellow like you, Jake."

Jake stood up and nodded, as a way of acknowledging Jim's apology without accepting it, and headed down the street to Wilson's tavern.

As he walked in the regular foursome at the first pool table stopped to take a long look at Jake. "Hi, Jake," said PeeWee Dunbar, a smart ass, smiling, winking to his partners. "How's our high-powered politician?" Jake didn't answer or slow up as he made a beeline for his almost regular stool near the end of the bar.

"Harry, who knew about this practical joke? Did you? If you did, cancel my mug of Pabst!"

"I heard Ryan was up to something about the election, but I never heard any names and certainly not yours. For a tavern, we're respectable here, but we're still a tavern. My customers and me are what I think you who know the big words would call the hoi polloi. Not a part of the Ryan coffee klatch.

"We don't vote in local elections unless there's a hot race for sheriff or mayor. Folks in here are one or two levels down from the lawyers and town leaders. Oh, I belong to the businessmen's association, and I probably could have found out what was up. But I didn't want those fellows to think I cared enough about what they were doing to ask them to let me in on it."

Usually conversation at Harry Wilson's was sporadic, punctuated by the click of pool balls, and a call now and again to "Rack 'em up, Harry." Tonight, among the twenty patrons huddled into six or seven pairs or groups, there was almost a buzz. "D'jya hear about that printer Jake Trickle, the guy talking to Harry up at the bar? He beat Si McDermott on a write-in for township supervisor here."

"You're shittin' me, man. How could he do that? Nobody knows him from Shinola."

"Something about a joke that ol' man Ryan wanted to play on his one-time buddy McDermott."

"Well, I'd say it's quite a joke. I hear that last year McDermott was elected head of some statewide association of politicians. Bet he's pissed off beyond belief."

"What ya' goin' to do about it, Jake?" Harry wondered out loud, not knowing whether he should sympathize with Jake or congratulate him, but doubting the latter.

"I'm going to track down this Ryan, give him a piece of my mind and tell him just where he can shove that supervisor's job."

Harry's tongue wrapped around his vile saliva-soaked White Owl (five cents apiece when not on sale) and rolled it over into the left corner of his mouth, the better to speak clearly. Once Harry unwrapped his daily cigar and popped it in his mouth, unlit, the cigar was never again touched by a human hand, not until closing time when Harry reluctantly pulled out the short remaining stub and pitched it into the brass cuspidor.

"That's just what he'll hope you do," said Harry dryly, in the quiet, knowing timbre of a counselor.

"What d'ya mean?" Jake almost barked back at Harry.

"I've been running this tavern for almost thirty years, first as a young pup bartender, and for twenty years as proprietor. I know both sides of the track in this town. On the proper side, where Ryan lives, people want respect, a bit of stature if possible and a sense of self-satisfaction about their place in life. And they don't like being embarrassed, which is what Ryan will be, mightily, if his prank results in very proper Si McDermott being bumped off the county board, where he has chaired the three-member finance committee—which runs the board—for the past ten years.

"Right now Ryan's joke is causing him a real nervous stomach, which he'd never, never admit. I can almost hear the churning from here. Si must be madder than a hornet with embarrassment, and his wife Margaret is up in her bedroom, mortified, blankets over her head. Ryan and Si aren't actually bad sorts. Ryan has quietly kept a couple of foolhardy young locals from the wrong side of the tracks out of the state pen. God, they would have been chewed up in there. Ryan never bragged about his savvy or pull on that one, nor got any money out of it, and there are other examples.

"And Si has done his share to help a couple of hard-working tenant farmers, who didn't have two nickels to rub together, to get a stake so they could buy a little land and start building some security for their families.

"But those two are so goddamned puffed up with themselves that you have to tether them to lamp posts to keep them from floating away. Now, you can bring them both down to earth if you make 'em squirm, keep 'em on tenterhooks."

"You don't mean I should follow through and take the post? Not on your life."

"Why not? As many books as you've read and as much type as you've set about county board meetings, you'd do all right. Be a heap better than half the members."

"But what about running the township? I don't know anything about maintaining roads and helping poor people out."

"Then learn. I could help and so could my buddy, Gordie Allen, at the other end of the bar. He used to be a township road commissioner before he went to work at Colgan's John Deere.

"You've been an outsider all your life, Jake. You must want something more out of life than work, a couple of mugs of beer and then back to a stuffy rooming house to read yourself to sleep before you start the cycle all over again. This ain't a bad town, all things considered. Yet it takes a lot of effort from all sorts of folks to make it that way. Ryan and Si need to be taken down a peg or two. The town would be better for it and so would they, if they can stand it. But those two are still better men than you, Jake, unless you make a contribution to the world around you, like they've done."

Jake drained his mug, cooled off as much by Harry, the barkeep philosopher, as by the beer. He walked down Main Street, headed to his room. As he walked by the paper's big plate glass windows, he saw the newsprint

announcement, hung by clothes pins from the wire: Town
Supervisor: Trickle, 284; McDermott, 244. Cars slowed as
drivers strained to catch the breaking news that the hanging newsprint always heralded.

One driver, window rolled down the better to read the
news, yelled at Jake, "Who the hell's this Trickle? Never
heard of him."

"Neither have I," Jake responded.

Jake tossed in bed until 2 A.M., then got up and drove
out to Ernie's place. "Ernie, what the hell should I do?"

"About what?" Ernie asked, always the last to know. He
poked around at the dying coals, threw on a couple of hot-
burning cherry logs from a load of new wood. Sherwin
Appenheimer had stacked it outside the week before as
thanks for babysitting his children a couple of evenings.
Jake, showing good judgment, turned down Ernie's offer
of some elderberry wine.

The two talked until four. Ernie thought long and hard,
appreciating that Jake needed a friend and that he may
have been the first real friend he had ever turned to.

"Whatever happens, Jake, keep your dignity. You've
earned that much in life. You weren't the object of this
joke, just the anonymous vehicle."

"Yeah, I wasn't even significant enough to be the butt
of the joke," Jake laughed, not quite bitterly. Ernie took
that for a good sign.

"I just feel used, humiliated. Tomorrow I know I'll feel
like I'm walking through town buck naked, everybody
talkin' about me, then chortling."

"So keep your dignity, then," Ernie said, his own anger
rising. They could just as easily have written in Ernie's
name, he realized. "Don't give the bastards the pleasure of
seeing it get to you. 'Why, thank you, sir, it was a nice vote,
wasn't it?' then move on as if nothing unusual had happened. You'll drive 'em nuts!" Ernie smiled, surprised at
the sagacity of his counsel.

"I can do that," Jake declared, beginning to get into the spirit of the situation. "But what should I do about the office itself? I'd make a goddam fool of myself. Then where would my dignity be?"

Jake had Ernie there. He sure wouldn't take the job, Ernie knew for certain, but then something he'd seen in Jake over the past weeks gave Ernie the sense that Jake could handle it.

"If you refuse the post, you do keep your dignity; but Ryan wins his little joke. And he and the boys won't have learned their own little lesson, that you can't make an ass out of an innocent bystander and get away with it."

No response. The two looked at the Franklin Stove as if it were a sitting Buddha who could emit wise counsel. Ernie opened the stove door so they could see the live show within, always mesmerizing, a neon peach-cherry glow, popping and crackling.

The stove's iron potbelly pulsated with dry heat that radiated right through the two loners. Shy people have more trouble resolving conflict like this than do the out-going types, because reserved, introverted folks tend to avoid conflict in the first place and so lack practice.

Jake never did respond to the conundrum Ernie laid out, and Ernie didn't push him. Jake did appreciate that he actually had someone to turn to, whether his friend's advice was sage or well-intended drivel. Ernie was struck that he had never had anyone to turn to either. Life gets lonely if you think about it like that. So Ernie was glad Jake drove his coupe out that night.

Next morning Jake was at Humphrey's counter the minute Bill and Margy opened for breakfast at six. Several tables and a booth filled up right away. Two regulars on the county highway crew took their places down the counter from Jake.

"I heard about the election, Jake," Margy said as she plopped a coffee and water down on the wood countertop.

She didn't know what else to say, whether to congratulate Jake or observe on what sons-of-bitches Ryan and his buddies were.

"Hasn't everyone by now?" Jake mused. And from the booth eyes were looking Jake up and down, then heads turned back to offer their take on the unusual election.

"Whatcha gonna do?" Margy asked, in a sympathetic tone.

"Keep my dignity, Margy. Keep my dignity and keep 'em guessin'." Jake finished his eggs and toast, took a final swig of coffee and slowly eased himself off the polished wood counter stool. He left the right change for the meal and walked out slowly, even nodding with a smile toward one of the booths, something Jake had never in his life done before.

At the newspaper office by seven, Jake was met by Harry Campbell and Dave Gelvin. Jim was already at his desk, typing out a couple of stories for the front page. The back shop fellows simply nodded to Jim and opened the door into their realm. The electric metal pots on the Linotypes, working through the night to keep the lead liquid and ready for the operators, welcomed them with a comforting warmth that was appreciated on this raw, blustery April day.

"Why don't you finish the ad guts and heads, Harry, and I'll run through the straight matter." Harry nodded. Dave was at the make-up tables, long counters three feet deep, polished stone tops, lined up with eight empty full-page iron chases to be filled with type, locked up and by late morning put on the press bed, four at a time.

Nobody mentioned the election, in deference to Jake, whom Harry and Dave liked. Not just because he was so damned competent but because he always carried more than his share without ever complaining.

Jake sat at the Model 8 and picked up the copy that he was to turn into type. He flipped through the quarter-inch-thick stack of newsprint copy, always on 5 1/2 x 8 1/2 sheets. Jake stopped at the one headed "ELECTion Story 1 1 1 1" and put the five sheets under the metal guide just above the keyboard. He began to tap away, each tap plucking loose an alloyed-steel matrix, or mat, which came tumbling down a chute from its steel magazine and into a neat horizontal side-by-side stack 12 ems (two inches) wide, the width of a column in *The Republican.*

In a stunning, totally unexpected upset, veteran Starke Township supervisor Silas McDermott was defeated yesterday 284-244 in his re-election bid by write-in candidate Jake Trickle, a master printer and machinist at *The Republican* for the past eight months.

McDermott had never been opposed in his four previous bids for town supervisor and member of the county board, nor was he publicly opposed this year.

Details are not clear at press time, but it appears that a write-in campaign was organized quietly on Trickle's behalf in the past several weeks. Since there was no opposition on the ballot for township offices in Starke Township, the largest in population of the 16 townships in Wílliams County, voter turnout was understandably light.

McDermott owns McDermott Farms. 'Si' McDermott is known statewide both for his prize-winning Angus cattle and his leadership role in the Illinois Association of County Officials, which named him president-elect at the December meeting of officials from the state's 102 counties.

In a Wednesday morning interview, supervisor-elect Trickle told this paper. . . .

JAKE, YOU TAKE IT FROM HERE!

JIM DUNLAP

Jake had been setting this story in his mind since he left Ernie's at 4 A.M. but never thought he'd get to say his piece. Jake had never done much writing. No family to write letters to. No schooling. But he had set these day-after-the-election stories since he was fifteen. And he thought of how Perfesser Jerusalem Styles from *Raintree County*, cynical yet not without hope, might write this story. He started a couple of times, then gingerly discarded the hot slugs of type. Finally, he continued:

"I am grateful for the confidence the voters of Starke Township have shown in my abilities," stated Trickle, "and I will do my utmost to see that confidence justified.

"Since I have never before held public office, I will look to the leaders and all the voters of Williamstown and surrounding parts of the township for guidance and support. Based on my introduction to the fine people of Williams County since my arrival just eight months ago, I am confident such help will be forthcoming.

"Actually, I was not even aware that my name was being put forward as a write-in candidate, or that community leaders were so dissatisfied with the service of Silas McDermott, a dissatisfaction, by the way, which I do not share, for I hold Mr. McDermott in the highest respect."

For the past 18 years Trickle has been a printer, type-setter, and mechanic in printing businesses and newspapers in several Illinois communities. Prior to coming to Williamstown this past August, Trickle had worked at the Pontiac (Illinois) *News-Leader* for four years. He never had an opportunity to attend high school, but Trickle is an avid reader and can be found at the Starke Township Public Library several evenings each week.

Trickle, 31 and a bachelor, resides in Williamstown. Trickle tried numerous times to enlist in the services dur-

ing World War II but was always rejected because of a birth defect that left one leg lightly shorter than the other.
IF YOU WANT ANYTHING MORE, JIM, HOLLER. AND THANKS FOR THE OPPORTUNITY TO SAY MY PIECE.

JAKE

The story written earlier by Jim went on to explain how township government worked and closed with the observation that:

While notice of the annual town meetings is still printed in *The Republican*, few if any citizens attend, so the supervisor and trustees approve the budget for the year without public input. Town boards meet monthly. As most readers know, the Starke Township Hall is located in Starke's Grove, one mile west and one mile south of Williamstown.

Jake finished setting the story, which ran about twelve inches in type, slid the still hot slugs of lead into a long metal galley and ran them through the proof press. He looked the story over as he took it to Jim.

"Just wanted you to see the election story, with my quotes. And thanks for giving me directions to the Town Hall. Didn't even know there was one."

Jim read through Jake's self-interview, then reread it. He looked up. "You're not really serious, Jake, about following through on this? You're pulling my leg. If you're not, you don't know what you're getting into. Both Ryan and McDermott will go higher than a von Braun rocket."

"Let them stew in their own juices, dammit. Ryan, whoever he is, deserves this and more. Clearly, he and his buddies have been getting too big for their own good."

"Oh, you'll find out who he is. Ryan'll figure he can stare you right out of town."

The phone rang. "Ziggy, Jake's here, but we've got a paper to put out, too. I can't have you bothering him on paper day." William "Ziggy" O'Connell was the regional reporter for the *Peoria Star*, working from a cubbyhole office in Kewanee.

"But Jim, this is a statewide story. Si McDermott is well known around this state. To be beaten on a write-in is unprecedented so far as I can tell. What the hell happened?"

"Call Lloyd Ryan, the local attorney, and ask him. He was the ringleader of what was a practical joke, though the joke may be on Ryan now. Ziggy, we've got to get back to work here. You're welcome to come down and read the proof for our story, talk to Jake briefly and use our phone to call in to your paper."

❖

Late on Tuesday night McDermott had learned the whole story. He needed just one call, to Irene Claybaugh, evening telephone operator at the Williamstown Telephone Company. Irene had worked as an operator since she graduated from the Williamstown High School in 1929. The Warren Dexter family owned the company and lived in a large apartment on the second floor of the small yet dignified burgundy brick building. There were two switchboards in the offices on the first floor and another in the Dexter apartment.

Irene was married to her switchboard. While it wasn't all that she might have dreamed for in high school, Irene basked in her role as "Central," the critical link to the outside world. Central told firemen where the conflagrations were. During the war Central connected servicemen to their loved ones in Billtown, and she carried the Good News and the Bad News into and out of Billtown, exulting and crying along with her phone subscribers. Irene also had that sixth sense, critical in the communications business, to know when to keep her mouth shut and when to fill people in.

Si McDermott was a person you filled in.

"Irene, what the hell's goin' on with the election?" Si thundered, about nine o'clock.

"Mr. McDermott, apparently Lloyd Ryan and your old coffee klatch wanted to play a joke on you, in hopes of drawing you back into the morning coffee gathering, and the joke worked too well."

"I'll be the laughingstock of Illinois, Irene. Don't those sons-of-bitches—excuse me, Irene—realize that I'm president-elect of the state association of county officials? I'm getting to a place where I can do our county some good. God damn them all—I'm sorry, Irene." McDermott hung up.

Irene immediately called out to the Catalpa Grove. "Al, get me Ryan. I have a message for him."

"Yeah, Irene, whatcha got?" Ryan barked into the phone.

"Si McDermott put a call through, and he knows about the practical joke you guys played on him."

"Thanks for telling me, Irene," Ryan said, hanging up without a further word, not bothering to ask how McDermott learned this. He assumed Irene had told him, based on what she had gleaned from other calls that traversed her wires.

Starke Township Hall

Chapter 4

A Switch in Time

Ryan went through the state's election code line by line. Yes, Jake Trickle could take the office. He didn't have to be registered to vote. Ryan called the county clerk, Tommy Jackson.

"Are there enough flawed write-in ballots to pull Trickle below McDermott's total?"

"No, Ryan, your associates must have been crystal clear in their instructions. Oh, I could throw a couple out for not crossing the X inside the box they drew but not enough to change the results."

Thursday morning Ryan went down to *The Republican* offices.

"Jim, I want to talk to this Trickle fella."

"Go into the back shop. Jake's locking up a printing job at one of the make-up tables."

Ryan was a banty-rooster. Five-foot-six with skinny legs, or so you guessed from the baggy pants legs, propping up a barrel chest that was beginning to sink. Ryan sported a thick, unruly mop of wiry black hair, and wild eyebrows like those of coal union boss John L. Lewis.

For thirty years Ryan had regaled customers at Catalpa Grove with his courtroom exploits. He did put on an eloquent show. Following each trial Ryan would restate the arguments of both sides, blow by blow, always fair to his opponents, as if the businessmen at the bar constituted the jury. He would provide the legal underpinnings of each side's arguments, and profile the judge and jury. Ryan would have been a great law professor.

One of his favorite cases was the successful defense of Art Parrish, who had torched his furniture store in nearby Galva for the insurance money.

"State Farm should never have sent over such a young lawyer if they really wanted to win. He was bright all right, but he didn't understand the jury, which liked Art a helluva lot better than they did State Farm."

"But did Art torch the place?" asked one of the barroom jurors.

"Of course he did, but State Farm could never prove it!" They all howled with laughter, and Ryan set up another round for the admiring assemblage, who appreciated having such a smart lawyer in their hometown.

This Thursday morning, however, Ryan had to size up a fellow he had made the butt of a joke.

"Mr. Trickle, I'm Lloyd Ryan, and I'd like to talk with you." Ryan had a burled walnut pipe clenched in his right jaw. He didn't bother to take it out.

"So you're the fellow I owe the pleasure of my election to office," Jake responded. He rubbed his hands on his apron and stuck his make-up rule in one of the pockets. Ryan hadn't offered his hand, however, so Jake put his against the stone make-up table.

"I've come to say that I'm sorry for having taken your name in vain," Ryan offered, pleased with his own capacity for humility, "and I hope you are man enough to put affairs back where they should be by turning down the office of supervisor. The incumbent is a good man and a statewide leader."

"Then why did you play such a trick on him, Mr. Ryan?"

Harry Campbell had been setting type for a purebred hog sale catalog, but the clack-clack of Linotype mats falling into line came to a halt, leaving only the soft whir of the Linotype's distributor. Harry wanted to hear this.

"Just a prank among old friends, Mr. Trickle. You know how it is. And what's this about you actually taking the supervisor's job? You're not qualified, and you don't know the town."

"You might have thought about that a little sooner, Mr. Ryan. I think I can handle the job quite nicely, though I'll have plenty to learn at first, just as anyone would."

"Now look, fella, don't get cute with me," retorted Ryan, apparently not reading this jury of one with much acuity. "If you try to follow through with this, I'll have Jim Dunlap fire your ass, and you'll be on your way in no time."

"Now don't get hot, Mr. Ryan. And if I'm going to be fired, I'd better finish this sale bill job first."

Ryan clamped down even harder on his pipe, turned on his heel and slammed the back office door.

"Jim, I want you to fire that smart-ass fella back there. We don't need his kind in our town."

"Wait a minute, Ryan. I need him more than he needs me. Good printers are hard to find right now."

"Then talk him out of taking the supervisor's job. Otherwise, Si will have to give up the presidency of his state association, and the whole town'll look foolish."

"I've already talked with Trickle," Jim said, "and he seems set on following through."

"Well then, dammit, don't expect any more of my printing business." Ryan left in a cloud of pipe smoke.

"Hey, Jake, you're going to pi the type if you don't stop hammering the shit out of that planer," Harry Campbell shouted back at Jake from the other side of the Model 14 Linotype.

"Oh, yeah, thanks," replied Jake, as he let up on his wooden hammer with which he had been mindlessly pummeling the wood block planer used to smooth the type in the job forms. "Better pay attention to my work while I still have it."

Jake's mind raced. Should he follow through on the supervisor's position and risk losing his job? He could always get work as a printer; but, hey, he had a date Saturday night with a beautiful lady, his boss's daughter.

"And what are Kay and I going to do Saturday night?" Jake wondered, as his mind darted to a more immediate challenge. Jake had eliminated the westerns and war movies, narrowing the choices down to two romantic triangles: Loretta Young, William Holden and Robert Mitchum at the Princess in *Rachel and the Stranger*, or Tyrone Power, Linda Darnell and Rita Hayworth in *Blood and Sand* at the Madison. Or they could go dancing to Eddy Howard at the Hub Ballroom. Jake smiled. If only he could dance.

Jake spent that Saturday morning with Charlie Durbin, one of the high school printer's devils, at the Model 5 Linotype, for his first lesson in how to set hot type. "You don't punch the keys—just tap them—and they release the mats—no force needed. The letters used most are at the left of the keyboard, near the space band release, so you move your left hand very little, just keep your fingers spread in a fan and tap each key with the nearest finger tip."

Jake got a lot of satisfaction from training printer's devils. This was true apprenticeship. Charlie had the mechanical aptitude and could see that there was a real craft to be learned.

"Take your time. When you get a line filled, let me look at it. If it's too loose, you'll get a squirt of liquid lead through the line. It will jam up everything and can hit your left leg, which you wouldn't appreciate, I can assure you. Better to do some hand spacing to fill out a line than risk a squirt."

By eleven o'clock Charlie was sending lines of mats up the first elevator and over to meet the metal pot without Jake looking over his shoulder. By noon both teacher and apprentice were feeling good about themselves.

In the afternoon Jake was feeling like the novice, as he anxiously prepared for his date. He took his coupe to Herb Murray's Phillips 66 station, where for twenty-five cents you could wash your car using Herb's hose, mitt, soap and chamois.

At the rooming house Jake surveyed his new wardrobe of dressy clothes and decided upon the grey herringbone suit jacket and the charcoal slacks. He came by Ernie's place later, both to have him check him out and teach him how to tie his tie. "You sure look handsome, just like an up-and-coming politician taking our community's best looking lady out on the town." Ernie smiled, almost wishing—more than almost—that he were in his friend's shoes and finery.

"And that's almost the way I feel, except for the politician part. I'm beginning to have second thoughts."

"Don't look to me for answers on that one. All I know is you are coming out of a shell. Whether it's meeting Kay or your anger at being humiliated, I don't know; but you're different, like all of a sudden you want to take on the world after a life lived in its shadows."

"Whatever or whoever I am, wish me well tonight. I feel like a teenager going to his first prom. Pleased with myself but awkward and unsteady as a newborn colt." Ernie did wish him well, because he did think a lot of this new fellow in town who had become his buddy.

Precisely at six Jake drove his spotless coupe up to the Dunlap home. New Stetson fedora in hand, he twisted the ringer on the door and waited. Jim opened the door.

"Come on in, Jake. Kay'll be down in a minute, or so she promises."

The men sat down in the living room. Jim turned down H. V. Kaltenborn and the news on his hulking RCA console, almost the size of the jukebox at Peachie's but in subdued walnut veneer.

"You look like a man about town. Never would have thought you a clothes horse."

"I never have been; but Kay is, well, you know, very attractive. Don't want to embarrass her."

Kay could be heard coming down the front staircase into the front room. "I hope you two men have solved all the world's problems." Kay's Doris Day smile lifted the hearts of both men. She looked like a million dollars, they thought. Straight burgundy skirt hemmed just below the calves, belted at the waist, topped with a solid eggshell rayon blouse and an over-the-shoulders burgundy jacket.

She took her long wool coat, a deep forest green with an empire collar, out of the hall closet, handed it to Jake, who was on his feet close by, fidgeting. "Please help me with my coat," she said while putting a cream wool beret onto her strawberry blond hair at a rakish angle.

"I guess we're off, Jim," said Jake. "We're having dinner at Maple Shade and then into Peoria for a movie. We shouldn't be late." Kay smiled puckishly. "We don't have to clock in with Jim, Jake. After all, we are adults."

"I just meant—oh, let's go."

In the car Kay turned to Jake. "I shouldn't be so forward, but this evening you look like Montgomery Clift." Just being mentioned with the dark, brooding but good looking young actor made Jake wince.

"Now don't get me flustered. I'm nervous enough as it is. I've never had a dinner date before, let alone with someone like you." He paused. "Feel free to teach me proper manners; I'll be all thumbs."

Maple Shade was a big country home with a wrap-around porch, converted into a steak and seafood restaurant, ten miles north of Peoria on old Route 88. The hot corn fritters, light, fluffy and dusted in powdered sugar, are known throughout central Illinois.

Jake hadn't thought to make a reservation, so the two were directed to the small bar where they found a tiny table for two. "I'll have Pabst, ma'am, and in a hurry, please—I'm new at this." Jake chuckled, surprised at his own humor. Kay ordered a Canadian Club with club soda. "Light on the CC, please," she added.

"This is fun. I haven't been out like this in years."

"You're kidding. I'd think the fellows would be lined up six-deep outside the Dunlap home."

"For several years after my husband was killed, I wasn't interested; and not many men are interested in reading all one thousand pages of *Raintree County*."

"One thousand and sixty-six, to be precise."

The hostess came in and led them to their table in what had been the home's original dining room. Six tables had been squeezed in, there was a small fire in the fireplace, and the room was warm with the banter and laughter of couples and foursomes enjoying Saturday night out.

Jake encouraged Kay to have the rock lobster tail, but she demurred because of the $5 tariff, instead ordering the fried chicken. Jake ordered a T-bone and another Pabst. "I'll Be Seeing You" was wafting into the room from a piano in the former living room.

"Kay, I'm pinching myself to see if I haven't died and gone to heaven."

Kay smiled, thinking that it was fun. And for his first real date, Jake was doing just fine.

"And now you're going to become an elected official, I read in our very own newspaper."

"And that's where the storm clouds blot out the sun in my life. Should I? On Thursday this guy Lloyd Ryan tried to scare me out of it. Said he'd have me fired."

"Jim would never fire you over that. He says you're the best thing to happen to the operation of the back shop in years, and he says you're as solid as the stone make-up tables."

"That's nice to hear, but I've always been the opposite of the hail fellow well met, and that's what being a public official is all about, isn't it?"

Just then a tall, good looking fellow came up to the table. "Kay Townsend, is that you? Of course it's you, just as beautiful as when you were a Chi O at Illinois."

Kay grasped his hand. "Bob Bowman, Sigma Nu. We double-dated for the White Rose Formal! See, I can remember those good old days.

"Bob, this is my friend, Jake Trickle."

"Pleased to meet you, Jake. Did you go to Illinois? What house were you in?"

"No, I'm afraid I never got to college."

Bob turned back to Kay, dismissing Jake. Bob was practicing law in Peoria with a firm that handled Caterpillar's legal affairs and practicing his golf game at the Mt. Hawley Country Club, which he had just joined.

"Kay, you must quit hiding your golden light under a basket. I'm going to call to see if I can talk you into a round of golf."

"You're thoughtful, but I'm afraid my golf game never graduated from the U of I."

"Better get back to my table. Good to meet you, Jake. Take good care of this beautiful lady."

"I'll sure try, Bob.

"Nice guy, I think," Jake said, returning his gaze to Kay.

"A little full of himself, I'm afraid, but I'm glad to see he's doing well. He and my husband were in the same fraternity, so we double-dated and drank lots of that beer you have in front of you.

"And you're doing well, too. You sure have thrown the town powers-that-be back on their heels with your plans to accept the supervisor's post. I'll bet Ryan is still smarting."

"You just can't treat people like they don't exist. That's what Ryan did to me. But as for doing well, I've never known what that means. I live in a rooming house— always have—and have been content with my printing and reading, my own private world of books and type. I've observed small towns, but I've never really cared about who was important and who wasn't.

"All of a sudden, maybe those things do matter. Maybe the big fish ought to get their comeuppance. Maybe a guy like me needs to jump into the fishbowl. What do you think, Kay? I sense that you're on the outside edge, too, in many ways. You have your teaching and your books—"

"And my father Jim. He's the dearest man in the world, and he needs me. His heart has never stopped aching over the loss of my mother when I was born. Father and I are muy simpático. My life will be as full as I could ever want so long as I can bring a smile to his big round face."

Dinner came, the hot fritters in a miniature wicker basket lined with wax paper. Talk turned to the movie choices. Jake said that Linda Darnell and Rita Hayworth appealed to him, while Kay countered with a preference for William Holden.

The second show at the Madison ended at eleven, and half an hour later Jake saw the green neon sign for the Hub Ballroom, off Route 88 in the farm village of Edelstein. "How could there be a ballroom in the middle of those cornfields?" Jake wondered.

"Oh, the Hub's a great place. An interesting story. The owners built the place to house an expanding John Deere implement dealership. Then they threw a thank-you dance for customers on their new hardwood showroom floors. It was such a hit, they gave another dance, then another, and finally moved the tractors and plows out all together. I wonder who's playing tonight?"

"Eddy Howard. I know, because I came across the ad as I researched plans for our date."

"Oh, a really danceable band. Could we stop by and listen to their last set?" She paused. "You didn't appreciate how bold I can be, did you?"

"But I've never danced in my life," Jake said as he turned off 88 into Edelstein.

The Hub sits on the slightest rise among a huddle of white frame homes, surrounded by a tabletop expanse of rich black Sable soils, purplish in the moonlight. With only half an hour remaining the ticket-takers had abandoned their posts. The half-acre dance floor was crowded with couples who moved slowly to a Howard classic, "Careless, Now That You're Gone From Me, I Care Less." Eddy's thin tenor voice crooned to the pole microphone he embraced, and the four saxophones wailed softly behind him.

Unfolded wood chairs circled the dance floor. Jake and Kay found two, then decided to stand.

"I sure wish I knew how to dance. I'll bet Bob Bowman could twirl you around the floor like a whirling dervish."

"Come, let me show you." Kay took Jake by the hand and pulled him to face her. Oblivious to the accomplished dancers near them, Kay took charge.

"Stand straight. Put your right hand, fingers spread, on my back, a bit above the waist. Come on, there isn't much time.

"Now take my right hand and hold it out straight, like this."

"Couldn't we just hold it right like this, say for several days?" Jake suggested, almost euphoric with the simple touching. Kay's back was firm, her curled, soft hair at his face.

"Now you make a simple box with your feet, leading with your left foot, and pulling your right up and then over to the right. Then back with the right and pull the left back and to the right to complete the box."

Kay pulled Jake forward and through the box with Jake stumbling along. They tried again; this time Jake stopped when he should have started, and Kay tumbled into him, face against his neck, her body against his. They remained that way for a moment, Jake too excited and perplexed to know what to do.

"Oops, I'm sorry. I'm afraid your pupil goes to the back of the class."

"I'm enjoying this, but we could use more practice."

The band continued with Howard's signature tune, "To Each His Own," (I've found my own, my one and only you), which signaled the last dance. At the door to the Dunlap home Jake said simply, "Kay, this is the best time I've ever had in my life. Thank you. If there is any chance we could do this again, I'll go back to my room thinking I'm about the luckiest fella in the world."

"Of course, it was fun for me, too, though I will have to look into surgery for my toes," she laughed. Kay leaned forward, hands grasping Jake's arms, and gave him a peck on the right cheek. Then she was through the door before Jake knew it.

⧗

Jim Dunlap waved Jake to his desk as the fellows came out of the back shop Monday afternoon. "If you're really serious about becoming township supervisor, here's a book you'd better start reading up on." Jake took the small book that Jim offered and read, *Guide and Duties of Township Officials, 1948.*

"Thanks, Jim. I looked for something like this at the library, but Ernie and I couldn't find anything of much use. Kay was going to do some calling around as well to see what she could come up with."

"There's a lot more to the job than most folks appreciate. Poor relief, and fifty miles or more of township roads.

Our library is also operated by the township, not the city, as most people think."

That night at Harry's, over two mugs of Gipps, Jake pored over the township officials book. Illinois has fifteen hundred townships, most of them perfect six mile squares. Each township elects a supervisor, four trustees, clerk, assessor and road commissioner. The supervisor and trustees comprise the town board.

In 1949 township government was a last vestige of pure democracy, like its model, town government in New England. At the Annual Town Meeting on the second Tuesday in April, all electors—registered voters—are authorized to participate. The electors elect a moderator for the annual meeting and then set about approving the property tax levies and budgets for the relief, road and library funds. If the town meeting wants to cut last year's poor relief budget by half, they can do it. In 1949 the citizens could make all the big decisions for the township. In reality few citizens show up at the town hall for the annual meeting, but any organized group could take over the meeting if it had the numbers.

Newly elected officials like Jake, elected on the first Tuesday in April of an odd-numbered year, are sworn in after the annual town meeting later in the month. "So Si McDermott will handle the meeting coming up," Jake realized, relieved.

As Jake read on, he began to think anxiously, "What in the devil have I gotten myself in for?" This is complicated stuff—making decisions on whether to grant grocery and rent and doctor's office vouchers to applicants for poor relief; approving the road commissioner's budget; appointment of the library board and approval of its budget; maintenance of the township cemetery; control of noxious weeds and Canada thistles. "What the hell are Canada thistles?" wondered Jake.

"Election and appointment of Assistant Supervisors." The section jumped out at Jake. "I could sure use an assistant," he thought, smiling.

"In townships of more than 5,000 population, one assistant supervisor shall be elected for every additional 2,500 persons, or part thereof. The assistant supervisor's sole duty shall be to serve as a full voting member of the county board. . . ."

"Harry, how many people are there in Starke Township?" Elbows on the bar, Jake cradled his half-filled mug in front of him, eyes peering over the mug. Harry was leaning against the bar, arms spread out.

"Around 5,000, I'd guess. The city has 4,000, so there'd be right about 5,000 or a few more."

An idea was coming to Jake. "How could I find out for sure?"

"Where else do you think? The library, you dummy. As much time as you spend there, you'd think you'd know."

Jake finished his beer in one big draft and headed for the library. It wasn't quite nine.

Five thousand three hundred and twenty four, declared the 1940 report of the U.S. Census Bureau.

⌛

Saturday morning Jake put in three hours at the office, coaching Charlie Durbin at the Model 8 Linotype. "When Charlie gets out of high school, with my training, he'll have a good middle-class job for life, anywhere in the country," Jake thought, feeling good. "I'll set some ad guts Sunday afternoon," Jake continued to himself, realizing that he'd have to take off at three on busy Tuesday afternoon to attend his first Annual Town Meeting. Then on the spur of the moment, he took a walk the mile west of town to the Starke Township Hall, turning over in his head the idea that came to him at Wilson's earlier that week.

The town hall, built in 1892, was a simple white clapboard building of the neat rectangular proportions idealized by the Greeks, single-pitch, straight slant roof, chimney up the back wall, three modest vertical windows on a side. Half a dozen forty-foot evergreens provided a stately backdrop. "Like a thousand town halls and country chapels and one-room school buildings," thought Jake. A '49 Buick sedan, ruby red, was parked on the gravel drive.

Jake tried the door and entered. Bars of sunlight coming in the south windows cut sharply across the hall, illumining shafts of dust particles. Wood folding chairs were set out in eight rows, five on each side of a single aisle that led to a platform, raised maybe six inches. This third of the hall was separated from the rest by a low, polished oak railing. American and State of Illinois flags hung from wood poles in each of the back corners. Behind, at a large desk off to the left, sat a fiftyish man in a herringbone jacket, leather elbow patches, wearing polished tan boots.

"Come on in," he shouted, in an offhand manner. The fellow continued arranging papers on his desk. Jake walked to the railing.

"How can I help you?"

"I'm Jake Trickle, and I'm guessing you're Mr. Silas McDermott."

"So you're the new supervisor. Yeah, I'm Si McDermott, just getting the books ready to hand over to you after the annual meeting. You sure you want this job?"

"I'm sure I don't want to back down from Lloyd Ryan's making me the butt of his joke."

"Hell, you weren't the butt of his joke. I was." McDermott snorted, looking like the prosperous farmer everybody said he was. Ruddy face, thick dark hair in a short brush cut, almost a crew cut. Just fleshy enough to suggest that as a young man he had done the farm work but now had the luxury of turning that over to tenants.

"Then he made fools out of both of us," Jake said. "I didn't deserve what I got."

"Well, just maybe, I did," McDermott responded, looking back across the hall out the north windows.

"Local government is important work, though most folks take it for granted, Mr. Trickle. At any time, I have twenty-five to thirty cases of poor folks who don't know where their next meal is coming from. We provide groceries, rent, coal. And the sixty miles of township roads right here, and a thousand times more statewide, are critical to getting farmers' crops and livestock trucked to elevators and markets, and school children to school on the yellow buses. And the library, which I'm told you frequent, is our responsibility.

"And then there's the county board duties—more roads, of course, the county farm for the homeless, the sheriff's operation, the county hospital, on and on—big business—and I enjoy the hell out of it, Mr. Trickle. And dammit, I'm good at it."

"Everybody I talk to says that's so, Mr. McDermott. And I don't want to make a fool of myself right off the bat. That's why I wandered out here, halfway hoping I'd find you." He hesitated briefly.

"You know the population of the township, I'm sure, Mr. McDermott."

"Yeah, five thousand, plus a few."

"Five thousand three hundred plus, according to the last census," Jake noted. "So why don't you have an assistant supervisor for the township, Mr. McDermott? You're entitled to one."

"Well, we're just over the population threshold, and we'd be the only township with more than one member on the county board, so I never pushed it. Didn't want the other supervisors to think we were being uppity."

"Well, how about, at the town meeting on Tuesday, I refuse to accept the supervisor's job. What would happen then?"

"Well, I'm confident the town board would appoint me to fill the post. Why do you ask? I thought you said you were going to take it."

"Mr. McDermott, this local politics is all new to me. In fact, just being out and around like this, talking with you as if I belonged here, is all new to me.

"But all of a sudden, I burn to do two things—teach that Lloyd Ryan a lesson and get a little respect. So I was thinking last night, what if I refused the supervisor's job, and you were restored to the post. And then," Jake paused, "then the town board named me to the assistant supervisor's job, which I could handle because I could learn from others on the county board, like you, as we went along. Then wouldn't everybody come out a winner, and wouldn't it look like I patched back together what Lloyd Ryan had torn apart with his prank?"

The wheels turned in McDermott's head. "God damn but that's a nifty idea, Mr. Trickle. You sure you want to do it that way?"

"So long as we have a deal about the town board naming me assistant supervisor."

"You've got a deal, Mr. Trickle," McDermott said, beaming.

"Call me Jake. May I call you Si?"

⌛

"Are you and Jake going out again this week?" Jim Dunlap asked from behind the slim Saturday *Chicago Tribune* he was glancing through. Kay was also in the living room, flipping the pages of the new *LIFE* magazine. Minnie White was in the kitchen, washing dishes after having served breakfast.

"Jake's taking me to the Lariat Club for dinner and then to the Inglaterra Ballroom, where Griff Williams is playing."

"Another expensive evening in Peoria. Guess I'll have to boost Jake's wages, so he can afford you." Jim smiled, though his face was still hidden by the newspaper, which he held straight up.

"Do you think that's a problem?"

"Not really. With his long hours, he probably earns as much as you do teaching, probably more, now that I think of it; and what else does he have to spend it on? Earl Turner at the bank told me—I'm sure he shouldn't have—that Jake had moved a nice savings account to the bank. And I can't think of a better object for his lavishness. Do you really like Jake?"

"Well, I don't know what you mean by 'really,' but I do like him. Jake is different from the college boys I remember at Paul's Sigma Nu fraternity. They were outgoing, brash, devil-may-care types, but often rather hollow, I thought.

"Jake is so reserved. He gives you the sense that he's standing several feet behind where he actually is. Yet he's so alive to learning and not just from his books. He's coming over here this afternoon, an hour before we leave for dinner, so I can teach him the basics of dancing, something he's never done before. Last week he asked me, sincerely, to correct him on his table manners at dinner. Can you imagine one of the Sigma Nu's, so confident on the surface, ever asking a girl to correct him?

"It's as if Jake has lived all his life in a shell, and only now at, what, thirty or so, he's beginning to peck himself out to meet the world. And I think he likes what he finds, so far anyway."

"So you do like Jake. As for that shell, let him peck out at a reasonable pace. Otherwise, like Humpty Dumpty, he may take a great fall."

"You don't think he's that fragile, do you? He seems quite strong to me."

"A tough outer skin is often needed to protect delicate innards, Kay. Now I don't know if that's true, but it sounded good. Anyway, I think we should assume that about people." Jim had put the newspaper in his lap, feet stretched out on the ottoman. "Kay deserves to have some fun," he thought. "And maybe she also is beginning, finally, to pull down the walls she built up around herself after her husband was killed."

⧗

Kay led Jake up to the third floor of the old Dunlap home. "This is the ballroom, at least that's what it's always been called. If this old house were really grand, then this room really would be a small ballroom. But, it's enough for us to learn to dance."

Kay kicked back a dusty old rug that covered the hardwood floors, put a big 33 rpm record—Horace Heidt—onto the turntable and put the needle on near the edge. The strains of "I Don't Want to Set the World on Fire (I just want to start a flame in your heart)," filled the room.

"This tune has a good lilt." Kay turned to Jake, who just stood there, admiring. "Well, remember how to hold me?"

"Yes," Jake declared, and he moved to her.

"Later, when we've got the steps down pat, you'll be able to turn me with your left arm, using your right arm—remember firmly against my back—as a kind of fulcrum."

"But I just want to repeat our stumbling act, where you fall into me," Jake joked, playfully pulling Kay closer to him. He breathed deeply of her cologne. To Jake, it was truly intoxicating. He kissed her hair without quite touching it, wondering if he were doing that right.

"We'll stumble plenty, I'm sure," Kay laughed.

⧗

At the end of the evening Jake walked Kay onto the Dunlap wraparound porch that enveloped the front door. "Say goodnight to me in the vestibule. It's cold out here. And thanks for another fun evening, this time of real dancing. And not much stumbling."

"Not enough stumbling," Jake inserted.

"Now, put your arms around me and kiss me, darn it."

"The arms I can do"—and he did—" but I've never kissed before—"

Kay put her arms around Jake's back, high up, reached up, and kissed Jake hard and long. Jake responded.

Jake's back felt muscled and taut, even through the blazer. It had been almost a decade since she had held anyone. Finally, she pulled back.

"This was a great evening. Let's do it again—soon."

Jake nodded, a little unsteady, and turned back through the front door into a bracing mid-April evening, oblivious to the world around him.

Jake drove out to Ernie's cabin. It was 1 A.M. and Ernie was asleep, the embers in the Franklin stove still providing a smidgen of warmth.

"I'm sorry to bother you, but I have to talk with someone, and you're about it. I just had the most wonderful date known to man. Kay is the most incredibly beautiful and wonderful woman in the world; and she said, 'Let's go out again—soon!' And I kissed her, really kissed her. And I'll never forget her cologne. It's like lilac with a punch. I'm walking on air, and I had to tell someone."

"That's wonderful. You're a lucky guy," Ernie said, happy for Jake, a tad envious of a situation that he had never known and didn't expect to.

They sat up for a couple of hours. Jake recounted the dinner and dancing, and how he had learned how to jitterbug, if just a little at this point. He filled Ernie in on his deal with Si McDermott, which did sound brilliant to

Ernie, untutored though he was in politics. Jake was a new Jake Trickle.

They agreed to take a long walk on Sunday morning along the banks of the Spoon River. Ernie promised to enlighten Jake about the warblers and wildflowers that would be appearing soon. Maybe not to compare with dancing, Ernie said, but a close second. After all, Ernie had seen a gold-crowned kinglet this past morning, so the colorful warblers were only a few weeks away. Jake wasn't listening, but that was okay with Ernie. He hummed to himself, "Ah, sweet mystery of life, I've found you."

Ernie had also long been inebriated with love but had never shared that with anyone, not even the person he loved.

⧗

The Annual Town Meeting for Starke Township came off without a hitch. Jake looked downright impressive in his grey herringbone suit with a wide silk tie of giant paisley design in gold, red and navy. Twenty-five people attended, primarily the township officials and their wives and a few retired farmers with time on their hands. Ethel Gray whispered to Ruth Hollister as to how the new young man reminded her of the actor, what was his name, the loner with the distant blue-gray eyes. "Oh, Montgomery Clift, you mean," Ruth said. They smiled in agreement.

Jake had worked hard to memorize his short speech. He stammered at first, but that was engaging to folks who themselves weren't comfortable with public speaking. Jake said he realized what a distinguished leader the township—indeed the whole state—had in Silas McDermott. Therefore, though he had a strong desire to serve the public, he, Jake Trickle, was refusing to serve as Township Supervisor, and he hoped the town board would see fit to appoint their longtime leader, Silas McDermott, to that important post.

The audience, which had been clued in beforehand by an appreciative McDermott, broke into hearty applause when Jake sat down. Si McDermott then explained that under the law Starke Township was authorized one assistant supervisor because its population exceeded 5,000 persons, according to the last census. He expressed appreciation for the magnanimous gesture made by Jake Trickle, a fine, capable newcomer to the community, and proposed that Mr. Trickle be appointed to this post, new yet authorized to Starke Township, by the annual meeting of the town's citizens.

"I nominate Jake Trickle to the job," thundered Larry Foglesonger, a retired farmer. Jake was voted in by acclamation.

McDermott then presented the budgets for the several town funds for the coming year, which were approved without comment. Road commissioner Rusty Smith asked the town meeting for authorization to buy a new Caterpillar road maintainer. "The John Deere we have is twenty years old, and the engine and transmission are both close to shot. We have money in the road fund, and if you want me to keep the roads graded and clean of snow, then I need a new machine."

Rusty had cleared this with McDermott in advance, and the request was approved without dissent. McDermott ran a tight ship in his little fiefdom. After the meeting the wives of the four town trustees served coffee and cookies, and Si introduced Jake all around. Everyone stood on the riser near the fireplace, which was stoked with coal to warm at least the back of the hall on a raw spring day.

"What committees would you like to serve on at the county board, Jake?" asked Foglesonger, who had been on the board in the 1930s. "I always enjoyed the license and

liquor committee," he went on. "In one evening the committee would tour the five establishments in the county
that we licensed to see that there were no problems. Every
owner set us up with drinks, and by the last place we were
three sheets to the wind."

"Oh, pshaw," broke in his wife, Carolyn, looking every
bit the proper Baptist matron and attractive at that. "If
you had been, I'd never have let you back in the house."
Larry just winked at Jake, savoring the good old days.

"I haven't given much thought to the question," said
Jake, "but I do enjoy a glass of beer now and then. First,
I'd better do my homework on the problems facing the
county board and how I might contribute."

Jake was feeling good as he headed back to the office
at five-thirty. Since he had missed work that afternoon,
the day before the paper came out, Jake now had to pay
for his civic service by catching up on page make-up and
printing the first section of the paper. He carefully hung
his suit, shirt and tie on coat hooks and slipped on work
trousers, shirt and a clean, starched printer's apron just
back from the laundry.

"That was real legerdemain," declared Jim, after Jake
recounted the annual meeting.

"But only because you gave me the township guide-
book."

"Why don't you try your hand at writing—or setting—
the story. I'd like to see how you'd like it said."

"I'll give it a shot, but this writing is new to me. I've set
enough palaver written by fellas like you, though, so
maybe I can kind of fill in the blanks from those stories."

Jake went back to the Model 8. The back shop was still
buzzing with activity. The printer's devils were sawing and
routing lead "cuts" that had been cast to represent the
illustrations for the grocery and automobile ads, and to
announce the new lines of John Deere and Allis Chalmers
spring planting equipment. Four-row corn planters were

the newest advance, replacing the two-row equipment that had been standard for years.

Harry Campbell was hunched over the Model 14, pumping out both ad copy for the big grocery ads and heads for the one- and two-column news stories. Dave Gelvin was atop the newspaper press, which clanked and rumbled as he neared completion of side one of the first eight-page section. The air was prickly dry and pungent with inks and gasoline rags.

Jake took a big pull into his lungs and loved it. "Ah, great for the nasal passages," he observed. Then he began tapping on the pluck-release keyboard.

Silas McDermott of rural Williamstown, and president-elect of the Illinois Association of County Officials, was appointed to a full four-year term as Starke Township Supervisor on Tuesday afternoon, in a surprising but much appreciated action at the Starke Township Annual Meeting.

"Too wordy and not punchy enough," Jake thought, "but I don't want to embarrass Si in what I say either." He picked up the four lines of type he had set, still hot, rolled them around briefly in his left hand to avoid getting burned then pitched them on the floor with the lead shavings trimmed off each line as they came out of the hulking machine. Jake started over.

Starke Township Supervisor Silas McDermott was appointed to a fifth term in that post Tuesday at the

township's annual meeting. This action followed a surprise statement by supervisor-elect Jake Trickle that he
would decline the office if he could be assured that
McDermott would continue to provide leadership locally
and in his role as president-elect of the Illinois Association of County Officials.

Trickle was then appointed by the citizens assembled
to serve as the township's assistant supervisor, who is to
have a full seat on the Williams County Board. This is a
new post for Williams County.

Any township with more than 5,000 population is
authorized by state law to elect or appoint an assistant
supervisor to the county board. Starke Township, home
of county seat Williamstown, with a population of 5,300,
is the only township in the county with more than 5,000
residents. Starke is taking advantage of this option for the
first time.

Following these actions, McDermott thanked Trickle
for his gracious action and pledged to serve the township,
county and state to the best of his abilities. McDermott
went on to predict that "young Mr. Trickle will add sound
judgment and energy to the county board."

"How does this read, Jim?"

After looking it over, Jim said, "You appear to have a
knack for this. I think I'll call it in to Ziggy O'Connell at
the *Peoria Star*. Because of Si's standing in state politics,
this ought to make the wires.

"Now, please, get back to the shop, Mr. County Board
Member, and let's get the first section put to bed before we
get out of here. Then I'll buy you a beer at Harry's."

LINCOLN HALL

University of Illinois

The Lincoln Lodge

Jake picked Kay up at 6 A.M. on a beautiful May Saturday. The sun was shooting between the large frame homes that lined the street. Robins and finches chased their kind hither and yon in a mad courtship frenzy. Kay met Jake at the door, small suitcase in hand. She kissed him lightly.

Jim Dunlap had told Jake that the state's leading student of local government was Prof. Philip Monypenny at the University of Illinois. Jake used the *Republican's* phone to call the university, where he reached the professor. Monypenny would meet with Jake on the following Saturday morning in his office in Lincoln Hall.

"Kay, would you be my navigator on this trip, as you must know where Lincoln Hall is, and we could go out to dinner . . . and even stay over?" Jake added, with great hope in his voice.

"What a great idea. You learn about county government, and I introduce you to my old haunts on campus. Then we have a romantic dinner at Katsina's, if it's still hidden away in downtown Champaign."

Kay suggested that they stay at the Lincoln Lodge on University Avenue, a new yet rustic, low-slung hostelry in the motel style that was catching on. "You'll have to call ahead to make reservations for our two rooms, as it's quite popular."

They drove beyond Peoria on US 150, giddy, like college freshmen on a walk-out. They talked nonstop from one farm town to the next, then were comfortably silent till the next town, drinking in the crisp, sun-warmed air that streamed in the car windows, opened an inch.

"I can't wait to show you the U of I. I spent four wonderful years there, and this is the first time I've been back. I hope it hasn't changed too much."

"And this is where you met your husband." Not really a question, as Jake knew it to be the case.

Kay looked wistfully straight ahead at the bleached two-lane pavement that rushed under the coupe at 55 miles an hour.

"Paul, my husband for three days, was tall, slender, boyish looking, yet handsome. For some reason, I'm recalling—for the first time since 1941—an exchange where my sorority and his fraternity came together for dinner. It was Wednesday evening, which was date night, so after eating we went with several other couples to Prehn's, a popular hangout. We drank beer and sang bawdy songs at the tops of our lungs. I can still see us, standing on our chairs, who knows why, singing endless verses of 'Roll Me Over in the Clover.' What marvelous, innocent times for people who could afford college, even if just on a shoestring.

"Our junior and senior years, Paul and I had the best of all times. We were bright enough to do well with our studies and still act as if life were created for football and basketball games, exchanges, beer busts and picnics at Turkey Run, over near the Indiana line.

"I get a little misty-eyed just thinking about it."

"I envy you. At that time I was perfecting my life as a kind of working hermit. The printing shop—which I loved, and still do—followed by supper, the library, a couple of beers and back to the room."

"Well, let's both have fun today and tonight. I'm feeling like a coed again."

With Kay navigating, Jake weaved through Champaign into Urbana on Green Street. They found a parking spot on Wright Street, just in front of Kay's Chi Omega sorority house, across the street from venerable old Lincoln Hall, a tile-roofed, Italianate classroom building that could have been a major government building in Venice or Florence.

"Gosh, I wonder if the housemother is still 'Mrs. B,' and if she'd remember me."

Kay grabbed Jake's hand and they went up the three steps onto the colonnaded porch. Two blonde coeds in sweatshirts, pedal pushers and saddle shoes were on their way out, rubbing sleep from their eyes.

"Yes, Mrs. B is the housemother," one said, looking Kay over to see if she would pass muster as an alum of the house. They concluded to themselves she would.

Jake waited on the porch while Kay stepped inside.

As the two coeds went out to the sidewalk, they gave Jake the once-over. In the world of Greek fraternities and sororities, Kay explained later, much time is spent sizing up other people to see if they fit a style set somewhere, nobody knows where, by the most confident and carefree of that age, and adopted slavishly by those less confident, who feel a need to belong.

On the plus side, friendships are forged over four years that often last a lifetime. And for the upwardly mobile middle class, and even working-class sorts who have natural beauty or athletic skill, the system imparts many of the social graces that the upper classes would pick up at home or at their Ivy League schools.

"He's handsome, in a rough sort of way, don't you think? Reminds me of Montgomery Clift."

"Yeah, but he looks a little uncomfortable, don't you think, as if this isn't his world."

"I don't care. I could see scrunching with him against the vestibule wall at closing time."

Kay returned with Mrs. Mary Barnhill. A sprightly seventyish lady of great southern charm, Mrs. B had been housemother for twenty years, since her husband had died unexpectedly, leaving her with little but her charm. They exchanged pleasantries, and Jake began to think his natural shyness among strangers worked nicely when combined with the quick, engaging smile that Kay had brought out of him. No need for lots of talk on his part, just punctuate the conversation with a smile and a nod here and there.

"My, what a handsome gentleman you have with you, Kay," said Mrs. B, extending her hand, which Jake took, nodding, smiling. "You two must come back soon, maybe this fall for a football game, Kay, ya' hear now!"

Kay took Jake's arm this time, guiding him across the street onto the grassy campus Quadrangle. The Quad was the heart of the university, framed by stately classroom buildings, anchored at the south end by a plump domed auditorium, which looked more like a seated Buddha than the Roman Pantheon it sought to reflect.

"This isn't a beautiful campus, not when compared with those at Indiana University or up in Madison at the University of Wisconsin. Too flat and unadorned by lakes or woods. Yet for me it was the experiences and the friendships that endow the campus with its enduring mystique. Thanks for bringing me. I'm coming alive again."

Kay dropped Jake off at Prof. Monypenny's office, a long hike up to the third floor of Lincoln Hall. She was then off to Gregory Hall, where she had taken many courses.

Hmmmmmn! "Come in." Hmmmmn! Philip Monypenny beckoned Jake. The large, high-ceilinged office was in great disarray. His large wooden desk and two library tables in the room were piled high with textbooks, file folders and assorted papers. Monypenny himself looked to be in disarray. A thick shock of straw-colored hair tumbled down his forehead. His vested, grey pin-stripe suit was wrinkled, Phi Beta Kappa key dangling on the fob from the vest watch pocket. He was apparently at work grading hourly exams, even though the final exams were only two weeks away.

"Good of you to come in, Mr. Trickle." Hmmmmn. The professor unconsciously filled the breaks in his speech with back-of-the-throat humming. "Not many elected officials look me up for advice. I wish there were some formalized training for new board members, as many of the business practices of local government are antiquated or nonexistent. If they are not improved, the federal government will someday, using that as the rationale, sweep in with all its money and take over much of local government's work." Hmmmmn.

Jake listened, almost transfixed. He had never heard a professor before, and it appeared he was in for a nonstop lecture. "This eccentric man is not much older than I am. Must be descended from Plato," Jake mused, smothering the hint of a smile.

"The key to understanding government lies in the budget. Where does the money come from, and how is it spent? Is it spent on the right things, and is it spent wisely, efficiently, honestly?"

Talking nonstop, hmmmns serving as paragraph markers, Monypenny handed Jake a copy of his small book on *Local Government in Illinois*. He was saying, "Illinois has more units of local government—taxing units, that is— than any state in the nation. So we have lots of democracy. Too much, if you ask me, because citizens can't monitor all of them, no matter how hard they try; and the antiquated accounting practices increase the possibilities of hanky-panky. Please remember that, Mr. Trickle. While I'm not saying that Williams County is corrupt, mind you, I am saying that clever officials can easily hoodwink not only citizens but also their fellow officials, who often just go along with matters the way they have always been done.

"So," hmmmn, "ask plenty of questions about why your county is doing what it's doing. For example, how many inmates are there in the county home, or poor farm, as it's often unfortunately called, and could they be cared for more humanely in another setting and at less cost to taxpayers? And how much is the county spending to build and maintain its roads, and how much is it paying for road oil, and hot mix? Few board members ask, or know how to compare costs, so I think a good new board member would want to become an expert on the budget, because that's the heart of any government."

At one o'clock Kay finally knocked on the professor's door, after standing in the corridor for half an hour. "This could go on all afternoon," she thought.

"Come in." Hmmmn. "Well, how do you do, miss? How can I help you? Are you in one of my classes? I don't recognize you." Hmmmn.

Jake explained the situation, thanked the professor for the book and the advice, and asked if he might call or write with follow-up questions. The kindly—even as a young man he seemed kindly—Monypenny said he would be delighted to respond.

"Just remember the budget; become the budget expert if you want to help modernize your county government!"

"Wow, is that what college is like? I couldn't get a word in edgewise at first, although later I just blurted my questions into the conversation. He knows so much, and I'm so ignorant. But he's a great guy, I think."

"Oh, you'd have loved college. Instead, you're putting yourself through a kind of college with all your reading and now your visits to college professors."

"I'd never have made the fraternity set, I'm sure, with my background and lack of social graces. But you're my tutor in all that, so you have the challenge of polishing me up." Jake laughed, and looked at Kay as if she represented the Venus on the pedestal at the central atrium of Lincoln Hall.

Prehn's was an architect's joke for a Moorish castle. Burgundy tile roofing over cream stucco, all doors and windows done in the traditional arches, tiny minarets jutting up here and there for no reason. Inside, stone flooring, high archways leading from large rooms into smaller nooks and crannies, high-back dark wood booths tucked here and there.

"I spent half my college years at Prehn's. We rallied here before and after varsity games, came here after study dates at the library, and almost took the place over for exchanges. God, but we were carefree—until the war came along."

Hamburgers finished, Kay took Jake's arm for a tour of the campus. Jake liked best the stacks in the Main Library. "I've never seen so many books," as they climbed the narrow stairs through the six compact stories of books that went on endlessly, to Jake's mind. "I'm looking for the American Lit section, which used to be on the fourth level. In my senior year, they awarded me use of a carrel, a study nook, like those along the outer walls, where I worked on my honors paper on Edna Ferber."

"Quiet, please!" harrumphed a professor from his own carrel; or maybe it was a graduate student struggling with a dissertation.

Next came a stroll through the Greek ghetto, where imposing three-story brick fraternity and sorority edifices in Tudor, Federal and Greek Revival styles tried to outdo each other in their grandeur. Kay had dated one or more fellows in the Beta, Phi Delt, AKL, Acacia, Sigma Chi and SAE houses, if Jake caught the names right.

"Each of the houses had its own singing chorus. When one of their fellows had offered his fraternity pin to a member of our sorority, they would come to our porch at night, after our closing hours, to serenade. I know I'm corny, but I still get a chill when I hear Bing Crosby sing the 'Sweetheart of Sigma Chi,' even though he couldn't touch the renditions done by the Sigma Chi house

here. . . . 'Oh, the girl of my dreams is the sweetest girl
. . .' " Kay sang the opening line softly and squeezed Jake's
arm.

Kay directed Jake out to the Lincoln Lodge. "Now I'll
pay for my own room. No arguments about that."

They signed in, and Jake carried their suitcases—Jake's
purchased the Tuesday before—to rooms 23 and 24, the
last two rooms on the second floor, at the far end from the
main lodge. Each door opened to the outside, in the new
style of roadside motor inns.

Katsina's restaurant was tucked away down a narrow
side street in downtown Champaign. The dark interior
was illumined primarily by tall candles at each small
table, the hot red wax melting like miniature lava flows
onto the straw baskets of the chianti bottles below.

Lex, the solicitous owner, greeted them warmly, telling
Jake his lady was so beautiful that he must seat them at
one of the two window tables so passersby could admire
her.

"Now you know why I insisted we come here," Kay
laughed as they were seated.

"And for you lovers—I can tell it in your eyes—a bottle
of my best Chianti Classico, on the house." Lex popped the
cork with a flourish and filled the small chianti glasses at
the table, white linen dinner napkin draped over his left
arm, hugely pleased with himself at his generosity, hoping
the tip would reflect same.

Over dinner the "lovers" talked about Edna Ferber and
her strong heroines, the Kinsey Report and whether
Americans have sex as often as reported, which they
doubted, and even about what would happen in China
now that the communists had pushed Chiang Kai-shek off
the mainland.

"I'll bet your U of I is relieved not to be playing Bradley
this year. The Braves would clobber the Illini. With
Billtown's own Paul Unruh on the team, we ought to go to

a Bradley game, but I don't have any ins for tickets. I'll bet your college friend Bob Bowman has tickets."

"Do I detect a note of jealousy?"

Kay looked absolutely smashing, thought Jake, his desire warmed by the Chianti and the candlelight. And Kay kept thinking the real Montgomery Clift couldn't hold a candle to her lover. She rather liked Lex's characterization.

"How can I be jealous of Bob Bowman when it's me you're with this weekend? I just wish I could sing the 'Sweetheart of Sigma Chi,' or that I had a jeweled pin to offer you."

"Thanks, but don't think a thing about my sentimental recollections today. It was simply a magical time and worth remembering. Do you have any magical memories?" As soon as she asked, Kay wanted to swallow the question.

Jake's eyes turned dark for a moment, then brightened. He lifted his chianti glass to Kay and said, "You're damned right, I do. Peachie's, Maple Shade, dancing at the Hub, Katsina's." Jake reached for Kay's hand, which she extended. He held it tight, his eyes glistening.

They returned to the Lincoln Lodge.

Jake and Kay embraced and kissed outside Room 24. "Thanks for a great day, Kay." At a loss for further words, Jake said goodnight and slipped over to Room 23. Five minutes later, minus coat and jacket, he was at her door.

"May I come in?"

"Yes." She opened the door into her dark room.

They made love, awkwardly at first, more passion than satisfaction. A little later, they made love again.

Jake buried his face in Kay's neck and shoulder, silent, for minutes. "Are you okay, Jake?" Kay asked, still holding Jake. "Yes, it's just that I never imagined a fellow could feel—I feel so alive, so happy, so, I don't know, so complete." They remained quiet, listening to their breathing. Soon they were asleep.

Williams County Courthouse

Chapter 6

A Taste of Politics

The Williams County Board of Supervisors met the second Thursday of each month in the second floor courtroom of the handsome Greek Revival courthouse built in 1856 when that dignified style was in vogue. The supervisors seated themselves around two large walnut tables, used by the plaintiffs and defendants on court days, and pushed together for county board meetings. Elected county officials sat in the first row of courtroom seats on the spectator side of the railing. The exceptions to this were county clerk James T. (Tommy) Jackson, who was seated next to county board chairman Col. Ernest M. Hazen (Colonel Hazen to almost everybody), and state's attorney James W. Emmerson, seated on the other side of Hazen, all three at one end of the joined table.

Members started gathering at nine o'clock for the important business of gossiping over coffee before the meeting, which began promptly at 9:30 A.M. The elected county officials rotated the chore of providing coffee and sweet rolls in the back of the courtroom.

Jake had butterflies as he walked down Main Street to the courthouse. Margy Humphrey had complimented him on the downright handsome figure he cut in his herringbone suit, declaring that Jake looked "just like a big city lawyer." Kay had given him a silver stick pin with a good-sized opal setting which had belonged to her late husband, Paul. Jake stuck it into the tie so that the opal rode on a swatch of navy, setting off the luminous pastels of the stone.

At the post office two men nodded to him, one even saying, "Mornin,' Mr. Trickle." At the courthouse on the portico of thick, beveled, Ionic columns, Si McDermott grabbed him by the arm. "Howdy, Mr. Supervisor. I'd like to introduce you to your new colleagues upstairs."

Si McDermott ran the show, no doubt about that. The longtime chair, Colonel Hazen, was a beloved 75-year-old war hero of sorts, a staff officer to General John J. (Black Jack) Pershing in World War I. The Colonel presided at the meetings, but he delegated all the work and key decisions to McDermott. Si made every member feel important in some way. If Harry Winans, who was in his second term, lamented about not being a committee chair, then Si would recommend to the Colonel that a new committee on public health be created, with Hank as chair.

McDermott also made the members feel good about themselves. They thoroughly enjoyed the annual Central Illinois County Officials Day, a golf outing and dinner held in August at the Williams Country Club for county officials from twenty counties. Si saw to it that no expense was spared. County suppliers ponied up to pay for the dinner and door prizes, and everybody came away with something—a new putter, a box of balls or a briefcase. The drinks flowed freely, and Congressman Everett McKinley Dirksen and the area state legislators always put the day on their calendars. Everyone in the know called it "McDermott Day," and the Williams County supervisors enjoyed reflecting their colleague's prominence.

The county board was a social as much as a political entity. Several leading farmers of the county represented their rural townships. A retired school teacher and an insurance man, John Enslow, also served. These men enjoyed their monthly gatherings but had enough to do as township supervisors. They were glad to leave the county-level thinking and decision making to Si.

So, the members were genuinely interested in meeting this Jake Trickle fellow. After all, he had rescued them from the task of picking up the pieces had their leader been removed from the scene, and ignominiously at that, which would have embarrassed them all personally.

"Good to meet you, Mr. Trickle," effused Dale Doubet of Truro Township, "but I imagine we have lots to teach you about the problems us farmers have out in the country." He laughed, pleased with his good-natured jibing.

"Si McDermott simply told me to follow his lead in all things and I'd look brilliant," Jake retorted, equally pleased. Everyone in the group around Si and Jake guffawed.

Colonel Hazen, who filled the George Washington role for the board—dignified, courtly, a bit distant—called the meeting to order. County Judge W. W. Wright was asked to swear in the nine new members, after which the Colonel conferred on each a parchment certificate of office. Each certificate was cleverly embellished in red sealing wax with the county seal, courtesy of Tommy Jackson, who was duly thanked on the record.

County government in Williams County was big business. With Williamstown the only community of any size therein, county government was seen as the natural unit to deliver general services. In addition to highways and law enforcement, the county operated a county "poor farm," technically known as the County Home, and also the Williams County Hospital, a 50-bed general hospital that was the pride and joy of county government.

The primary order of business was the election of a chair and the appointment of committees for the ensuing two years. Colonel Hazen was nominated by Si

McDermott and re-elected by acclamation. The Colonel thanked the board stiffly but with genuine appreciation and then announced the committee appointments.

Si McDermott would again chair the three-man Finance Committee, which set the budget and property tax levy and paid all the bills. Si had been on the finance committee since he had been elected sixteen years earlier. He had chaired it for the past twelve. Service on the budget committee was coveted, and for the past eight years Si had the loyal support of Kirk McDowell of Copley Township and Max C. Webber of Osceola Township. These men, who like Si raised cattle on their farms, were his proteges. They liked his bluff, self-confident, sometimes grand style.

Jake was appointed to the County Farm and State Legislation committees, which suited him. Jake had often wondered what life was like for the residents at the "poor farm," who resided in a stately Georgian red-brick home three miles south of Williamstown on the "county farm blacktop." The county owned the surrounding half-section of land, which was farmed to support the inmates. Those few of fairly sound mind and body helped with the farm work and gardening.

As might be expected, Si was also a member of the State Legislation Committee, which traveled to Springfield at least once during the biennial sessions of the General Assembly to lobby for bills of interest to counties generally. Colonel Hazen and Ralph ("Lightning") Mannix, nicknamed for his stolid deliberateness, were the other members of this committee, also a prized assignment. Indeed, the Colonel announced that the committee would be traveling to Springfield the following Thursday for the lobby day of the Illinois Association of County Officials. Jake winced, wondering how he would finish the 64-page new product catalog job for the casket hardware company in nearby Galva, which was staring him in the face at the office.

At noon the board and county officials adjourned to the Williamstown Methodist Church basement, where dinner was served. Over chicken potpie, overcooked green beans, fist-sized golden buttery rolls and cherry or Dutch apple pie, Jake began the process of getting to know his fellow board members. Not such bad fellows, he concluded, but their overweening pride in agriculture as an industry—no, a religion—was a bit hard to take. "Don't they appreciate the roles of other fundamental industries?" Jake mused. "Hell, they wouldn't be getting whatever bushels of corn they were bragging—and probably lying—about, if it hadn't been for good ol' Gutenburg, movable type and the printing press, which made the spread of scientific knowledge possible." He told the farmer supervisors just that over coffee, to their blank, uncomprehending stares.

After dinner the board members all went over to the county treasurer's office to be paid their $9 per diem for the board meeting, plus mileage for those who drove. Then it was back to work for Jake.

⧗

Jake stopped at Ernie's cabin less often now, what with Kay, the county board and late hours at the office to make up for time lost to his governmental chores. But Ernie and Kay helped Jake set up his first apartment that May. Kay had told him that the carriage house on top of the huge detached garage behind the Mills Tingleaf manse had been vacated after the death of the elderly groundskeeper who had lived there for decades. Mills Tingleaf was a banker whose enterprise had closed its doors during the Bank Holiday of 1933, never to open again, much to the chagrin of the depositors, who never saw their money again either. Not everyone blamed the Tingleafs for the losses, as the Depression was larger than even many bankers; but then again, why didn't the bankers try to make good over time on depositors' losses?

The Tingleafs became recluses, living quietly in their biggest-in-town manse, complete with two turret spires, on a modest bluff at the west edge of Williamstown overlooking the Indian Creek valley. The carriage house, which was indeed over the old 1890 carriage and horse stable, also commanded the same refreshing view. And Jake could put his car in a garage space below, all for $50 a month. A steal, Kay said, especially in the secluded setting, shaded by stately oaks, walnut and hard maple trees, the valley unfolding below the 40-foot bluff down to the winding creek.

Kay took charge of decorating the large, sunny single room, tall double-hung windows on three sides. She pointed out a household goods auction coming up where Jake (with Ernie at his side providing shaky counsel) was successful bidder on a bed, sofa, chair, small kitchen table and chairs, all for $53.50. Kay asked Minnie White to sew straight pleated window curtains in a sturdy, masculine chocolate brown duck cloth, and Kay contributed the area rug that since childhood she had rolled up in "the ballroom" so that she could dance.

Kay was enjoying all this immensely. She took Jake and Ernie shopping at Miller's Hardware to get basic gear for the tiny galley kitchen. She and Perry Miller pondered over how many pots and pans were needed at a minimum. Ernie understood why Jake was head over heels in love with her. "Now, Perry, don't try to sell Jake the whole store," she chided, laughing as she did so.

"But now that Jake's an elected official," Perry insisted, "he's going to have to entertain now and then." He explained this to Kay rather than to Jake and Ernie, who remained on the periphery of this dealing.

With housekeeping all set up, Jake invited Kay and Jim Dunlap, Ernie and Minnie White to be his guests for lunch the following Saturday. Minnie had to beg off, as her ailing husband demanded all her free time. That was really a blessing because Jake had just four straight-back chairs for the kitchen table. Ernie brought two bottles of his best apple wine and a large sack of morel mushrooms, picked that morning in the woods behind his cabin. Jim brought a housewarming bottle of Courvoisier brandy. Kay baked a peach pie for the occasion. They all wondered what Jake might prepare, given that he had not so much as boiled a potato in all his thirty-plus years.

In fact, with some coaching from Harry Wilson's wife, Esther, Jake had covered chicken pieces with two cans of cream of mushroom soup and one of milk, and baked it all slowly in a casserole. Ernie sauteed his mushrooms on Jake's stove, and when they sat down, Jake ladled the chicken gravy over white and wild rice. Kay poured the wine, which appeared to go down well with everyone. Quite a repast. The windows were open, and the sweet air of springtime, yeasty with the scents of buds, blossoms and the turned earth of fields nearby, moved freely across the room. All was well.

Jim had finished a second slice of pie and moved to the overstuffed sofa. Kay sat with him. "Can I have another glass of wine, please?" Jim asked. "You ought to patent that stuff, Ernie."

"I'll accept the compliment, but we all know that it's as raw as gasoline. On a day like this, however, it seems to work quite nicely." Ernie mused that maybe the stuff wasn't so bad as he had always thought, if Jim Dunlap could compliment the wine with a straight face.

"How'd your first county board meeting go, Jake?" Jim asked, surprised the topic hadn't come up sooner.

"Fine, I think. Si made me feel right at home, as did the other supervisors, though they don't know how to talk to people who aren't farmers. But then, who am I to talk, as I've never been a great conversationalist myself.

"I do worry about the time the job will take, but I'll make sure I get my work done at the office. Colonel Hazen announced, for example, that the State Legislation Committee would be going to Springfield next Thursday, and we'd come back Friday morning."

"That's not a problem. You can just work all weekend," Jim chuckled, half-seriously.

"No, he can't either," Kay protested. "We're going on a picnic next Sunday at Lake Calhoun, if the weather's decent."

Jake smiled. He appreciated being fought over, a truly novel sensation.

Jim was content indeed to see his Kay so exuberant, following years of living pretty much to herself and just going through the motions of life. After a second coffee, Jim thought it time to go. Kay said she'd stay to help Jake with the dishes, so Ernie also excused himself.

As the two men left, Jim joked that soon the whole town would be talking about Kay and Jake. "I don't give a damn if they do," he added, but then asked, "Ernie, is Jake as solid as I sense he is?"

"Almost too solid. He doesn't brook two-faced people, or so I gather from our talks. And even in local politics, he'll soon find that people aren't always as they try to appear. I wonder how Jake will handle that?"

⌛

The State Legislation Committee departed at 7 A.M. for Springfield. "Lightning" Mannix had offered to drive Colonel Hazen's big new Packard sedan on the three-hour trip to Springfield, the state capital. And Jake looked forward to his first day of lobbying the legislators, as Si put it.

"Right after we arrive—if Lightning knows how to get us there—I chair the executive committee of the Illinois

Association of County Officials," Si explained. "This will be at the Abe Lincoln Hotel, where we're staying, just two blocks from the capitol. Jake, you and Lightning can check in and then go over to the capitol and watch the House or Senate, if you want. They will both be in floor session."

Then they were to be back at the hotel for the five o'clock reception for legislators. "The Speaker of the House and the Lieutenant Governor, who presides over the Senate, Jake, have assured me they would adjourn so the fellas could be at the reception on time. After the reception, the Williams County delegation—that's us fellows—and my state executive committee will host the Senate Local Government Committee for dinner at the Red Lion Restaurant in the Leland Hotel, just a block east of the Abe Lincoln—so you shouldn't get lost, Jake." Si laughed.

On the drive down the three farmers critiqued the planting, which by mid-May was in full swing. "That fellow over on the right, Si," pointed out Lightning, "he's putting in soy beans. Wonder if there'll ever be much of a market for beans? They say you can squeeze lots of oil out of those little buggers, but nobody much knows what to do with the oil yet."

Lightning, who looked about 45 and strong as a bull, was in his glory at the side of Si and the Colonel. He was more than happy to drive, take care of the car, help in any way he could, just like an aide-de-camp. Lightning had a good tenant on one small farm his wife owned and a reliable farm hand on his own 240 acres, so he didn't feel too guilty breaking away right in the middle of planting. Of course, he would have preferred a rainy day for the trip, when no field work could be accomplished.

Jake smiled as they drove by a Burma Shave jingle, one line after another nailed on fence posts:

Ben met Ana

Made a hit

Forgot to shave

Ben-Ana split

Burma Shave

The State Legislation Committee from Williams County soaked in the sights. The towns all appeared to bask in the post-war prosperity. Soon they were snaking through Canton (pop. 12,000). "The International Harvester plant here is paying big union wages and going great guns. Everybody in this town sure appears to be middle class," observed the Colonel.

"And strip-mining for coal west of Canton, with even bigger union wages than at I-H, is creating a real bonanza," added Lightning. "But it makes you sick to see how they're ruining the farmland, just to get at a three-foot seam of coal sixty feet down. Si, I sure as hell hope we don't have to face that problem in Williams County, because there doesn't seem to be any way, so far at least, for local governments to keep the mining out."

"But we will face it, fellas," said the Colonel. "The Illinois Geological Survey down at the U of I says that two-thirds of all Illinois is underlaid with strippable coal. With the skyscraper-tall draglines and shovels Bucyrus-Erie is building, it's a helluva lot less expensive—and safer—to scrape off the top layers for the coal near the surface than it is to drive shafts way into the ground for coal deeper down."

Farther south on 78, as Lightning drove carefully over the hump-backed Illinois River bridge into Havana, the Colonel continued, "This town is wide-open, Jake. Gambling, girls, anything you want."

"For awhile maybe, Ernie," responded Si, who was the only person in Williams County who called the Colonel by his given name, "but that new fancy-pants Governor Stevenson claims he's going to shut the town down, and everyone like it. We can't have any fun at home, and soon we won't be able to kick up our heels out of town either. But let's have some fun tonight in Springfield, dammit, while we can."

In the lobby of the Abe Lincoln, the hotel where most of the Republican legislators stayed, Si seemed to know everybody. Democrats stayed at the St. Nicholas, three blocks north. Si was dressed in a proper three-piece business suit, but instead of the Stetson fedora that was obligatory for businessmen, Si wore a tan suede cattleman's hat, just different enough to be noticed; yet it sure fit him and his style just right, thought Jake. Instead of wingtip business shoes, McDermott wore supple black boots, spit shined, with one-inch heels.

"How the hell are you, Johnson?" Si called out to the county board chairman from Winnebago County. "And Walt, you old son-of-a-bitch, great to see you." Si was in his element, loving it.

"Si's an important fellow down here, Jake, as you can maybe tell," said Lightning, with a note of pride. "That's why so many of us appreciate what you done after that fluke election."

The capitol sat on the only rise in a city of 81,000 situated on a tabletop. The capitol's dome soared 150 feet, higher than that of the U.S. Capitol. Inside, Carrara marble, polished to a glassy finish, lined the floors and walls. On the first floor school teachers organized third graders in queues, in readiness for a perfunctory tour of the building, and brief visitation to the galleries of the House and Senate. The children comprehended nothing, nor did the adults for that matter.

"The governor's office and those for the other state officers are on the second floor, Jake, and the legislative chambers are on three."

But Lightning asked the elevator operator to go to four. "Si told me how to get copies of the legislative calendars from the bill rooms for each house, which are on four. This way we have scorecards as to what's going on."

By mid-May in the odd-numbered legislative session years, the Illinois General Assembly had a head of steam up. Legislative proposals had been heard in committees, and scores of these bills now awaited action on the full House and Senate floors. From the gallery seats that overlooked the House chamber, Jake saw nearly 200 desks arranged in a semicircle, facing a raised podium. "The Speaker of the House controls things from up there," advised Lightning.

"Sure doesn't seem under control," remarked Jake, as he watched a not-so-friendly shoving match between two lawmakers, off to the right side of the chamber. Elsewhere, cliques of three or more legislators huddled in conversation. Other members were reading the *Chicago Tribune* or the *American*. A clerk, standing beneath the Speaker's podium, droned on, just barely above the buzz from a score of conversations on the floor. Every so often Jake could hear the clerk sputter out a bill number. Jake could now see a member at his desk, standing, as if speaking to the Speaker. Across the aisle that separated the half sphere into two equal quarters, another member stood, apparently ready to respond.

"Now you see why having a scorecard helps. They're on Second Reading now, where amendments are offered to bills that have come out of committee. They have to plow through all the members' amendments before they can consider the whole bill on its final Third Reading." Jake watched, mesmerized. He thought of the channeled chaos of the Spoon River rolling along, the water not knowing where it was headed but determined to get there anyway.

Across the rotunda the Senate, with only 51 members rather than the unwieldy 153 of the House, was quieter, more dignified. The senators were at ease, waiting for a huddle between the majority leader, a Republican, and his minority party counterpart, to resolve an issue. Sen. Fred Rennick, cousin of the Williams County state's attorney and the senator for Williams and five other counties, noticed Lightning and Jake enter the gallery above and behind the presiding officer's dais.

"For what purpose does the gentleman from Bureau arise?" asked Lieutenant Governor Sherwood Dixon of Senator Rennick. "To introduce the Senate to a distinguished guest in the gallery, Mr. President." Pointing toward Jake and Lightning, he said, "Please acknowledge the presence of Mr. Ralph Mannix and his colleague. Mr. Mannix is the chairman of the Williams County Board of Supervisors State Legislation Committee, here for the biennial reception of the County Officials Association." Lightning, a bit embarrassed but mightily pleased, nodded to the perfunctory applause and waved to Rennick.

"So you're a big shot, Lightning," noted Jake, half in jest, half in compliment.

"I'd like to think so, but Si probably mentioned to Fred that we might be in the gallery today. Si's a real operator, and I'd be kidding you to say I didn't appreciate the introduction, even though we know it doesn't amount to a tinker's damn."

At the reception Jake continued to watch Si McDermott operate. At five o'clock, four hundred or more county officials and most of the legislators began to fill the ballroom of the Abe Lincoln. In the center, under a crystal chandelier, a groaning board of appetizers glistened seductively.

There were mounds of shaved ice festooned with huge fresh shrimp stuck into the ice with toothpicks. Chicken livers and water chestnuts wrapped in bacon and skewered with toothpicks were heaped into steel serving trays.

A giant black man, who looked seven feet tall in his puffy chef's hat, carved from a massive round of beef, placing slices on onion rolls or rye bread. In each corner of the ballroom bartenders at an open bar poured highballs for the thirsty crowd from bottles of top-of-the-line booze. A seven-piece Dixieland band played "Tin Roof Blues" from a small, portable stage against one wall of the room.

"Quite a shindig, eh, Jake," commented Lightning. "Si knows how to put on the dog." Jake and Lightning had filled their small plates with goodies and moved slowly around the room. Jake held the neck of a Reisch beer, the local brew, in his right hand. Lightning saw a couple of fellows he knew from counties near Williams, and he introduced Jake. Si could be seen near the entrance to the room, greeting legislators as they arrived.

"That's Senator Jimbo McCarthy from Chicago over there with Speaker of the House Paul Powell, who's from way down south in Vienna. Real powers, both. Jimbo helps protect Chicago's interests, and Powell does the same for deep southern Illinois. Lots of trading goes on between the two. And Si gets along great with both of them."

By seven the legislators had moved on, in groups of three or four and in the company of lobbyists who would pick up the tabs. Now it was on to the Red Lion for dinner. Jake followed Si past the long mahogany bar in the Leland Hotel, which was anchored at one end by a twenty-pound block of cheddar cheese and a bushel basket filled with Ritz crackers. Lightning snatched a loose slice as they walked by, toward the private room at the back.

"How in hell are we going to eat dinner after all we downed at the reception?" Jake wondered out loud.

"I knew this was coming, so I haven't taken solids in three days. You'll know better next time."

Si presided at dinner with the Senate Local Government Committee with goodwill and light-hearted charm, making everybody comfortable. The highballs didn't hurt any in that regard. Si thanked the lawmakers for their sacrifices and hard work, and for their support of the County Officials' legislative program.

Following prime ribs that lapped over the edges of the plates, Si displayed a reproduction of the chairs used by members on the Senate floor. He noted that each member of the committee was being sent a similar chair for use back home in the senators' offices or studies. Each chair would be emblazoned with the State of Illinois seal, the member's name and notation of gratitude from the County Officials' Association. The members were delighted. While gifts weren't unusual, this one would hold special meaning for the lawmakers. "No wonder Si usually gets what he wants down here," Jake thought.

After dinner Si directed Lightning to get the Packard. "I want to take you fellows out to the Lake Club, so you can see where the action is. Jimbo said he'd join us out there." The Colonel begged off, saying he would struggle back to his hotel room "under the great weight of all I have consumed."

The Lake Club wasn't on a lake, but it was where legislators and lobbyists so inclined went to whoop it up in the later hours. A parking valet offered to take the car off Lightning's hands, but he said "no thanks," playing his assigned role to the hilt. Inside, Jake adjusted his eyes to the subdued lighting and smoke, saw maybe twenty tables around a good-sized dance floor, and beyond, the only lighted spot in the place, a dance band identified on the music stands as George Rank and His Music Makers.

Jake recognized many of those at the tables from the reception at the Abe Lincoln. Jimbo McCarthy came in behind them with four attractive young women in tow. The senator introduced the young ladies as his secretary and three of her associates from the Senate steno pool. "Cute, in their early twenties," Jake surmised. "Would have made saucy flappers twenty-five years earlier. Too bad hemlines went down so far this past year," he lamented.

Si asked the host, who embraced Si like a long-lost friend, if he could put together a table for eight. After a short wait they were seated. Based on the way Jimbo's secretary, Irene, grabbed his arm as they headed for the table, Jake mused that she was probably more than a stenographer for the fiftyish McCarthy. Jake ordered yet another beer, a premium Blatz this time. "At least the sixth beer, maybe the seventh," Jake counted to himself. "Too many, whatever the number." He declared to himself that this would be his last drink.

The band struck up the Tommy Dorsey theme, "I'm Getting Sentimental over You," with George Rank playing a passable trombone. Jimbo and Irene were up and dancing. Si asked Marie (with a long Polish name) to dance. This left Jake and Lightning with Anne and Jo. "We're all from Chicago," Anne offered. "We work for the city of Chicago but Jimbo, Senator McCarthy, that is, invited us to work down here during the session. It's kind of fun, though Springfield is really a hick town. But we haven't paid for a meal or bought a drink with our own money yet. And Jimbo tells Irene he thinks we may get promotions when we get back to our regular jobs.

"Do you want to dance, Jake? You're really cute, you know, but so quiet." Anne took Jake's hand.

Jake smiled but declined. "I'm just learning to dance and wouldn't want to embarrass you out there." The place was jumping.

At 1 A.M., Si, Lightning, Jake and Marie, Anne and Jo piled into the big Packard. "Back to the Abe Lincoln for a nightcap," declared Si, his face flushed with liquor and the success of the day.

The girls were in a party mood, but Jake and Lightning were beat. Anne was crowded onto Jake's lap in the back seat, her arms around his neck, next to Si and Marie, who shared the back seat with them.

"You want me to stay with you tonight, Jake? Jimbo said to be good to Si's friends," Anne whispered, and nibbled on his ear. She had refreshed her cologne on a restroom stop just before they left the Lake Club, and the scent aroused Jake. His arms were around her lightly. There was no place else to put them. Jake's alcohol-befuddled mind danced about, weighing the pleasures offered against the hurt he could imagine in Kay's eyes.

At the Abe Lincoln Lightning resolved the situation to Jake's relief. "Si, we'll drop you and Marie off at the hotel and then take Jo and Anne back to their apartment. Jake and I have to get our beauty rest." The two men walked the girls to their apartment door, up two flights of stairs. Anne turned to Jake, hugged him, then reached up and kissed him. "Why don't you fellas come in and stay with us?" Anne whispered in Jake's ear as she nibbled on the lobe. Jake was tempted, but Lightning pulled him away and back to the car.

"Wow, is this Sodom and Gomorrah or what?" Jake asked, a bit breathless and unsteady as they got back into the Packard. "I never expected this kind of day when we started off this morning, or yesterday morning, that is."

"Those girls are called 'monkey' secretaries—they hang onto their jobs by their tails. Several of the Chicago lawmakers bring girls down for the session. They're not bad kids, just fun-loving girls who think this can boost their chances back in Chicago. I kind of worry about Si, though, and whether he ought to play around like he clearly is tonight."

"Si does love this whirl," Jake thought, "and enjoys throwing some real money around to burnish his image as a player."

The Carriage House

Chapter 7

Simple Pleasures

The summer of 1949 was a time of simple pleasures in Williamstown. Television was still a novelty. In the apartment above their implement store trendsetters Dean and Marie Blair brought friends up to watch the grainy test pattern and wrestling matches that heralded the questionable promise of a new medium. Evenings were spent instead on porch swings, pushing hand fans back and forth (courtesy of Kidd Funeral Home), creating a breeze in the still of the evening. Folks called out greetings from porch to sidewalk as neighbors strolled by after supper in the near dark of mid-evening. As night fell children were called inside from their rambunctious game of kick-the-can (with the can directly under the milky corner street light globe). Mothers threatened laggards with stern retribution from "Your Father!"

Saturday was market day. Stores stayed open till 9 o'clock. High school band director C. P. Patterson led the Williamstown Municipal Band every Saturday night from a wooden bandstand on the courthouse lawn. Folks parked their cars around the square early on Saturday afternoon so they could listen to the 8 P.M. concert from their cars, windows down, munching white popcorn sold in brown paper bags by young Jay Arganbright from his popcorn trolley in front of his father's grocery store.

Children hung from the barrels of the two Civil War cannons that stood guard before the front portico of the courthouse, and the little urchins tried in vain to climb the slick marble statue that commemorated the visits of Lincoln and Douglas, on separate days it had to be noted grudgingly, in that year of the momentous debates. Harry Wilson did land-office business at the tavern. Over beers young bucks tried to figure out what to do and where to go with the rest of their Saturday night. Maybe a drive "up the line" to the roadhouses near Kewanee. Farmers slipped in the alley door for a couple of brews while their wives shopped for groceries and sundries.

The Williams County Fair ran for one week in July at its grounds five miles west of Williamstown. Harness racing on the half-mile oval competed for fairgoers' attention with the aerial acrobatics of the Cole Brothers Flying Circus. No Dan Patches or Baron von Richtofens here, but the breeders and trainers of the standard-breds were area men, and Duane Cole himself grew up in Williamstown before going off to the Pacific to become a flying ace.

By dusk the sharp sweet-sour aromas from the cattle barn were masked by the fryers yielding up heaping plates of fried chicken for the sumptuous suppers served at the Methodist and Grange food tents. A thousand colored electric bulbs on the calliope and Ferris wheel created a dazzling blur of light, and the carnival midway was alive with the calls of barkers who seduced skeptical farm boys out of their hard-earned dimes and quarters. "Win a kewpie doll for your beautiful girl friend. Just knock over these three little milk bottles. Three tosses for a dime. Here, big fella." The carnival roustabout held out three baseballs, browned from a thousand sweaty palms.

In August the Williams County Old Settlers Association took over the courthouse square for a two-day festival that honored the county's illustrious forebears–or so they were proclaimed. Each year an octogenarian who had contributed much, or at least something, to the area was honored by having his photograph emblazoned on badges which were purchased and worn by nearly all attendees. Men turned up their long-sleeved white shirts two turns from the cuff and sat on long wooden benches which were moved around the courthouse green to catch shade from the mature maples and elms planted decades ago for just such a purpose.

The big event of Old Settlers Day itself was the chicken pot-pie dinner at noontime served right there on the courthouse lawn to more than one thousand persons, eating from long plank tables that rested on sawhorses, served from a special kitchen constructed right there for just that one meal and for the supper that followed. Of course, there were band concerts. C. P. Patterson was trim and resplendent in his cream-colored band director's uniform, while the high schoolers and adults in the band wore white shirts or blouses and dark trousers or skirts. And, naturally, declamations by the area's politicians. U.S. Congressman Everett McKinley Dirksen was always a big draw. His mellifluous tones and unruly blond curls reminded people of a melodramatic, turn-of-the-century thespian. The Baptist Church Strawberry Festival on the first evening of the gathering vied with the Congregationalists' Ice Cream Social for bragging rights over best home-baked pies and cakes. The blackberry and rhubarb pies always went fastest but only because many more apple pies were baked.

⌛

Jake and Kay took in these events at her insistence and to Jake's great enjoyment. Jake asked Ernie to join them for a day at the county fair, which Ernie always considered a treat. Kay insisted they first go through the stifling white clapboard Domestic Arts Exhibit Hall to see if Minnie

White's corn relish, pickled beets and bundt cake all received blue ribbons, which they did. Kay observed the judges would get an earful from Minnie if they hadn't.

The trio took a quick swing through the livestock barns, where 4-H teenagers tended their hand-raised calves and sheep. Si McDermott's daughter Samantha, sparkling in cowboy boots, jeans tucked into them, and red-checked blouse, starch not yet wilted, called out to Mrs. Townsend, her English teacher. "Come see Henry the Eighth, my black angus calf. He's going to win the grand championship." They all admired the pert youngster and her sleek animal. Jake wondered aloud whether Samantha or the hired hands really raised the animal, and Kay, sincerely angered, flared up that men just couldn't bear to give women any credit for anything. Chastened, Jake became quiet.

On the small carnival midway Jake tried to win Kay a stuffed panda bear, first at the shooting gallery, where his corks hit but failed to topple the Lucky Strike packages all in a row. "Damned things are nailed down," Jake declared to the barker, whose pained expression of "How could you think such a thing?" satisfied no one. They both tried to pop balloons with darts, again coming up short. "Oh, Jake, what will I do without a panda for my bedroom?" Kay leaned against Jake, laughing.

"Let me make up for my failings on the midway by treating for snow cones," Jake offered as consolation. Behind a tub of ice, a lady with a kewpie doll face of her own, red cheeks and frizzy hair, pushed big scoops of crushed ice into Dixie cups, poured thick red syrup over each and stuck tiny wooden spoons on top.

Jake saw two supervisors as they neared the grandstand. "Howdy, Jake," one of them called out.

"Howdy, Herman. See you got your corn laid by nicely and before the 4th. Looks real fine."

"Sure nice of you to notice," responded the lanky American Gothic look alike.

Jake introduced Kay and Ernie, and they moved on. "Why I would swear you're becoming a windbag politician like all the rest of them, Jake," observed Kay, and they all guffawed.

It was like this at Old Settlers as well, the band concerts and ice cream socials. Kay was her old self again, or so Ernie overheard some ladies remark when he was in the A & P one day. She was almost like a schoolgirl in her new-found exuberance. Jake was quiet but always pleasant, smiling and nodding, commenting on the weather, inquiring about crops with farmer acquaintances from the county board. They made a handsome couple, and the townspeople were grudgingly coming to think that maybe, just maybe, Jake was good enough for their Kay Townsend.

⧗

Jake much preferred to be alone with Kay, which wasn't all that easy to pull off in a small, always inquiring town. So when Kay mentioned her father's old canoe in the barn behind the house, Jake immediately ran out to Ernie to ask if he would drop them off the following Saturday morning where the county farm road met the Spoon River and then pick them up late that afternoon down the river at the village of Sturdevant. "Dave Gelvin tells me that would make a nice day's canoe trip, with plenty of time for a picnic along the way," Jake said, and Ernie concurred.

The gods smiled on Jake that Saturday. The day turned cool, at least by summer standards, breezy and sunny, so the mosquitoes wouldn't carry the two lovers away. Kay packed lunch in a wicker picnic basket, and Ernie contributed a bottle of rhubarb wine which they accepted with feigned pleasure. Kay wore blue pedal pushers, a man's white shirt, probably her father's, sleeves rolled up to her elbows and collar up. She wisely brought a wide-brimmed straw hat which she put atop the picnic basket.

"God, she's attractive," thought Ernie. He had walked the river banks in that area all his life and knew what the two would encounter at each meander. "Great day for a lovers' canoe ride," he thought as he walked back to the car.

Kay had instructed Jake on how to sit quietly and not rock the canoe. Jake paddled slowly with Kay up front, guiding as necessary with her paddle.

The hackberry, poplar, cottonwood, maple, ash and oak provided a cathedral canopy. "Look, Jake, ahead on the right, on the fallen tree trunk. Aren't they incredible?" Five painted turtles sunned themselves on the trunk, an adult maybe eight inches across and four youngsters. The adult raised its substantial head, bright green stripes on a camouflage green base. The shell in a similar dark green was edged all the way round in a bright red. As the turtles heard or felt the canoe, they plopped under water.

Belted kingfishers put on an aerial show for the lovers that far surpassed the Cole Bros. Flying Circus. With its long, slender beak extended, unruly cockade riffling as it flew, the kingfisher looked like a diminutive descendant of great prehistoric fishing birds. First one, then another kingfisher would swoop down from its tree perch and skim the river's surface for fifty yards in a search for minnows and fish, then climb sharply back to a tree limb perch.

Jake and Kay startled a Great Blue Heron, a mop on stilts. The ungainly yet elegant bird unfurled its five-foot span to rise slowly off the water, like a B-29 heavy bomber compared with the quicker dive-bombing kingfishers, settling high in a cottonwood at the far end of the water runway.

"Jake!" Kay could say no more. She just pointed. A snapping turtle, shell as big as a turned-over bushel basket, grasped a fallen tree trunk with claw feet, huge eyes sticking out from folds of ancient leathery skin. Jake and Kay coasted by silently.

By late morning Kay spotted a well-shaded grassy knoll which beckoned them to lunch. Jake secured the heavy canoe to a tree branch, and Kay spread out a big cotton blanket. Jake opened Ernie's wine, Kay held up two glass goblets and they chuckled, not for the first time, about how vintage June 30 was supposed to be a good year. Then they toasted their friendship to him.

Over soft cheese, French bread, apple slices, cold fried chicken, Minnie White's bread-and-butter pickle chunks and mustard potato salad, and second goblets of wine, Jake and Kay talked and talked. "So you feel sorry for Hemingway?" said Jake. "With his luxury lifestyle in sunny Key West, or whatever island he's on, not many would feel a need to send sympathy cards."

"He's on his fourth wife. He surrounds himself with movie stars and obsequious followers, and struts around like the Great White Hunter. I think he's wallowing in self-pity, afraid that he's run out of stories to write about."

"But what a storyteller. His affair with the nurse in *A Farewell to Arms* is the great love story of my lifetime. Time and again in my tiny sleeping rooms I have lived that love affair for myself. And now I'm having a love affair for real with an equally beautiful and desirable woman. I never thought it would be more than a dream."

Jake was resting his head on his elbow, looking down at Kay, who had her hands behind her head, looking up through the tree leaves at the blue sky. She turned her head, looking into his eyes. "Jake." They loved one another that afternoon on the thick, soft carpet of pasture grass. The sun flickered across them through the trees. A breeze caressed the lovers, and the rustling leaves sighed, like the faintest roar from a distant sea.

"Jake, I love you. Thank you for coming on a bus to Williamstown." Jake got teary-eyed and buried his head in her shoulder.

After a moment Jake cradled his chin in his hand and looked down at Kay, then away, then back at Kay. "Kay, I'm thirty-one years old, and that's the first time in all my life anyone has ever said to me, 'I love you.'"

Kay held Jake as tight as she could, for a long while, tears in her eyes as well.

Later, Kay watched her right forefinger skim across the water as Jake paddled. "Maybe those couples surveyed by Kinsey do make love as often as they claim." Jake chuckled to himself, not responding.

Ernie saw them come round the bend in the Spoon at Sturdevant, carried solely by the languid current. Ernie wished somehow that Jake and Kay would keep paddling—past him and the village, around the bend and on to a special world just for lovers—and out of his sight.

Jarred back to reality, the two bounded out of the canoe more friskily than prudent, almost sending Jake into the water. The three laughed outrageously at the near mishap.

Kay hugged Ernie. "Thanks for meeting us. But you should have given us another four hours, or four days, darn it." Ernie grinned, sheepishly.

On the way home they stopped at the 78 Club for supper, their treat to Ernie, Kay and Jake said. The two knew Ernie fancied the deep-fried catfish with corn fritters and sugar-and-vinegar cole slaw.

"Jake, I insist on buying the tickets because it was my idea, and anyway I'm a working girl living at home who doesn't have anything to spend her money on." Tommy Dorsey was coming to the Hub direct from appearances in Kansas City and St. Louis, and headed for the Aragon

Ballroom in Chicago for the weekend. Tickets were $5 per person, not per couple, which was unheard of, but Tommy Dorsey was worth it.

Jake and Kay were almost living together, although Kay never stayed overnight at Jake's carriage house. They did fall asleep one cold evening in late June, and neither awakened until 4 A.M. Kay was sure no one saw her slip back home. But as always happens in a small town, Kay's quiet trip home in her Pontiac coupe was duly noted. Mae Heaton, who couldn't sleep that night, saw the car, and closer to the Dunlap residence, Herb Murray lifted his shade to see Kay hurry from the garage into the family home.

The whole town soon knew of the overnight tryst and of the relationship at the carriage house. The community juries gathered to discuss this case at the Shackateria, Humphrey's, the bar at Midland Country Club and after the American Baptist services. They concluded, generously they thought, that these transgressions were forgivable because of Kay Townsend's tragic widowhood and the redeeming fact that her long-lost effervescence had been restored. The juries were still out, nonetheless, as to whether Kay and this passably handsome but unconventional printer would, or more important, should ever formalize their relationship.

Kay wore an off-the-shoulder midnight blue cotton dress with a deep décolletage that drew one's gaze to her alluring breasts, set off by a coppery tan unsullied by any strap lines across her broad shoulders. Her eyes danced as she twirled like a model, showing off in her new purchase for Jim and Jake. "My god, Kay, as your father, I can't let you go out in public like that. You'll be carried away by the gods to their lairs in the clouds." Jim was almost serious, as he gazed in great pride at his daughter. Jake, in his khaki Palm Beach summer suit with a wide silk tie of riotous colors, just smiled in appreciation.

The Hub was packed, the evening hot and muggy. Yet as advertised, there was "Always a breeze at the Hub," though not enough to deflect beads of perspiration from foreheads across the sea of dancers. Lanky Tommy Dorsey, trombone resting lightly in his left hand, stood to the side of his front line of four reeds, backed by three trombones and, on the highest riser, four trumpets. Vocalist Dick Haymes sat off to the side.

The crowd roared as Tommy opened with his solo lines for the signature tune, "I'm Getting Sentimental Over You." Then, after introducing himself and key members of the band, Tommy led into " Marie" (the dawn is breaking, Marie, my heart is aching), and everyone tried to dance, though squeezed together like sardines in a can. Jake and Kay laughed at their efforts, as they were jostled every which way.

"I think every man in this room simply wants to get a look down your front, Kay, and that's why they're all bumping into us," Jake chuckled.

"Oh, stop it. This is the style. Don't you know that women were liberated by the Great War. We're not going to be trussed in corsets and high collars anymore."

"Let's move to that corner where we first danced. There may be more room." A series of danceable standards followed. Jake and Kay moved slowly, playfully whispering the lyrics to the tunes. "Once in a While" (won't you try to give one little smile, to me).

"You make me smile even when I'm not with you," Jake said. "When I'm on top of the newspaper press, which makes so much noise you can't hear yourself think, I just smile and hum tunes like 'Blue Skies, smiling at me, nothing but blue skies do I see.' Because that's all I see since I met you in the library almost a year ago now. God, is it really that long—seems like but a moment?

"Then I whistle, 'I'll be seeing you in all the old familiar places, I'll see you in the morning sun, and when the night is new, I'll be looking at the moon, but I'll be seeing you.' And that's the honest-to-god's truth, Kay. God, how I love you."

"Jake, 'Let's Get Away from It All,'—let's take a trip to Nyack, in a kayak, let's get away from it all, Jake. . . .'The One I Love Belongs to. . .' Oh, no, Jake, it can't be true, this tune, I mean, you belong to me, don't you?"

"Didn't, I tell you, the one I love . . .lives back in Pontiac, Illinois, where I used to work, on a farm?"

"Why did I let 'My Foolish Heart' fall for an itinerant printer . . ."   The trumpet line from the Dorsey band filled the ballroom with a cascade of brilliant, golden, but almost melancholy sounds to "My Foolish Heart," and Kay nestled her head on Jake's shoulder.

It was a night of romance and music, little else. Kay saw Bob Bowman and a couple of his college buddies with wives and girl friends. They all chatted briefly, then moved on.

"Why didn't you move to Peoria or even Chicago, after your husband's death, Kay?" Jake wondered. "You could have had a much grander, livelier life."

"Don't, Jake, we've already covered that. Jim needs me, though he won't admit it—and maybe I've needed him. I love him so much I ache at times because he lost my mother just when life was becoming beautiful for them."

"But it wasn't your fault."

"Maybe not, but if I can fill the void a bit, I'll feel better about myself somehow."

After a break, the band returned with a series of sentimental wartime ballads. Kay and Jake made their way to their own little corner of the dance floor. Dick Haymes provided the vocals. "Don't Worry About Me," (I'll get along . . . somehow) and then "You'll Never Know Just How Much I Miss You" (if you don't know now), and last in the set, "I'll Never Smile Again" (until I smile at you. I'll never laugh again, what good would it do?)

"Those ballads tear me apart. Think of the thousands of couples who parted during the war, never to see one another again. Think of my father. I think his smiles often come with great effort. Let's never miss one another. Let's always smile—and let's sit down until they play something more upbeat."

"I wish we could always smile, but life is tough, as you've learned. Let's enjoy these moments and build on them. But don't build a sand castle in hopes there will never be any rain." Kay looked away, her gaze fixed on infinity. She understood what Jake was saying, yet wondered if she could handle any more rain.

Tommy Dorsey picked up the tempo, bringing on the Clark Sisters, four dazzlers patterned after the Andrews Sisters, to sing "On the Sunny Side of the Street." Kay's spirits brightened. Then came "That's a Plenty," "Boogie Woogie," the take off on Rimsky-Korsakov's "Song of India," and then the wild "Hawaiian War Chant," with its primal, jungle-like drum solo. Unable to find the space to dance, couples simply stood, cheering the soloists.

Closing came with the strains once again of "Getting Sentimental Over You," as Tommy Dorsey thanked the crowd in Edelstein—he kept saying "Edelstine" but nobody corrected him—"for a great evening in the corn-fields of America's Heartland."

▨

Jake never brought up the topic of marriage, haunted by uncertainty as to who he really was—an itinerant and loner, or a budding community leader. The latter still seemed improbable, yet was more and more appealing. Could a printer be good enough for Kay? He thought so, but . . .

Kay had thought about marriage but was relieved by Jake's silence. She clung to the surrogate role that she had created as mistress of the Dunlap household. Why couldn't she move in both orbits, the worlds close but never colliding—one man needing her, the other wanting her?

The Bismarck Hotel

Chapter 8

The County Poor Farm

"Glad to see you haven't totally abandoned your favorite beer emporium." Harry Wilson greeted Jake, who had slipped onto his favorite stool near the end of the bar about nine in the evening after a long day at the paper.

"I must confess I've found better company than you and your vile cigar, Harry, but for old times sake and the bite of a frosty brew, I'll stop by now and again."

"I was hoping you'd stop in. I have a piece of information I'd like to stick in the noggin of an elected supervisor. Great thing about a tavern, you pick up lots of gossip after tongues have been loosened by an extra mug. A little twerp was in here last night, first time in my place. Bookkeeper for Triple A Asphalt out on the edge of town. A buddy was consoling the little fellow here at the bar. They'd had too many beers, but hey, that's my livelihood, The twerp was madder'n hell at his boss, Andy Ashmore. In addition to playing around on his wife—Ashmore, that is—the little fellow bitched out loud—I'm sure I heard this right—'Why in hell couldn't the bastard help out a loyal employee, when he was selling the county road oil for forty cents a gallon?' "

"Yeah, and what's the point?"

"Later, out of curiosity, since forty cents a gallon for anything sounded high to me, I asked Jim Chamberlain, who used to be the township road commissioner down in Akron Township in a far corner of the county, what he used to pay for road oil. What do you think he said?"

"Dammit, you know I'm new at all this. I have no idea."

"Eight cents a gallon! He said the stuff was a residual waste product in oil refining and that companies sell it for little more than the cost of getting it up here from Texas. Several thousand gallons a year at that price and you're talkin' real money."

"Maybe the county buys a different kind of oil."

"Chamberlain said it's all the same."

"Well, what am I supposed to do about it?"

"You're my supervisor, and this sounds like a rip-off of my taxes, dammit to hell."

Jake was thinking back to Professor Monypenny's admonition: "Follow the money! Get inside the budget!"

"Okay, so I'll check into it, but I'm not on the finance committee. This Thursday, after a short county board meeting, I'm off to visit the county poor farm. That's the committee I'm on. We approve the budget later."

"All I'm sayin' is that such a big spread in prices might mean a little hanky-panky, so don't telegraph your inquiries."

"What? You think something's goin' on here?"

"Hell, government is just a game for some folks, even otherwise upstanding citizens. You don't have to be a cynic, just a fulltime skeptic like me, and you'll less likely be bamboozled."

"Okay, I've tucked the info away and the advice, too. I'll check it out. And I expect you'll be my pipeline for all manner of barroom patron complaints and charges."

"I'll be only too glad to oblige, honorable supervisor."

⊠

The Williams County Farm was eight miles south of Billtown on the aptly named County Farm Road.

Everybody called it the county poor farm, because since it was established in 1880 that's where the county put up the homeless and those mentally unbalanced folks who weren't so deranged as to need a straight-jacket in a state mental hospital but couldn't take care of themselves. Most jurisdictions had a county poor farm, sometimes called alms house, poorhouse, county home or infirmary. Bob Hepner and John Oliver explained all this to Jake as the three members of the County Farm Committee drove out for the committee's annual inspection.

Jake and Kay had driven by the farm before when taking blacktop shortcuts to Peoria that Kay knew. Jake had been impressed by the handsome redbrick Georgian edifice with four white pillars on a semicircular portico, standing between the two wings of the building, set back from the road and surrounded by a well-tended lawn. A small brick cottage stood off to one side. A tiny cemetery with miniature, dull gray tombstones could be seen beyond the cottage.

Kay had never been inside the county farm, she told Jake, nor had most people in the county. "Jim told me years ago that parents would drive their children by the county farm, tell them that evil witches, goblins and insane people lived there, and if the children failed to work hard and save for their retirement, they would end up in there with the witches and goblins. He says that it's an awful place and that it's a shame some people have to be put in there."

"The county leases the farm's two hundred and forty acres, and we put the rent into supporting the home," Oliver explained, as he guided his humpbacked '47 Ford sedan into the drive. "The inmates aren't capable of helping with the farm work, but several of them work in the garden out behind the home."

"I wish I weren't on this committee, to be honest. This place is so depressing," lamented Hepner. "Just thank your lucky stars you aren't in here, Jake."

The superintendent and his wife stood in front of their cottage where Oliver parked.

"Howdy, fellas. You know my wife Maud." Mark Montooth and his wife, who did the cooking, had been caretakers of the home and inmates for many years, ever since Mark lost his farm during the Depression. Mark and Maud looked tired and wan, but they tried to be professional for the committee visit. Jake thought they looked like adequately fed Joads from *Grapes of Wrath*, beat but with paying jobs and a nice cottage, even if it was next to the poor farm.

Jake wasn't prepared for what he encountered. "Men inmates occupy the south wing and women the north," the superintendent explained to Jake. "At present we have thirty-one men and fifteen women. Beds are upstairs, except for those who can't climb. For them we put the beds off to the side of the dayrooms on the first floor."

Two ancient men sat in rocking chairs outside in the shade of the portico, one on either side of the front door. They gazed at the visitors and tried gamely to nod their heads in greeting, mouths drooping open. The stench of excrement reached Jake before they got inside the front screened door, which Mark unlocked. He noticed Jake involuntarily wrinkle his nose. "Most of the residents are unable to take care of themselves, and my wife and me just can't look after every one of 'em, so it's not near so tidy as we'd like in the house. We do the best we can and allow those who have some of their wits still about them, like Lucius and Marvin back there on the porch, the freedom to move about. In fact, we help them get about when we can."

"You mean you and your wife are the only help here?" Jake asked.

"Well, Doc Johnson, the county physician, comes out once a week, and Maud has part-time help to keep the residents and the house as tidy as possible."

Jake had never been in an insane asylum or a nursing home, and this was a combination. In the men's dayroom the committee walked a gauntlet of old fellows propped up—some tied up—in straight-back wood chairs or lying on cots. A chorus of moans, mindless grunts and shouts, accompanied by stares, a few vaguely curious, most vacant. The bright sun shot through the small vertical windows, but the rays didn't spread out much so the room was a patchwork of light and shadow. The greenish plaster walls were unadorned, streaked here and there with bodily effluent of some sort, Jake imagined.

"How long do these men typically live here, Mark?" Jake inquired.

"We get them when they can't take care of themselves and have no place else to go, no one to look after them. Some live for a decade or longer. For most it's four or five years, I'd reckon. We take care of 'em as best we can, but we could use more help. It's kind of pitiful, really, I admit it."

The women's dayroom across the way in the opposite wing was a little less depressing because there were only half as many residents. The women were shriveled after a lifetime of backbreaking housework, childbearing and tough breaks. Jake tried to look through them, back into their earlier lives, but saw nothing.

"Maud, being a woman, devotes more time to keeping the women looking proper. She just thinks that's only fitting."

"What do the residents do?" Jake asked Mark.

"Do! Why those who can help in the garden do that, although nobody right now is able to be of much help to me. Those fellows on the front porch come out to the garden when I'm working there, but they're not much help. Three of the women are quite all right, nothing wrong with 'em but old age and no place to live. They help Maud in the kitchen almost every day and enjoy it. Otherwise,

I've got a farm to operate and a garden to tend, and Maud keeps the house up as best she can, so there's no time left to organize games or cards or whatever."

Bob Hepner asked about the crops and finances.

"As you can see, the corn looks pretty damned good, if I do say so, though the prices they're talking about for the fall won't come close to covering costs out here, is my guess."

Jake had more questions, but he wanted to escape to the outside first, feeling guilty about his desire to flee the netherworld he had encountered.

On the drive back to town, forearms on the back of the front seat, head thrust almost between his fellow committee members up front, Jake asked, "Can't we do more for those poor bastards at the poor farm? I never knew such awful places existed."

"Jake, our county farm is a pretty good one, all things considered. The residents are fed decent, and they have a roof over their heads," Bob responded, a bit defensively. "And you can see that the residents aren't in this world anyway, for the most part. To me, the real tragedy is the feeble folks of sound mind who have to share their last years with witless folks who can't take care of themselves."

"And we try to pay for the upkeep and care from the revenue from the farm, though we have to levy some additional funds from property taxes almost every year, which the board hates to do," contributed John Oliver.

"I guess I understand, but if you fellows took care of a parent or greataunt at home, I know you'd do a helluva lot better than that for them."

⌛

Jake took his concerns to Si McDermott. "Si, the conditions are deplorable. At the least the aged of sound mind should be given separate quarters so they can live in some degree of dignity."

"Maybe you're right, but it'll cost real money to build a separate wing or building, and property tax rates are as high as I'm comfortable pushing them. But do your homework. If you can come up with a reasonable plan, you can bring it to the whole board."

Jake took up Si's challenge. He came to Jim Dunlap, Kay, Harry Wilson, even Ernie, for advice. And he wrote Professor Monypenny. Jake had a unique way of corresponding. He set his thoughts down in lead type, on the Model 14 Linotype, in 12-point Bookman, then ran the inked type through the proof press on newsprint, pulling as many copies as he needed.

Kay and her father agreed to visit the county farm with him. Ernie went along to take photos. Harry grudgingly joined the informal visitation committee.

The superintendent and his wife were surprised by the unannounced visit one Saturday morning. When Jake reassured Mark that his efforts had Si McDermott's blessing, the superintendent relaxed a bit. The scene was just as dreary and depressing as on Jake's first visit but no more so. At least Mark and Maud hadn't presented a spruced up look to the county board committee.

Jim asked good, penetrating questions about the care and finances. Kay visited with the several elderly ladies who were of sound mind. The ladies warmed to Kay rather quickly and were soon telling her of the indignities of life with the mentally feeble majority. They lamented the lack of privacy and the intrusions into their dayroom by Herman Eldridge and Jonathan Wainwright, feeble-minded but physically strong men who terrorized but thus far hadn't harmed them. But the ladies had nothing bad to say about Mark and Maud, who were as helpful as they had time to be. The women cried; Kay cried.

Ernie got good shots of the stark conditions throughout while Harry carried his flashbulbs. Harry tried to talk
to Herman Eldridge, who had been a good customer at
one time, but Herman just kept repeating, "Hello. Hi.
Hello. Hi." Harry gave up and patted Herman on the
shoulder.

As Jake figured, they were all devastated by what they
saw. Jim seemed particularly downcast, as if he should
have known all along and maybe did somehow, but like
others had put it all out of his mind.

Jim didn't use many photographs in *The Republican*.
Half-tone plates had to be made from the photographs at
the *Peoria Star*. But for this story, Jim went all out, maybe
because he knew it meant a lot to Jake and thus to Kay.
Jim used four photos and ran them three columns wide
each, inside a story that filled page 3 in the August 24 edition, under the eight-column head:

COUNTY FARM A DISGRACE TO COUNTY CITIZENS—ACTION NEEDED

"Residents at the Williams County Farm live in
deplorable conditions that deny the dignity every person
in our society is entitled to," began the story under Jim's
byline, another rarity from a publisher who had always
scrupulously avoided controversy. The social norms of
Billtown held that the town and its citizens not be
upbraided or embarrassed publicly. When problems
arose, community leaders dealt with them quietly, by
consensus of the Main Street elite. With this story, Jim
knew he was going out on a limb with his longtime
friends on the county board and at the Shackateria.

In a separate box on the page, printer-county board
member Jake Trickle called for construction of a separate

facility for the elderly of sound mind, and for increased nursing and attendant care for all the residents. "The county cannot in good conscience consign its own citizens to a warehouse for dying, at least not without the dignity and support we would want for our own loved ones," Jake declared. "Most of these men and women are indeed 'our own,' having worked and lived throughout their lives in Williams County."

Ernie's photos attempted to capture on silver chloride the smells and disarray and hopelessness in which the residents lived. The gap-toothed, wild-eyed pleas of the sorriest of the residents made Ernie's job an easy one.

Jim was quick to absolve the superintendent and the county board of blame, like the preacher who chastises and forgives his flock in the same sermon, for the sake of his job. "The caretakers and the county have tried hard to do their jobs with limited resources, and they have been good stewards of the county purse. Yet all of us need to look anew at a problem that we have put out of sight and out of mind for too long," the story emphasized in boldface.

⧗

Si McDermott was livid. "What the hell has gotten into you two?" Si stormed at Jim and Jake in the front office of *The Republican*. "Goddammit, you've made the whole county board, and especially me, look like hard-hearted Hannahs."

"You told me to do my homework, Si. This is part of it."

"This isn't homework, it's a condemnation of me and the board, and you know it. And Jim, you know this isn't the way we do business in this county. Why didn't you

come to me with your concerns?" The soothing, diplo-
matic tone which had characterized McDermott in all
Jake's previous dealings with him was gone.

"You're right, Si, and I thought about it." Jim was
struggling with himself as he thought through his answer.
"But maybe the way we've done things in the past in
this county results in matters like this just being covered
over."

"Well, goddammit, it's a little late for you to be coming
to that way of thinking after years and years operating like
we always have around here. We take care of our problems in this county, better'n most."

"So let's do something about it, Si," Jake said. "That's a
hellhole out there and apparently has been for years," he
added, getting a little hot himself.

"I'm all for it if you can find out how in hell to do it
without jacking up property tax rates. Voters' hearts will
bleed for the down and out, Jake, so long as it doesn't cost
them anything. That's the magic combination you need to
find."

Jake found it. In response to his inquiry, a letter from
Professor Monypenny arrived. The states of Minnesota
and Wisconsin had begun granting federal-state old-age
and blind assistance to counties for residents in county
homes, so long as the counties agreed to bring their facil-
ities up to modern standards. If Illinois did the same,
wrote Monypenny, then Williams County could use the
income stream to finance a nursing home wing and provide full-time nursing assistance.

Jake took the idea to Si. "Can you get Springfield to
adopt this idea?" Jake asked. "If so, you and the County
Officials Association could become real heroes."

"Yeah, but only after getting egg on our faces for the
conditions that exist right now. Remember, what we do
here, bad as you think it is, is more and better than in
most counties.

"But you get more information from your professor friend about how it's working in those other states. I'll talk with my executive committee. If they like the idea, we'll take it to Governor Stevenson. It's too late for the legislature to do anything about it, and they don't come back for another eighteen months. Maybe the governor can make the change by executive order to the welfare agency. The problem is clearly money, but Stevenson is a bleeding-heart liberal if ever there was one, so he's going to like the idea."

The following week's *Republican* was more to Si's liking. The banner across page 1 read:

MC DERMOTT LEADS PUSH TO MODERNIZE
COUNTY HOMES ACROSS STATE.

Jim quoted Si McDermott at some length:
"County home residents are the forgotten folks of our great state. We are all responsible for the inadequate care they have been receiving. We must do something about it, and we can—without increasing your property taxes!"

McDermott announced that he had scheduled a meeting in Chicago with Governor Adlai Stevenson to discuss his plan for state payments for county home residents, and that in return the counties would, as soon as possible, bring their homes up to standards established by the American Public Welfare Association.

⊠

"Jake, you get your professor to come to this meeting, because he has the details. And you're coming along, too, 'cause you sure as hell got me into this. My county officials are royally upset with me, because they all have reporters snooping around, doing stories on their county homes, and as you know, the picture ain't pretty. And it's going to cost me a pretty penny as well in schmoozing to smooth it all over with the fellows in my association."

Si was referring to the fact that Charlie Cleveland, the statehouse reporter for the *Chicago Daily News*, had seen a copy of *The Republican's* story on its county home. Cleveland had talked his paper into sending reporters out into ten other counties across the state. What they found made the Williams County Farm look pristine by comparison. In Wilson County residents were chained to their beds, lying for days in their own filth. In Monrovia County, the *Daily News* found "a Bedlam of horrors beyond Dickens' worst nightmares."

Si and Jake boarded the Denver Zephyr at eight thirty-seven Friday morning at Kewanee. They hurried to the dining car for the last call for breakfast. The black dining car steward led them to a table for four with snowy white linen tablecloth and real silver service. Si insisted Jake order the "Mile High" French toast dusted with powdered sugar, with real maple syrup which the steward poured on generously.

They were half-finished by Princeton, where Bureau County chairman Tom Seidel boarded. He saw Si and Jake in the dining car from the station platform and joined them. "Have some French toast, Tom, on me," Si boomed out, as he rose and introduced Jake.

"Damn right you'll buy," barked Seidel, in a less than cheery tone. "What a pickle you've got us all in, Si. Folks are giving us hell for these county farm homes, when all we've been trying to do is save them their tax dollars. Nobody really gives a shit about these residents. They're nobody's kin."

Si smiled, glancing over to Jake to see that he appreciated his predicament. Si calmed Seidel down by Mendota, where the LaSalle County Chairman Tom Anderson, also a member of the executive committee, boarded. Si slipped the steward a dollar bill so that the fellows could continue talking over coffee, poured solicitously from a sterling pot by the white-jacketed black waiter.

Anderson was in no better mood than Seidel, but again McDermott absorbed the complaints and soon had the LaSalle chairman talking positively about meeting with Stevenson. McDermott never mentioned that Jake was the fellow who stirred things up in the first place.

It was only five blocks from cavernous Union Station to the Union League Club on West Jackson. Si was a non-resident member at the club and had arranged a meeting room on the seventh floor for the six-member executive committee. The clubhouse, as Si called the club's 20-story building, was grander than anything Jake had ever seen. The carpeting was inches deep, the walls dark oak panel-ing throughout and original art work in ornate gilded frames was displayed throughout. "That's a real Monet, Jake. A famous French artist," Si bragged. "Best art col-lection in the midwest outside the Art Institute."

The staff all knew Si and called him "Mr. McDermott." "We could stay here overnight, but the association gets a special rate at the Bismarck, and that's across the street from the Well of the Sea in the basement of the Sherman House hotel, where we're all meeting Jimbo McCarthy for drinks and dinner.

Professor Monypenny was already waiting in the club's lobby when the group arrived. "Good to meet you, Mr. Chairman." Hmmmmn. Monypenny introduced himself to Silas as he fiddled absent-mindedly with the Phi Beta Kappa key on the fob of his pocket watch.

The executive committee meeting went smoothly. The six members were evenly divided by geography and party, three each from the central-northern part of the state, three from southern Illinois; three were Republican, including Si, and the three from southern Illinois were all Democrats.

Si introduced Jake as a member of his county farm committee. "Jake made contact with Professor Monypenny, who is fast becoming the state's leading student of state and local government," said Si. He asked Monypenny to explain the concept that Si McDermott was proposing the committee take to Governor Stevenson that afternoon.

"County homes, poor farms, almshouses—whatever they might be called—are under fire across the country, gentlemen," Monypenny started. "As our population lives longer, the number of mentally and physically infirm grows, so county farms have been transformed from residences primarily for able-bodied homeless into nursing homes for the elderly. The traditional superintendent and his wife are not generally capable of caring properly for these types of residents."

Before Monypenny could get too deeply into welfare theory through the ages, Si broke in and asked the professor to focus on the policy option that he had earlier outlined to Jake.

"And what's the cost going to be, Professor? That's the big question a governor will have to answer," drawled C. L. McCarthy, from Johnson County, 400 miles to the south of Chicago.

"The federal government will not allow its portion of the old-age grants to go to governments like yours but only to individuals living independently. A governor can, however, grant the state portion of the assistance. Based on my estimate of 8,000 county home residents eligible for old-age and blind assistance, at $400 per resident per year, the cost to Illinois would be $3.2 million a year, or twice that for the biennium."

"Damn, that's big money, Si. Do you think Stevenson can find that in his next budget?" asked C. Wallace Cunningham of Marion County.

"That's what we have to convince him of this afternoon, gentlemen. And he'll want something in return. He won't let us use state money to replace local dollars. He'll want a commitment to improve our standards."

"But these national standards the professor talked about may well cost more than we'll get in new money, Si," Cunningham retorted.

"We're on the hot seat because of that *Daily News* series about some of our counties," Si responded, "and the conditions are worse than I thought they were, so we've got to do something. And we'd better come out looking like the good guys, even though some of our members may not give a damn about the folks in their county homes."

Agreement was reached, grudgingly, to ask Stevenson for the help in return for modernizing. Si excused Jake and Monypenny so the committee could continue with other business.

On Monypenny's recommendation the two walked three blocks into the center of the Loop for lunch at the Berghoff, "a great old German restaurant, Jake."

Over schnitzel, ham hocks, red cabbage and steins of beer, their talk came back to budgeting.

"Professor, I've heard a rumor from a good source that my county is paying forty cents a gallon for road oil when the going price is only eight cents. How can I check this out? When I asked Si about it, he said that couldn't be right, and he'd take care of it. I hate to push him, but I'm elected to know these things."

"Please call me Phil, Jake," hmmmmn, "and thanks for getting me into this county home issue. I'm from the University of Minnesota and have been in the state only a year now, so getting to meet with the governor and this association is great for me. And by the way, you're sure moving fast in this local politics game. When we met a few months ago, you were as green as grass."

"I still am, uh, Phil, and that's what worries me. I'm way out of my depth, but I sure feel strong about the county farm issue. I can't believe civilized people can treat fellow humans that way. As a single fellow without any family anywhere, I could see myself in such a place one day. I've been having nightmares about it. I think I'd shoot myself first."

"There are lots of people who fall off this flat earth of ours, Jake, and are forgotten forever. If you think the county homes are bad, you should visit a typical state home for retarded children. They tend to be far off the highway at the end of tree-lined drives, as if leading to fine country homes. Quite reassuring to the passing motorist. But inside the cottages, they cram hundreds of children where a few dozen could be housed comfortably, with little or no professional care. Enter a cottage and you'd think you had entered a hell vacated by the Devil himself as unfit for man or beast.

"But we can do something about the county farms and in the next year or two—if your county association will just buy into reforms in return for additional state dollars. You've got to convince the county officials that it's the right thing to do, and they can also look good politically and feel good about it."

"Si says it'll be a tough sell. Local officials hate state-imposed mandates, and they're scared that it'll require property tax boosts. But I'll push the executive committee when I have dinner with them tonight. Now, back to the road oil question."

Hmmmn. "Five times the going rate for road oil. Was the road oil put out for bid? Is there a written contract? How much has the county been spending for road oil each year over the past decade? How much do other jurisdictions pay for road oil? You need to answer those questions; but if the information you have is true, my guess is that your poking around won't be very popular.

"Each county is required to have a public hearing on its proposed budget. You can ask questions then and also at the board meeting when you vote on the budget. Of course, it's best if you know the answers to your questions before you ask them. I can do some checking for you through some highway officials I know up in Minnesota as to competitive prices and maybe get some recent budgets for counties up there about the size of yours, to give you some base of comparison with other counties. But as for Illinois, I don't know enough players yet."

Jake and Professor Monypenny joined Si and the executive committee at two forty-five in the tiny reception room outside the governor's Chicago office on the 16th floor of the State of Illinois Building. Jake and Phil had to stand, as the others squeezed into two low-slung leather sofas. Jake had never met with a governor, of course, and was a bit nervous. So were the county board chairmen, but they would never let on. Adlai Stevenson was an Ivy Leaguer and international lawyer who had spent most of his life on the East Coast. He had wanted to run for the U.S. Senate, and University of Chicago economist Paul H. Douglas had wanted a shot at governor; but Chicago's political bosses switched the two because they wanted a World War II hero—which Douglas was—in the top spot on the ballot.

So the courtly, urbane, cerebral Adlai Stevenson found himself back in Illinois, meeting not with heads of state but with heads of rural counties. The governor's Chicago secretary led the delegation into Stevenson's modest office, and they sat around a small conference table. Si took the lead in introducing everyone to the governor. Stevenson, who had been briefed by a young lawyer-like aide, recalled how he had enjoyed campaign stops in the southern Illinois counties of the Democratic members of the delegation.

The governor was aware of the county farm issue and wanted to do something about it. "Gentlemen, we can't let these appalling conditions continue," he declared, adding dryly and with ironic intonation, "not that they do exist in your counties, of course." Jake was impressed.

"I'll put per capita state grants into my next state budget—fifty dollars a month for each certified elderly resident who needs nursing care—for each county that meets the federal standards of the American Public Welfare Association within three years."

Si expressed his appreciation for the governor's concern, but parried that six hundred dollars a year per eligible resident would probably not cover the costs of getting up to standard and that three years wasn't enough time for some of the counties to comply.

"Your counties should already be up to the standards, Mr. McDermott. This has traditionally been a local government responsibility, not that of the state. You are the ones on the reporters' hot seat at the moment, and properly so. I can well use the money I'm talking about for the state's mental health hospitals, which are also in dire condition."

"And the governor's office will want to make any announcements to the press about this offer," inserted the bespectacled, bow-tied aide, "but, of course, we would be pleased to have you gentlemen with the governor at such a time for photos. And of course Governor Stevenson will need a commitment of strong support from your association, Mr. McDermott, as we'll have to get this through the Budgetary Commission and then the House and Senate."

Jake thought the governor's assistant, probably not yet thirty, was being pushy with the older county board chairmen, but Stevenson remained quiet, smiling.

"As you might imagine, Governor, this will be a tough sell to many of our county board chairmen, especially in southern Illinois where the property tax generates so little revenue." Si was looking for recognition of this reality from Stevenson. He didn't get it.

"I'm told you're an impressive, highly persuasive leader, Mr. McDermott. I'm confident you can win broad support for this important partnership between the state and its counties. My assistant here, Mr. Harrison McKeever, will work with you on a press announcement and photographs." The aide stood up, a signal that the meeting was over, which even Jake understood.

After pledging to work at building support, Si thanked the governor for his time. Stevenson walked around the conference table, shaking hands with each of them. "Oh, Professor Monypenny, I found your paper on the need for local government consolidation to be quite persuasive. Now if you can just convince the multitudes of local officials, like these gentlemen, to your point of view, maybe we could make some progress."

Everyone laughed at the governor's humor, as Si responded, "That's an idea, sir, that even with all the power of your office, you'll never get through the legislature." They all laughed again.

"Ah, yes, Mr. McDermott, I recall the words of Niccolo Machiavelli to the effect that, 'There is nothing more doubtful of success than creation of a new system . . . because of the enmity of all who profit by the preservation of old institutions.' "

"Well, I don't know this fellow—sounds like an Eye-talian, Governor," rejoined C. L. McCarthy, "but he sure sounds like he understands southern Illinois politics." More guffaws, and the delegation departed.

⌛

Sen. Jimbo McCarthy had already taken a big table in the bar of the Well of the Sea in the Sherman House, across the street to the east of the State of Illinois Building. Jake paused for a moment to adjust his eyes to darkness in the restaurant that sprawled across the basement of the popular hotel. He saw a huge illuminated glass aquarium that formed the back of the bar, separating the bar from the restaurant. Foot-long ornamental gold carp moved slowly along the glass wall, as blasé about their surroundings as the regular customers were about them.

Jake also saw Anne, Marie, Irene and three other young women with the senator. After a moment's awkwardness, Jimbo directed the girls to sit boy-girl around the table with the county board chairmen. "These young ladies all work over at City Hall, and I invited them to come wet their whistles with our visiting firemen from the County Officials' Association." Jimbo shouted to the ceiling for Harry, the waiter, to come take their drink orders.

Si McDermott motioned to Harry that he would take the check when they settled up. "Senator, you're always in such good company. I don't know if we'd be nearly so enthusiastic about joining you for a drink if you weren't," Si joked.

"My, my," exclaimed folksy C. L. McCarthy, as his Coca-Cola was set in front of him, "this is wonderful hospitality, Senator and ladies. I just pray that none of my hard-shell Baptist constituents see me having so much fun. Here's to y'all." C. L. lifted his glass to the senator and waved it around to all the girls, who didn't know whether to be impressed with C.L.'s charm or put off by his countrified ways.

Jake looked into the foam on his glass of Meister Brau beer, a Chicago product not available in central Illinois. Anne seemed genuinely pleased to see him. She was appealing in her simple dark skirt with white blouse, her trim, neat figure squeezed up against him on the crowded banquette. Anne introduced the other girls.

"The senator said that all of you men—with the exception of Jake here, of course," Anne laughed, "were important public officials and that we should show you all a warm Chicago welcome." C. L. raised his glass to Anne, as did his colleagues.

Si told Jimbo of their meeting with the governor. "I don't know, Senator, if all our counties could meet the national standards that Stevenson insisted upon in return for a commitment of state funds."

"That pin-striped mother's boy should never have been our candidate," Jimbo retorted. "We just thought nobody could beat your Governor Green, Si. I can help you guys with the money part next session so long as there's something in it for Chicago. And we can water down the standards in the legislature."

"That's why we enjoy working with you, Senator. You're a man of action and common sense," Si said, pleased.

"But, Si," Jake broke in, "our whole purpose is to upgrade the standards and provide better care for these poor folks."

"Jake, we'll improve conditions," Si responded soothingly, "but we've got to move slowly. Many counties lack the resources and the willpower to make big improvements immediately."

"Then we'll have to force those counties to make big improvements quickly," declared Jake, a flush coming to his pale face.

"Now, son," C. L. interjected, "we want to keep the state's nose out of our business, but we could sure use some of the state's money down in southern Illinois. God, boy, most folks don't have two nickels to rub together where I come from."

Harry brought another round of drinks. Si and Jimbo began to confer privately at their end of the table. The other county board chairmen compared notes on road work in their counties. The girls listened politely. Upset by the talk of watering down the reforms, Jake turned to Anne, as if for some support.

"Jake, I don't know anything about county farms, but I sure like that fire in your eyes." Anne rested a hand on Jake's knee and massaged it for a moment.

After dinner—and more drinks—across the street in the Swiss Chalet of the Bismarck Hotel, C. L. and the other county board chairmen excused themselves from the girls and returned to their hotel rooms. "Now don't you all stay out too late," C. L. admonished the table.

Si again picked up the check and left a tip that generated a smile and deep nod of appreciation from their waiter. "And now a nightcap at the Tip Top Tap," Jimbo proposed. As they came out of the Bismarck, a long black Packard rumbled up to the curb.

"My carriage and driver, gentlemen." Jimbo waved them into the sedan. "I think we can all fit. Take us to the Allerton, Charley."

Jake asked if this were really his personal car and driver. Si explained. "In addition to being a senior state senator, Jake, the senator is also Deputy Commissioner of Buildings for Chicago, and all deputy commissioners are provided car and driver. It's one of the perks of his job." Anne was on Jake's lap in the backseat, her head resting on his shoulder. Jake took a deep breath to draw in the remaining scent from her Evening in Paris cologne.

The Tip Top Tap was, fittingly, atop the Allerton Hotel on North Michigan Avenue. From a height of twenty-two stories, customers had a commanding view of Michigan Avenue and Chicago's business district to the south and up Michigan Avenue to the north. A picture of Don McNeill, host of the Breakfast Club show, greeted them. The program was produced each morning in the Tip Top Tap for a national radio audience.

"Isn't this a great view? That tall building to the north, with the beacon, is the Palmolive Building," said Anne, feeling as if she were on top of the world. Jake was overwhelmed by this high style living—chauffeur and car, and special treatment wherever they went. Yet he couldn't forget the glib dismissal of the standards for county farms, which he thought was the purpose of their trip. And he thought about Kay and what she would think to see him doing the town with the flirtatious young Anne.

Jake downed two more beers, which he didn't need. Charley, the huge black chauffeur, took them all back to the Bismarck. It was midnight. Jake was reeling from all he had drunk but knew he had to get to his room. Anne offered to help him find the way. The others went down the street to the Well of the Sea for yet another nightcap.

Jake was out of it. Anne helped him into his room, undressed him and put him into one of the twin beds. He was asleep immediately. "At least he didn't get sick," she thought. Anne undressed, kissed Jake good night on the cheek, sighed and slipped into the other twin. She and Marie had expected they would spend the night downtown, so she had packed the bare necessities in her large purse.

⌛

At seven, Anne turned toward Jake. "Time to get up, you sleepyhead. Didn't you say you and Si had to catch a 9 A.M. train?"

Jake didn't move, just opened his eyes to slits. "Where am I?" Jake moaned. "Oh, god, what a headache." He closed his eyes and tried again to orient himself.

Anne was standing in her slip, smiling down at her sad sack date. Then he struggled into the bathroom. At eight, Anne and Jake emerged from the room, just as Marie and Si came out from theirs across the hall.

"Well, how ya' doin,' Jake? Ready to conquer the world?"

"I feel terrible, Si. And," looking at Anne, embarrassed, "I don't want you to get the wrong impression, Si. We, we. . ."

"Had a fabulous time, Si," Anne finished the sentence.

"No, we didn't, Si. I mean Anne. . .I mean Anne helped me. . ."

"Don't worry, Jake. We need to hustle to catch our train. Ladies, great to be with you again." Si grabbed Marie by the waist and kissed her lightly. "Kiss your girl, Jake." Jake mumbled his thanks to Anne, and she kissed him on the cheek. "Get going, you two."

Jake was in no condition to talk much on the train back. It was just as well. He felt confused and distressed about Anne's overnight stay—and Si's awareness of it—and angry with himself for drinking too much. And Si disappointed Jake for agreeing without even a protest to water down the county farm reforms that Governor Stevenson laid out as his price for state aid.

Si, on the other hand, was pleased with himself. In the club car at the back of the Zephyr, he paged through the *Tribune, American, Daily News* and *Herald*, Chicago's daily papers. "I'll get some credit for the county home reforms that Stevenson will announce, with me present," Si thought to himself. "And I can tell the association later that we'll be able to live with what comes out of the legislature. And what an energetic filly Marie is! Ooh, yes."

But Si frowned when he thought about the costs of politics. He had to pay out of his own pocket for all that nightlife for Jimbo and friends and for the executive committee. "Oh, well, politics is expensive. That's part of the game," he thought.

When they arrived back in Billtown, Jake went to Jim Dunlap to tell him he felt miserable and was going home to bed but that he'd work all weekend. "You're going to have to, Jake. We have to deliver the sale catalogs on

Monday. I'll have the printer's devils work all weekend with you. And how'd the meeting with Stevenson go?"

"Oh, all right. He wants to help. I've never met anyone so polished. I have to go now. Please tell Kay that I'm sick, and I'll get in touch with her tomorrow."

Harry Wilson's Bar

Chapter 9

Road Oil and Romance Don't Mix

"Your friends are right, Jake." Hmmmmn. Phil Monypenny was on the line to the newly installed wall phone in Jake's apartment. "Road oil sells on the market for eight to ten cents a gallon. If your county pays forty cents, you're getting ripped off."

"Then I can't believe we are paying that much. McDermott is chair of the finance committee. He's too savvy to get ripped off. But how can I find out without causing anyone to think I'm casting doubt on his judgment?"

"Well, the county superintendent of highways would order the stuff." Hmmmmn. Monypenny was launching into a lecture. "McDermott's committee would receive the bill and approve payment. The county clerk, acting as the agent of the board, would order that the county treasurer write a check to pay the bill. If the product is contracted for and put out to an open bidding process, then the finance committee would review the bids and recommend an award of contract to the full board, which the board would act upon. At least that's the way your county should do it. Unfortunately, most county board members are either bored or mystified by the budget, so they leave it all to the clerk and finance committee."

The next day Jake took off a few minutes before noon so he could get to County Clerk James T. (Tommy) Jackson's office in the courthouse before it closed for the noon dinner hour. The lanky Jackson stood at the far end of a long oak counter, where a nervous young couple was filling out a marriage license application. Flanking the large one-room office to the ceiling on all sides were stacks of oversize cloth- and leather-bound books, which recorded the economic and social history of Williams County since its founding in 1836—quit claim deeds, mortgage recordings, military discharge records, and of course, marriages and births. The slowly decaying paper, yellowed and crinkly at the edges, gave off a musty scent. Jake liked it—the dignified aroma of history.

"Hi, Jake," Tommy boomed, as he moved in Jake's direction along the counter. "What can I do for you?"

"Oh, I was talking with an old friend in Pontiac about the cost of road oil, of all things, so I said I'd find out what we paid at the county and report that to him. I was hoping you could pull out a bill for road oil and tell me how much we pay per gallon."

Tommy looked perplexed for a moment. He turned to his two female assistants who sat at desks behind him. "Time for lunch, ladies. Why don't you let the supervisor and me talk in here." They took their cue and were out the door.

"Afraid I can't do that, Jake. The finance chairman says the specific bills are the domain of his committee alone, pursuant to the full board's approval of the budget ordinance, which you and your colleagues sign-off on each fall."

"Well, I am an elected official, Tommy, and all I'm asking is to see a simple invoice that is paid for with taxpayer dollars."

"I have my orders. You'll have to talk to Si. If he says okay, then it's fine with me."

Jake returned to the office feeling a little foolish. He didn't want to confront Si and have him think he doubted his judgment, or worse, which he didn't. But Jake didn't want to lose face with Harry Wilson, his favorite bartender and now his political counselor.

⧗

Si McDermott rang up the Dexter Phone Company and heard the familiar, "This is Central. How can I help you?"

"Irene, please call the Illinois County Officials office in Springfield."

"That's Springfield 426, isn't it, Mr. McDermott?"

"Right-O, Irene."

"By the way, Mr. McDermott, you know I shouldn't mention this, but the other day somebody was asking about the price the county paid for road oil. I wondered why anyone would be interested in that, and I recall you said once that knowing of public concerns about county matters would be helpful to you–"

"You're so right, Irene," Si broke in, a bit abruptly, "about it being helpful to me in my work. Who was it, Irene?"

"Oh, I couldn't tell you that, Mr. McDermott, but the call came from a fellow who used big words. What I'd expect a professor to sound like, if ever I met one. The guy called with information about road oil prices. I must go now, Mr. McDermott. Your call is ringing through."

"Must be that professor from the University of Illinois and Jake Trickle," McDermott thought. "What would prompt them to be interested?" He made a mental note to slip Irene another five spot when he saw her next.

⧗

As assistant supervisor for Starke Township, Jake had no responsibilities at the township level. Nevertheless, he felt he should attend the monthly meetings of the town board in order to learn more about its functioning. The board met on Monday evenings because a couple of the trustees had trouble getting away during the day. Jake was invited to sit at the large library table with the four town trustees, clerk, road commissioner, assessor and, at the head of the table, Si McDermott. The slat-back oak chairs creaked and scraped noisily against the unfinished wood flooring as the board was called to order.

McDermott gave a dozen or so invoices to town trustee Larry Foglesonger, who sat to his right. "I think these are all in order, fellows, but take a look at them and let's approve them. I'm going to talk with Dutch Arganbright and ask him to itemize the groceries purchased, rather than just put down a total amount. He knows better than that. Must've been busier'n hell this month."

The township roads were in good shape, declared Rusty Smith, the road commissioner, and the noxious Canada thistles on the roadsides in the south part of the township had been cut before they went to seed. "I tell the farmers that they're legally responsible not only for their fields but also for the roadsides next to their fields, but except for Merle Holmes, who's one good guy, the rest ignore the roadsides since they can't farm them.

"Don't blame them a bit," trustee Timothy Shambaugh, a farmer, commented dryly. The others smiled and said nothing.

"Didn't think I'd get much sympathy from you guys," Smith smiled. "Next year, Si, I'd sure like to upgrade the old Snareville Cemetery road from gravel to oil-and-chips. I already oil the gravel in front of the farmhouses along the road to keep dust down."

McDermott let the board trustees discuss the proposal, and they concluded that Smith and Si should work it out, so long as the cost wouldn't hurt maintenance elsewhere. "Just be ready for lots more requests to do the same thing on other roads, fellas," warned Trustee Foglesonger.

McDermott reported that there were thirty-two active poor relief cases in the township, one less than the month before. "Jim Smith's leg has finally healed enough for him to go back to work at the canning factory. They're giving him light work and paying him the same wage as before, so Jim and his family will, after a year out of work, have some money coming in."

"They sure as hell ought to pay him the same wage," boomed the voluble Foglesonger. "Jim'd never have gotten his leg caught in that conveyor if it had had a simple cowl over it. Unsafest goddam place in the county to work."

Jake expressed surprise that there were thirty-two families in the township in need of groceries or coal or help paying Doc Williamson for doctor visits. "Where are they located?" he wondered out loud. "You sure don't see them in town."

"Take the road over to Sturdevant some day, Jake," Foglesonger said. Sturdevant was a tiny unincorporated village of 300 or so, hidden behind the Spoon River five miles south of Billtown in the county's only rolling, wooded terrain. "It's like you're going into the hills and hollers of Appalachia. Lot of inbreeding and cases of the mental slows."

McDermott brought a note of levity to the proceedings. "I got even last week with Art Wotan, the supervisor in Rock Island County, the practical jokester. Remember this spring when he bought bus tickets to Billtown for a couple of bums he wanted out of town? I had to get them on the bus to Peoria right away. Cost us a couple of meals and the tickets, but Art thought it was great fun.

"Well, Tuesday last this floozy from Indianapolis, of all places, gets off the bus in town for unknown reasons, probably having slept off a drunk. She's broke, goes to city hall and asks for help; so they call me up, and I meet with her. She's seen better days but once was a looker, I'm sure. Says she's an exotic dancer, and we both agreed there was little potential for her trade here in Billtown.

"So I act real concerned, buy her a bus ticket to Rock Island, give her money for lunch first and tell her to look up Art Wotan, with my compliments, and that I was confident Art would find her work."

"Knowing supervisors' interests, he'll probably put her to work right there in his back office—in return for some grocery money," chortled Foglesonger.

They haw-hawed loudly around the table. Jake forced a smile. "God," he thought, "this community will take care of its own, after a fashion, even the halfwits in Sturdevant; yet they treat out-of-towners like they aren't real people, just pawns in their practical jokes." Jake shivered.

McDermott adjourned the meeting, and the board wandered out, still chuckling. "Jake, hold on a minute, will you?" McDermott called out before Jake reached the door. The two of them sat down again at the table, the exposed, green shaded light bulb hovering on its cord above them.

"I hear you're interested in what the county pays for road oil?" McDermott put it as a question. He caught Jake at the wrong time.

"Yeah, I was going to talk with you about it some time." Jake decided to dissemble. "A friend of mine back in Pontiac where I used to work heard I was on the county board. He's a new township board member, and he wondered what we paid for road oil. Said I'd find out. Simple as that. But it seems that board members aren't allowed to find out such things." There was an edge to his comment.

Now McDermott was beginning to get out of sorts. "Whaddaya mean by that?"

"I stopped by Tommy Jackson's office and asked to see an invoice for road oil so I could tell my friend what we paid; but Tommy refused, saying that on your orders, such is off limits for lowly board members."

"Now, whoa, Jake, you're getting a little testy, I think. Nobody's interested in the budget, and I run a tight finance committee that keeps expenditures under revenues, which is all folks want. If we allowed members to go over every bill we got, like we do here in the township, we'd have a million dumb questions and the meetings would last forever.

"Look, I appreciate to hell and gone what you did for me after the last election fiasco, and I've tried to involve you quickly in important and enjoyable activities. In fact, some of the old timers had wanted on the legislative committee and are kind of honked off. But I can't have you or anyone else telling me how to manage the budget. You got me in enough hot water already with the damned county farm issue.

"I can tell you that we're getting good work for our money from Triple A Asphalt. Andy Ashmore's a classy local guy who wouldn't screw us. Now that I recall, Andy doesn't break out the road oil charges, instead billing us on the basis of road-improvements per quarter mile or fraction thereof, depending on whether it's oil only, oil-and-chips or hot mix."

Jake hadn't even seen an annual appropriation ordinance yet, which was in fact the budget for the county, let alone any individual bills; but Si's response sounded vague. Jake recalled Phil Monypenny's admonition to "follow the budget."

"Guess I'd like to become something of an expert on the budget, Si, like you are, over time of course. That's the heart of government—and politics—isn't it?"

"Sure is." Si tried to figure out what Jake was getting at, if anything. He shifted gears. "By the way, you ever hear from your friend, Anne, in Chicago?"

Startled, Jake looked around and saw they were alone.

"She's no friend, you know that. We just talked those two nights you and Barney took us out on the town." Jake thought of Kay and how she would react if she heard about Anne from the wrong source.

"Yeah, sure, Jake," Si smiled.

"And what about you and Marie? You're a married man." Jake shot back, still defensive about Anne, thinking he'd better tell Kay what happened, before she heard about it elsewhere. Small towns are all ears and tongues.

"Since we're alone and friends, let me take you into my personal confidence, so you understand about me and Marie." Jake said nothing. "My wife has been frigid since our daughter was born fifteen years ago. My wife and I have an agreement. I can see a friend like Marie, so long as it's way out of town and always in the company of others. In return, I don't bother her about such things. That's just one of the reasons I like heading the state association. Hell, just between you and me, I'm thinking about running for the board of the national association, then moving up the chairs to the presidency."

"That would take a lot of time and money, wouldn't it?"

"Yeah, but it'd be worth it. And it could bring attention and maybe some good things to Williams County."

⌛

Early on Saturday morning at the office Jake put on his apron and went directly to the old newspaper files. It was January or February, he recalled, when as required by law, they published in the paper the county's annual appropriation ordinance. Jake found what he was looking for in the January 26, 1949, edition. He pulled two copies out from the twenty that had been saved for that week. Then he went back to the same period for 1948 and 1947, as far back as the loose copies went, found the budget ordinances for those years and pulled out two copies each.

Charlie Durbin and Ronnie Blevins, the printer's devils, came into the back shop a little after eight, rubbing sleep from their eyes, saying nothing. Jake sat Durbin down at the Model 8 Linotype and gave him the weekly copy from the farm and home extension advisers. "Durbin's going to make a good operator some day," Jake thought. He told Blevins to start on tearing up last week's newspaper page forms. Then the high schooler would have to melt the lead into pigs for use the coming week. Blevins groaned.

Jake smiled. Blevins came from a family that owned lots of farmland. He owned a better car than Jake's. Blevins would go to college. He didn't need to learn a trade he'd never use, so he got the grunt jobs, but he never really complained.

Jake went into the front office, sat at Eileen Benedict's desk and scribbled a note out to Phil Monypenny. "Please take a look at the last three appropriations ordinances for Williams County, which are enclosed. Is there any way to compare the budgeted amounts with those in other counties to see if they are in line? Does the amount budgeted for the county highway superintendent's operations appear reasonable or maybe too high?"

Jake went on. "I just can't seem to get a straight answer to the question of how much the county pays for a gallon of road oil. Apparently the invoice for road work is submitted on a per-quarter-mile basis, rather than broken out in more detail. And the county clerk said I couldn't look at specific invoices, per instructions of the finance committee chair, who is my friend Si McDermott. Shouldn't any taxpayer be able to see the bills? Thanks for any help, and for all the tutoring in the past. Jake."

Jake knocked off work at two, walked over to Harry Wilson's and found Harry at the end of the bar, reading the *Peoria Star*. "I need a Gipp's, Harry, and some counsel."

Harry wrapped the White Owl cigar in his tongue, rolled it into the left corner of his mouth, the better to talk. A shock of white hair slipped onto his forehead as he moved to the cooler. "Comin' up, honorable supervisor."

"Harry, I'm not getting anywhere in my pursuit of an answer to the road oil question. The contractor apparently doesn't bill for road oil separately. But what really ticks me off is that Tommy Jackson blocked my efforts to take a look at some invoices, apparently on an old McDermott directive."

"Welcome to cozy government arrangements among friends. Do you know Allan Andrew Ashmore of Triple A Asphalt?"

"I see the trucks rumbling through, that's all."

"Andy Ashmore runs a big operation, does all the state highway, county and much of the township road work for thirty or more miles in any direction. No competition. He and his fellow road builders long ago carved up the state into fiefdoms. Each reigns supreme in his own territory. Great way to make money. Andy also owns Ashmore Buick here in town and who knows what else. Until Si McDermott was admitted last year, Andy was the only local who belonged to the snooty Peoria Country Club."

"So what are you telling me, Triple A can charge any price it damn well pleases?"

"You got it, son."

"But Si knows what it costs to build roads. He's been active in the state County Officials Association for years, and those fellows compare notes all the time over bourbon-and-branch water. I saw that in Springfield."

"Maybe he does, maybe he doesn't. Maybe he does know and doesn't say anything about it. Who knows? But you're the supervisor, and I think you should get the biggest bang for each hard-earned property tax dollar I have to cough up every summer for the privilege of owning this miserable saloon."

Harry stopped. The desultory click-click of ivory pool balls colliding on the two tables filled the void.

"Well then, where do I go from here, counselor? Maybe that fellow who was in here mumbling about the 40 cents a gallon was full of bullshit."

"Remember I told you that little twerp had been the bookkeeper for Triple A? Later I found out why he had gotten likkered up that night. Seems he had, shall we say, borrowed $500 from Triple A, apparently because his wife had a big hospital bill. Anyway, he hadn't repaid the so-called loan when Ashmore discovered the shortage. The twerp pleaded his case and promised to repay with interest, but Andy told him to clear out of the office and out of town by the next night, or he'd have his ass in jail.

"I remember now the little fellow was bitter as hell about how he was treated after fifteen years of loyal service, and with the wife's problems and all. I hear from one of the regulars that the guy is in a small town in Colorado, and his wife has joined him.

"Maybe, just maybe, if I wrote him that Ashmore was bad-mouthing him all over town, maybe the guy would tell us what he knows."

"Yeah, but who'd believe an embezzler over Andy Ashmore?"

"Maybe nobody, but it'd still be interesting to see what he'd tell us."

"Then go ahead, track him down; but sometimes I wish you'd never brought it up. All I want is to woo my beautiful girl friend and be a good citizen in a decent little town. At least I think it's a decent little town."

⧗

That Saturday evening Jake picked Kay up at five. They headed for Harbor Lights, a restaurant on a harborless tiny lake just north of Galesburg, and then into town to the Rooftop Garden of the Weinberg Arcade, atop a four-story business and professional building. Tiny Hill and his Orchestra were appearing. Tiny looked like the squat, smiling ol' King Cole, jet black hair slicked back with plenty of pomade. Tiny had a wildly popular regional band that played a lilting prairie swing tempo to tunes like "Angry" (please don't be angry) and "Skirts" (how I luvva those skirts, they're such a big attraction to me).

The two had a great time dancing to almost every tune. The evening was warm, but summer's humidity had already begun to fade, and the air was sweet.

On the drive home Kay nestled against Jake's shoulder. Jake suggested they stop briefly at what passed in central Illinois for a hilltop knob that overlooked Lake Calhoun, eight miles west of Billtown. A breeze rustled stately white oaks.

"Kay, I need to tell you something before you might hear it elsewhere—and hear it wrong, I'm sure."

Kay sat up. "What is it, honey?"

Jake took a deep breath. "You remember when I came back from that trip to Chicago with Si McDermott? How I wasn't feeling well and went straight to bed? Well, I was hung over, really hung over."

Kay didn't say anything.

"Well, the night before, Si took the county board chairmen and me out on the town with his buddy, a state senator from Chicago named Barney Connelly. Connelly brought along half a dozen young women from City Hall. Si insisted I join him and Connelly and three of the girls for a nightcap at the top of the Allerton Hotel. I must admit it was fun to zip around the city in Connelly's chauffeured limousine. Like me, the girls, cute kids not many years out of high school, got a big kick out of it.

"Well, anyway, I had several more drinks than I should have—I must have tried all the beers brewed in Chicago and Wisconsin—and finally, who knows when, the driver takes us all back to the Bismarck, where Si and I were staying.

"All I know is the next morning I come to, and one of the girls is in the twin bed next to mine. She must have decided to stay over since it was so late, and she worked literally across the street."

Kay still said nothing. She was staring a hole right through Jake.

"Nothing happened, of course. Couldn't have, in my condition. As soon as I realized where I was, I told her she has to get out, and she told me I'd better hurry as well, or I'd miss my train. Anyway, when we both came out of the room, there was Si McDermott coming out of his room next to mine. He's joked with me about it a couple of times." Jake thought of mentioning Si's friend Marie but thought that might complicate matters even more.

Kay sat silent for a long time.

"I'm really sorry. The whole thing was completely innocent. I don't know why I got drunk. That hasn't happened to me in years and years. Guess I got caught up in the fast pace of the evening. I am really sorry for letting the dumb incident happen, but there was nothing to it."

Finally Kay asked, "What was her name?"

"Huh, oh, Anne, I think." Jake hated himself for shading the truth.

Kay got out of the car, walked a few feet forward to the edge of the modest promontory, arms folded together, as if she were chilled, looking out at the lake. Jake followed slowly.

"I don't need you out here," Kay said firmly, not changing her gaze. Jake said nothing, standing a few feet to her side, also looking out at the water.

Above, braced by a stiff breeze, the oak leaves rustled furiously, generating a muted roar that rose and fell with the winds. After what seemed like hours to Jake, Kay spoke. "Jake, I liked you from the first because I thought you were strong. I'm not strong. People in town think I am, but I'm not. I'm fragile, maybe even brittle. When my husband was killed, my world ended. So I came home to take care of my father. Dad's not strong either. His world collapsed when Mother died having me, or so I've been told by people in town. Other folks can bounce back from tragedies, but for some reason it takes an ungodly long time in my family."

"Kay—"

"Don't talk. You've talked too much already tonight. You're not strong, you just look strong. You don't care about me. I should never have helped bring you out of your shell, should never have gone past hamburgers at Peachie's and our books."

Abruptly Kay turned back to the car. "Take me home."

They drove in silence. Jake, forlorn, tried to think of something to say but couldn't. Then, in desperation, "But you do believe me, don't you, that absolutely nothing happened?"

Kay hadn't looked at Jake since they stopped at the lake, and she didn't look now. "Women don't believe such stories. We've been hurt too often. I don't know whether to believe you, but it shouldn't have happened."

Jake pulled up in front of the Dunlap home. Kay jumped out, slammed the door. "Don't call!" was all she said.

"I have to call, Kay. I love you." Jake fairly shouted the words out after Kay through the open car window. She must have heard him. The neighborhood must have heard him. The screened door slammed behind Kay.

The next morning Jake went out to Ernie's cabin. In town folks were headed for church. Ernie had already communed with his friends along Indian Creek. Ground squirrels scurried underfoot, mourning doves cooed, a cock pheasant had heard Ernie's footfall and responded from deep in the brush with his rasping squawk; quail called to one another: bob-WHITE, bob-WHITE.

"I don't envy my little friends at all," Ernie was thinking. "For them life is one short, scary struggle, requiring constant vigil. Nor, for that matter, would I change places with my friends in town in their church pews. Religion can apparently be comforting, and that's valuable," Ernie thought. "But there aren't any answers inside the tabernacles of faith, not for me anyway. I just wish I could find some out here along the creek."

Jake's approach brightened Ernie's unsatisfying reverie until he saw Jake's hangdog expression and sagging shoulders.

The cabin was stuffy that morning, so he pulled two rickety chairs out under the broad maple shade tree. Here no sunlight would strike them, and Ernie's great tree friend would brush any wisps of air across the two men.

Once again Ernie felt inadequate to help counsel Jake, as he thought back over his miserable lack of experience with women. There had been no loves in his life, he observed. "Oh, I have loved women in the abstract, like Kay Townsend," Ernie thought, but he wasn't about to mention that to Jake. "With my gigantic proboscis and painful shyness, I had never approached Kay or anyone else." During the war the younger guys in his unit had dragged him along to the whore houses, but expectations were never fulfilled in those sordid, sorry places.

"I don't know what to tell you. For her sake, as much as for yours, you have to pursue her; but how you do that, I don't know. Maybe Kay's 'Don't call' really means 'Wait a few days before you call.' If you had told me a year ago that you were coming to town to have a love affair and get into local politics, maybe I'd have read up on both subjects; but who would have taken that bet?"

Jake picked up a small dead branch and was aimlessly digging it into the dirt. "That's just it. Kay has opened up a new world for me, something I never dreamed I'd be a part of. And my little political adventure, well, I'm getting a real kick out of it. My problem is I still don't know how to operate in these worlds. I walk on eggshells, worrying about screwing up, like I did in Chicago."

"Maybe somehow you need to tell Kay exactly that. I'm amazed—and not a little envious—at where you've gone since we met at the library. So, take a long walk, like Lincoln used to do when he had the blues; then, like your friend Johnny Shawnessy in that book you love so much, bounce back for the next chapter."

Jake seemed to feel a little better when he left, Ernie thought, so he felt his friendship was of some use. "I envy Jake so much," Ernie realized, without shaping the words, "that I yearn to feel even his lover's heartache." Ernie took a second morning's walk down along the creek floor. He hoped to spy a red-tail hawk soaring high above his own lamentations.

🗕

On Monday Jake lost himself in his work. The Model 8 machine was frequently squirting lead for no apparent reason, each time locking the Linotype up with congealed metal. It was a pain in the ass to clean up. He spent an hour underneath the machine and finally found an errant shaving that was preventing a tight fit between the lead pot and the line of typeface mats.

Late in the day, as others were leaving, Jake sat down at the Model 14, engaged the steel auxiliary magazine of large 24-point grocery ad type, and set a note for Kay:

I LOVE YOU, KAY. MY HEART ACHES THAT I HURT YOU. I'M STILL LEARNING HOW TO MAKE MY WAY IN THIS WORLD YOU OPENED UP FOR ME. FORGIVE ME. WITH LOVE FROM RAINTREE COUNTY,

Jake took several sheets of ivory, seventy-five percent rag content Hammermill paper, almost like linen, inked the type, and ran sheets through the proof press until he had it just right. He signed the note, put it in a matching envelope, breaking a full box of five hundred envelopes, and hurried to the post office so it would be distributed in the morning mail.

At his apartment there was a letter from Monypenny.

> I compared your county appropriations ordinance with the one here in Champaign County and also with a couple of year-old ordinances for Minnesota counties that are similar in size to yours. Trying to calculate the number of miles in these counties and the budgeted amounts, it appears, very roughly, that Williams spends twenty-to-thirty percent more for roughly the same work. I hasten to add, however, that there are so many variables in all this that what I've told you proves absolutely nothing.

The letter went on. Jake could almost hear the hmmmns of exclamation points that the professor issued as he typed the letter

> Possibly more interesting is that in each of the last two years in Williams County the amounts budgeted for roads, insurance and some other line items have gone up almost fifteen percent a year. That's much higher than has been typical elsewhere. I'm betting that land values in your county, with its rich farmland, have been going up about that much as well, so you can budget more, a lot more, and the actual tax rate doesn't go up. But the tax bills go up, so if the increases continue, the farmers will start squawking. They should, anyway. Finally, I couldn't find anything in Illinois statute that requires the county board to disclose individual invoices and payments, which amazes me; but then I'm finding

that Illinois protects the politicians more than
Minnesota does. There are, however, a couple of court
cases in other states that forced local governments to
open up their records, so you could make a stink
about it. Let me know what more you want.

Phil

Jake took the letter with him to Harry Wilson's. The
September day had been warm and humid, so Harry was
doing land-office business. Several fellows were going to
be late getting home for supper. They seemed not to mind.
Jake reread the letter. No proof of anything wrong here,
though somebody should ask tough questions at the
required annual public hearing on the budget coming up
in a few weeks. Jake planned to attend.

Harry caught up with his orders, for a minute anyway,
and came down to the end of the bar with a schooner of
Pabst for Jake. "This one's on me, honorable supervisor,
but don't breath a word to anyone. I'm out of frosted
mugs, sorry. Dear God,"—Harry looked up to the ceiling in
mock reverence—"if you keep the weather like this until
December, I promise I'll darken the door of the Methodist
Church, should you be willing to reclaim this wretched
soul."

"Harry, quit your blathering, and read this letter
from my professor friend and tell me if you see anything
in it."

Harry had to reach into an empty Emerson Cigar box
on the back bar for his reading glasses. He read the letter
slowly, then observed: "I can almost see why the road
spending would go up quite a bit each year, trying to catch
up with work not done during the war; but still he says it
looks like it's higher than in the other counties. What gets
me is why insurance would go up so sharply each of the
past two years. I'll bet all the county's business is with

Mark Cummings, who's an old buddy of McDermott and the local worthies.

"And hey, I found out where the bookkeeper twerp is located. I sent him a note—first letter I've written in years, honorable supervisor, and all for you—and told him his former boss was saying truly vile things about him all over town. I mean from the gutter to this twerp is down, I said, so far as Ashmore is telling it. Good letter, if I do say so. Just sent it off end of last week. Provided my address and phone number. Now that I think of it, shouldn't have given him my phone number, 'cause Irene Claybaugh and the other telephone operators have awfully big ears. But he won't call; too expensive to call from Colorado."

Harry got Jake another beer. "Pay me for this one, Mr. Politician. Don't want locals to think I'm bribing you."

Jake went home, not knowing what to think, except that somebody ought to ask tough questions at the hearing. "I don't want to be a pesky burr under Si's saddle," Jake thought, "but I sure don't owe Si anything. Si does know his government, a real expert. Yet he seems to enjoy the schmoozing and politics as much as the government work; but they all go together, I guess, at least at the higher levels." Jake's mind went back and forth. Should he make an issue of the budget, with the little information he had? Nobody else was going to, Jake was sure of that.

Thoughts of Kay would then crowd out the local politics for more than a moment. "I'm going to call her. When should I call her? I could go over to the house. No, don't do that now. Wait to the end of the week and call. Maybe Kay will want me to call by then. Oh, damn, I hope so. When Kay said, 'I love you,' I thought my heart would burst, as if day one of my previously miserable life started that moment." Maybe there would be holidays to celebrate some day, even children to spoil, he thought. "Even if I never see Kay again—god, don't think it—but even if, I can now and forever dream those dreams, because for one moment anyway, they seemed within the realm of possibility. I'll call Kay Friday after work."

Jake called. Jim answered. "Kay's not home. Went to Chicago for the weekend to visit a sorority sister. Needed a break before the school year got too busy, she said. She's sure been down this week, Jake. You two have a fight?"

"Yeah, I guess you'd call it that. Please tell her I called and want to talk with her. I'll call again. . . Say, now that we're talking, could I sit down with you to talk over the county's budget? I have some questions about it and I don't know where to turn."

Jim seemed to hesitate, then said, "Sure, I'd be glad to, though I'm no expert on the county budget and don't know how I could help you. I imagine we'll both be in the office tomorrow morning. Come out front whenever you want."

And Jim wasn't very helpful. Jake let him read the letter from Monypenny, but Jim pretty much dismissed it. How can you compare counties in different states and climates and sizes, he wondered? Too many variables, he said. Anyway, Si McDermott is an acknowledged expert on county government. He wouldn't be president of the state association if he didn't manage the county prudently. "I think you're barking up the wrong tree," he said.

Monday after work, Jake called Kay. She was gone again, some card party and supper, Jim said, which didn't sound like Kay's style. Jake said he'd try the next day. When Jake got off the phone, it rang. It was Harry Wilson. "Your phone's been busy, dammit, and I have a letter I want you to read. I'll buy the first beer only, and I have frosted mugs tonight if you get down here quick."

When Jake arrived Harry said, "I'm amazed at how fast the mail is. Of course, this little twerp in Colorado and us are both close to the main line of the CB&Q, which goes straight as a shot to Denver. Anyway, I got this letter today. 'Dear Mr. Wilson,' it says, written in the neat tiny hand of a bookkeeper. Here, you read it."

Jake held it up in the dim light of the tavern and read:

> Mr. Allan Andrew Ashmore is a miserable, ungrateful son-of-a-bitch. I worked for him for fifteen years, without missing a day, at wages Bob Cratchit would have rejected, while he was getting stinking rich by bilking the state of Illinois and local governments all over the region. He doesn't know I know, but I do. Several years ago, Si McDermott came into Ashmore's office, and called him on bills the county had been getting for our road projects. Seems McDermott had gone to a midwest conference on local government, talked with some highway people from Iowa, over drinks I suppose, if Iowans drink, and they told him what they were paying for road projects.

Jake turned to the second sheet.

> McDermott wanted a breakout from Ashmore on a couple of bills: how much for labor, how much for rock, how much for road oil. I can hear through the walls pretty easy, and they started talking loud anyway. Ashmore hemmed and hawed, went through some files, gave McDermott a figure for rock, then I hear him say, "and forty cents a gallon for road oil."
>   That's when McDermott hits the ceiling, saying road oil can't be worth that much. Ashmore says to his old friend—you know they went to high school together— to settle down. Then the talk gets real quiet, and I can't hear them anymore. But, I also did the books for Ashmore Buick as well, which he owns, I'm sure you know.

Since then—I think it's been about four years—
McDermott trades in his big Buick every year for a new
one—and no money changes   hands, like it costs him
nothing. So now you see who the real criminal in all
this is—Allan Andrew Ashmore and all those bastards in
bed with him, taking a little here and there to keep the
scams quiet. I'd come back there and tell the whole
damned town about this, but I've got a sick wife out
here, and who would believe me against Ashmore
anyway? At least you know, and I feel good about telling
someone.

Sincerely,
Wendell Hawkins

"See, I thought something was rotten in Denmark,"
Harry said. He straightened up and ambled toward the
other end of the bar, pleased with his sleuthing. "Aw-right,
I'm comin.' Whad'llyahave, fellas?'"

"Why did I get involved in all this?" Jake mused, as he
waited for Harry to come back. "Improving conditions at
the county farms is more important than a few bucks
under the table, and I can't get anywhere on that without
Si's help, even if he is already thinking about watering
down the reforms. And why make a ruckus here in
Billtown if you can't prove it?"

Harry returned, put his palms, stiff-armed against the
bar, looked down at Jake, shock of white hair falling down
to near his eyebrows. "Well, honorable supervisor,
whadda' we do next?"

"That's my question to you, counselor. We don't have
any proof. We have an embezzler who won't—can't—come
back to talk. I could ask some pointed questions at the
public hearing on the budget next month, but Si will run
rings around me with explanations that I won't be able to
counter, and I'll forevermore be on his shit list."

"I just want some justice, Jake. All my life I've watched the Ashmores and the town gentry take care of one another, and act holier than thou while screwing the little guys, like this little fella who was run out of town for helping his sick wife."

"Yeah, but he shouldn't have put his hand in the till to do it."

"Damn it, what options did he have?"

"Harry, your great grandfather must have been at the ramparts of the Bastille in the French Revolution, or more likely, leaning against the bar in Madame LaFarge's tavern, shouting out directions to the poor bastards taking the grapeshot."

"So you're going to walk away from all this corruption!"

"No, Harry," Jake sighed. "Just let me think it through. Can I have the letter, or are you going to keep it?"

"I'm not sure I trust you with it, not till you sign on to the revolution." Harry smiled, handing him the letter. "I wish there were some way to copy it."

Jake finished his second beer, thought about a third, decided against it, the hangover from Chicago still in his mind. He walked toward his carriage house apartment down South Franklin under mature elms and maples, their branches reaching out above the street. Underneath the canopy the dim lighting from the corner street globe cast a yellow tone on the concrete street intersections.

"To confront, or not to confront. That is the question," thought Jake. "Maybe I ought to show the letter to Si, to gauge his reaction. But that would show my hand without making him show his."

Jake picked up his pace, thinking there was still time to try Kay again.

"Hello. Oh hi, Jake," Kay answered, after more than a week of Jake's calls.

"Kay! Thanks for answering. I'm sorry for hurting you. I love you. Please let me see you." Jake sounded like a sophomore, which he was in some ways. "Could we go out this Friday?"

Kay agreed, sounding cool, yet maybe a little pleased at the prospect. "Let's go to a movie and cool off. Will this hot, sticky weather never end?"

They went to the seven o'clock showing at the Wanee Theatre in Kewanee, which advertised its new air conditioning system. In addition, John Wayne and the young actor, Montgomery Clift, were appearing in a new release, *Red River*. Kay had mentioned more than once that Jake reminded her of Clift, whom Jake hadn't yet seen other than in *LIFE* magazine.

The drive to Kewanee was relaxed, to Jake's relief. Kay's sleeveless starched white cotton blouse offered good evidence of her shapely bust without being showy about it. Jake's being stirred.

"Do I really resemble this guy?" Jake whispered as Clift came onto the screen, a reserved, brooding, skeptical fellow with high cheekbones, slightly hollowed, deep blue-grey eyes and jet black hair. "Not bad, if I do," Jake mused.

"Shhh, we'll talk later. Anyway, just a slight resemblance, the hollow cheeks, I think." Kay smiled brightly, looking at the screen. Jake smiled, too. "Maybe I'm out of the doghouse," he thought.

They drove from the Wanee Theatre to the Waunee Farm Restaurant, a big old home with wraparound screened porch. Now turned into a roadhouse, the place jumped on the weekends. "This Wanee must have been some big-deal Indian chief. There are more things named after him around here than after Lincoln in Springfield—though at least 'Lincoln' is always spelled the same." Jake was feeling good.

They were lucky and got a table on the screened porch. Inside, near the horseshoe bar, Louise Gherkin was at the Wurlitzer organ, which was raised maybe a foot above the small dance floor. A medley of World War II favorites wafted out onto the porch. With a pretty but thin voice, Louise started with "There'll be Bluebirds over the White Cliffs of Dover," and then, of course, "I'll Be Seeing You."

Jake ordered a Schlitz beer and Kay asked for a Walker's DeLuxe and seltzer. With Jake's second beer they ordered deep-fried turtle and chicken baskets, separately, with fries and cole slaw and garlic toast. "Turtle tastes like a blend of five different meats, you know, Kay."

"No, I didn't know. What are the five meats?"

"Well, I have no idea; but that's what I heard in Harry Wilson's, so it must be true. I'll try to identify them when the basket comes."

Jake gave a nod of the head and a smile to Dave Keener and his wife Madge, who were just finishing dinner. "Dave's the supervisor from Orion Township, a farmer, which goes without saying. I'm one of the few non-farmers. He's a decent guy, quiet, go-along type, which also seems to be typical. Seems like two-thirds of these fellows are on the board so they can come to town and catch up on what's going on. They're delighted to let Si McDermott run things."

Jake suddenly knitted his brow.

"Now you're really looking like Montgomery Clift. What's the matter?"

"Oh, nothing. Well, I shouldn't say this, even to you, but I've got a suspicion that something in our county operations may not be on the up-and-up."

"You're kidding. Not with Si McDermott in charge. He's a paragon of virtue and civic leadership, according to Jim."

"Maybe so. I hope so. Sure would make my life a lot simpler. I just don't know where to turn for counsel. My buddy Ernie is no help on this, and Harry Wilson wants to start a revolution.

"Would you mind if I told you what I think I know, to see what you make of it?"

"Of course not, but I'm no student of such things."

Jake went through the original road oil charge from the bookkeeper, as Harry overheard it, and then through the budget evaluation that the professor did. Finally, he pulled the letter from his shirt pocket and handed it to Kay. Kay read through it.

"It's hard to believe that Andy Ashmore would bilk local governments or that McDermott would keep quiet in return for new cars. I can tell you want and need good advice. All I can tell you is, do what you think is right, Jake, or you won't be able to live with yourself."

"But what the devil is right? I can't prove anything, and this letter wouldn't hold up, yet I'm becoming convinced that something's not right. Of course, don't mention this to anyone, which I know you wouldn't. And why should I stir things up and probably turn folks against me—just when I may have found a town where I could settle down?"

Jake looked at Kay. She returned his gaze momentarily, then looked over his shoulder and changed the subject.

"Down there at the end of the porch is a young couple just married a few months ago. Maybe it's been a year already, and they're celebrating. Anyway, they were both students of mine. It's great to see my students grow up. Those two were awfully good students, could have gone on to college, as more and more graduates are doing; but they just wanted to settle down and rear a family."

Kay beamed her light-up-the-room smile past Jake toward the young couple, waving when she caught their glances. Jake took a deep breath, twisted slightly in his booth seat, as if straining on a leash.

As they left, the organist was bouncing into "Let's Get Away From It All." As a singer she was no Sinatra, but they loved her at Waunee Farm.

On the fifteen-mile drive to Billtown, much as he wanted to, Jake didn't even suggest that they go to his place. At the Dunlap house Jim's bedroom reading lamp was still on. Jake walked Kay up to the unlocked front screen door. Not a sound stirring. They embraced and kissed. "Thanks for a great evening and for seeing me again. I'm sure not perfect, and I have a lot of learning to do, but I do love you more than you can know."

Kay put her arms around Jake's lean waist, leaned back just enough to look into his eyes. "I must admit I kind of missed you the past couple of weeks." She reached up on tiptoes, kissed him quickly again and slipped inside.

⧗

When Kay came down the next morning for breakfast, Jim was reading the *Chicago Tribune*. Minnie White was pouring him a second cup of coffee. "Minnie," Kay said, "I wish you'd let me get our breakfasts. You shouldn't have to come over here every morning just for this."

"Don't listen to her, Minnie. We all know she doesn't mean it."

They laughed. Tiny, thin as a wraith, grey hair pinned up, Minnie brought Kay three buckwheat cakes, a Saturday morning tradition, with Aunt Jemima syrup. It was true. Kay rather enjoyed the luxury of not preparing the meals.

While Minnie was out in the pantry, Kay asked Jim, "Do you think any of the businessmen in this town are capable of cheating or bilking customers?"

"Oh, probably not more than two hundred percent of them. Why do you ask?"

"I'm serious."

"So am I. Every businessman looks for an advantage. That's how we build profits. Guess it depends on your definition of 'cheating'."

"Wouldn't it be unethical," Kay asked, "to charge twice as much as necessary for your work and then pay off somebody to keep it quiet?"

Jim's eyes narrowed. "What are you talking about?"

"Oh, nothing, I just sense that Jake thinks something's amiss in county government."

"Jake came to me about that. In a nice way I told him he was basically crazy. Listening too much to that professor friend of his." There was an edge to Jim's tone. "Nobody of Si McDermott's stature would do anything that wasn't up-and-up. Jake's beginning to take himself too seriously."

They dropped the topic. "There's never anything in this Saturday *Tribune*. They shouldn't waste the trees to put it out, dammit. The ol' Colonel, though, he sure can't stand our new Governor Stevenson. I get a big kick out of how his editorial writers and even the reporters look for opportunities to bash him."

"But Jake was impressed by Stevenson. Said he had a grasp of the county farm problems and wanted to help. Oh, and whatever you do, please never mention to Jake that you and I talked about this. It would upset him, I know."

"And harrumph to you, Kay!" he responded. Jim's gentle, intelligent round face was full of fatherly, widower's love for his only child—who just happened to be a beautiful young woman, if he did say so himself. So Jim worried a bit, not about where the relationship between Kay and Jake might lead but about whether Jake knew what he was getting into.

Later that same morning Jake was driving along US 150 to Morton, which was about halfway to Champaign-Urbana. Ernie rode shotgun. They were to meet Professor

Monypenny at one of Ernie's favorite cafes, right there in Morton. Great chocolate meringue pie, four inches from the flaky crust to the gold-tinged curlicues on top.

Earlier in the morning Jake had put the printer's devils to work and had Dave Gelvin come in for some overtime to clean up several printing jobs the merchants wanted first of the week. Jake was by now basically running the back office at *The Republican*, and that was just fine with everyone, including Jim Dunlap, who could now sit up front without worrying.

Hmmmn, Jake and Ernie heard, as they opened the cafe door, which jangled a little bell. The professor was lecturing the waitress about the Illinois Constitution. She shot Jake and Ernie a look of "Who is this guy?" But she was clearly fascinated by his big words, and his suit and vest on a September weekend.

"Jake, I found an Illinois appellate court decision—not your appellate district—but still a strong decision, saying that a taxpayer has the right to review bills submitted to local governments for payment." Hmmmn. Monypenny was pleased with himself. "So you could wave this citation in front of the county clerk if you had to."

"Yeah, but do I want to? What would I find? If the bills lack detail, what could I prove, except to make everybody mad. The deeper I get into this, the stickier it becomes." He handed Monypenny the letter from the little twerp, as Harry insisted on calling him.

Hmmmn. . . .hmmmn, as he read. The waitress looked over and smiled quizzically, not seeing many professor types in the cafe.

"Yes, I can see that it's awkward, even daunting," the professor observed, "to think about shaking things up without knowing what if anything would fall out. Yet it sure looks like there is some hanky-panky.

"Let me tell you what more I know. I talked with some faculty in civil engineering, and we figured for a county your size, which has lots of county highways, you could use several hundred thousand gallons of road oil in a season."

"You're kidding. That could mean thousands of dollars in possible overcharges. That's huge money."

Ernie ordered another piece of pie. Jake and the professor continued, hunched over their Green Rivers.

"As for the rest of the budget, I already told you that the insurance charges are twenty-to-thirty percent higher than in a couple of counties of comparable size, but even there we may be comparing apples and oranges. And for the rest of the budget it's almost impossible to do meaningful comparisons, except for one that I'm almost hesitant to bring up."

"What's that?"

"Well, the printing and legal publications charges look real high."

"You're kidding, of course."

"Again, could be apples and oranges, but they sure look high when I butt them up against Champaign County and the two like-sized counties in Minnesota. We're not talking really big money, of course; maybe four to six or seven thousand dollars more than I'd think the total charges might be, based on the other counties."

"Holy shit, I don't want anything more to do with this," Jake exclaimed. The waitress, taking a cigarette break on a counter stool, jumped a little. "We must be barking up the wrong tree. This Jim Dunlap is as straight a shooter as they come. Great boss, great guy, everybody likes him, respects him."

"You asked me to evaluate the budget. I'm giving you my best assessment. And I could be all wrong."

"I'm sorry. You're great. All this time you've taken, which can't have any payback for your university work, is sure appreciated. But what do you think I ought to do now?"

"That's tough, and it gets into the realm of politics. And we political scientists don't know anything about politics, you know. But, since you asked, you could go to McDermott and tell him you simply wanted to look through last year's bills, just so you can learn about what comes in, to get a feel for the budget. Do it in a non-threatening way. Or you could go to the public hearing on the budget and ask tough questions about the rapid growth in the budget, about road spending versus that in some other states. I could help with the questions and some follow-up questions, on the assumption he'd have convincing-sounding answers for you."

"And how will Si react to these options?"

"If he's smart, and I think he is, and since the bills are probably not very detailed, I think he'd say, 'Okay, Jake, you can look the bills over, but if you have any questions, bring them to me, not to the public hearing.' "

"And what would I say to that?"

"First of all, what does McDermott think of you? That is, does he think you're a straight arrow, or a political comer who wants on the inside or what?"

"I have no idea. Haven't thought about it. But so far I've been a go-along, get-along type. Hell, that deal I made to keep him on as supervisor now looks like a masterstroke of politics, though at the time I just wanted to get back at Lloyd Ryan somehow. Maybe, with my reserved, cagey Montgomery Clift looks—or so I'm told—Si thinks I want in on whatever's goin' on." Jake smiled, not knowing if he were half-serious or half-joking.

"And what happens to the county farm issue," Jake went on, "if Si turns on me? That's about people, not just money."

"You may put that issue at risk, although it has probably taken on a life of its own. If the governor sees that as a popular issue with real emotional appeal, Si probably couldn't stop it even if he wanted to." Hmmmn.

Monypenny pushed a shock of straw-colored hair off his forehead and ran his fingers back through the rest of his tousled, unruly mop. The shock of straw came back down to just above his dancing blue eyes.

They went to the cash register to pay the bill. Monypenny insisted on buying, over Jake's and Ernie's protests. The waitress took his dollar bill and asked, "Are you a professor? I've never met a professor."

"Why, yes." Hmmmn. Philip Monypenny, University of Illinois, political science. Why do you ask?"

"Oh, no reason. I just hope our daughter goes to the U of I some day. She's very smart. That's why I'm working here. Saving all I make. And," she added quickly, "you look like a good man. I'd like her to be in your classroom sometime."

Hmmmn. "Why thank you, that's very kind."

As they parted, Jake and Professor Monypenny agreed to keep in touch. Ernie promised to send a bottle of "my best" rhubarb wine with Jake the next time they met, in return for the two pieces of pie. Jake laughed, and added, "Yeah, and Ernie tells me that his June 1949 vintage was a very good year for rhubarb wine."

The McDermott Livestock Farm

Chapter 10

You Can Learn Too Much

Jake took off from work at four the following Thursday and drove to Kewanee. He had already put in three eleven-hour days through Wednesday getting out a big harvest celebration issue of *The Republican*. Jake hoped to catch Ziggy O'Connell, the *Peoria Star's* regional reporter, in his office. Jake bounded up three flights of stairs in an office building filled with doctors, dentists and bookkeepers.

At the end of the third-floor corridor he found the masthead of the *Star*, clipped from a front page and taped to the clear glass window that looked into Ziggy's cubby-hole office. Just room for a desk, a Corona typewriter, telephone and a four-drawer oak file cabinet. On the wall above the clutter of old newspapers and copy paper were photos of Ziggy with prominent politicians who had come through the territory on campaign swings. Small town reporters like Ziggy needed to shore up their hinterland postings by showing that they also hobnobbed with the big shots.

Jake had met Ziggy at his first county board meeting. They had talked a couple of times since. Jake thought him a fair, objective reporter who had his eyes peeled for a good story. Anyway, Jake didn't know where else to turn.

Ziggy, no bigger than Eddie Arcaro, sat on two canvas pillows in a swivel chair, peering at a piece of copy paper in his Corona. "Well, Supervisor, to what do I owe the honor?" Ziggy smiled.

"Ziggy, I need a favor. In return, if anything comes of what I'm involved in, I'll let you have the story first."

"Why not give it to your own paper?"

"Well, yours is a daily, and who knows when it might break? And it's probably not Jim Dunlap's type of story. You know better than me that the county seat weeklies are primarily booster papers. They play down any local negative stuff, which is okay.

"That's all I can tell you right now. Maybe nothing will come of this. I almost wish it wouldn't, but something inside me is pushing to find out what I can."

"Okay, I'm willing to wait. I've got enough to do covering this crazy Kewanee City Council. Had a fist fight last night. The mayor decked a commissioner, and the esteemed audience booed the commissioner when he failed to get up before the ten count. That's what you get in a small manufacturing town full of tough Lugans, Poles and Belgians. Sure never would happen down in your staid Wasp territory. What's the favor?"

Jake handed Ziggy a sealed envelope. "All I want you to do is sign this on the outside to show you've received it and put today's date on it. Inside I explain what I'm planning to do, something out of character for me. If I'm accused of something later, you can open this letter then. I don't know if people will believe it, but at least you can vouch for the circumstances, and it could even become part of the story.

"All I ask is that you put the letter away . . . somewhere that you can find it," Jake added, as he looked around the disheveled office. "Later, over a beer, I can tell you all about it."

"Sounds fair to me." Ziggy opened the top left drawer, slid the envelope in and slammed it shut. "Now I've got to head out to talk with a couple of school board members. They want to build a new high school. Big bucks, Jake." He reached around Jake and pulled his grey fedora off the coat tree behind the open door. There was indeed a press card sticking out from the satin hatband. Ziggy played his role to the hilt, even if he was just in hog and corn country.

⧖

"What do you want to see me about, Jake?" Si McDermott and Jake sat over coffee mugs on Saturday morning at Lola's Shackateria. Since the election fiasco, McDermott made an appearance there every now and then, though he couldn't bring himself to rejoin Lloyd Ryan and his coffee klatch. The two said their howdies to folks they knew, which even for Jake now meant just about everybody, and Si joshed with ladies at a table nearby. Then they could settle down to talk.

"So you still want to go through the bills? I can assure you, you won't find anything interesting there."

"I'm sure not, but I'm really liking this government stuff. And the trips to Springfield and Chicago, that's the kind of life I like. But it's not cheap, I know that. Who knows, maybe someday, like you, I'll try to move up the ladder. I'm never going to get rich as a printer, and I'm thinking it'd be great to have enough going to be able to marry someone like Jim Dunlap's daughter."

Si wasn't sure what he was hearing. "Nobody ever makes any money in politics, let me tell you."

"Probably not, but I need to figure out how to get to a place where I could buy a new Buick every year like you do. What's that cost you to trade in every year, a pretty penny, I'll bet?"

"Huh, oh not so much. Thank god I've got my prize herd of cattle to keep me in the clover." Si decided to probe Jake a bit. He lowered his voice. They were at the corner table. Nobody was in earshot. "Am I hearing you say that if there was a way to make a few bucks in politics—which there sure as hell isn't around here—that you'd be willing to play the game? If you are, you're playing with fire, you know."

"I guess maybe that's what I'm saying. What's so wrong with wringing a few dollars out of the system if that's what it takes to get ahead in politics? I'd repay it many times over by bringing projects and funding back to my territory. But as I could see in the capital and in Chicago, you've got to have a place at the table before you can get anything done."

Si measured his response. "You're a keen observer and a quick learner, I'll say that, but don't try to run before you can walk. I'll give you as many opportunities to participate as I can without riling the older guys who have been patiently waiting their turns. After all, we're just a small county, and after many years I'm just getting to the place where maybe I can do some good for folks back here at home.

"So go ahead," Si went on. "Look through as many of the goddammed bills as you want. Tell Tommy I said it was okay. He can call me if he has any questions. But promise me you'll take any questions you have directly to me, not to the public hearing on the budget. Nobody attends that but the supervisors and a couple of reporters. You'd just confuse everybody, and I'd have the answers anyway, the answers I'll give you when we talk about it between you and me. Is that a deal?"

"Yep. I just want to learn, and this is a good way to get started. Thanks, Si."

Tommy Jackson had already been alerted by Si when Jake came in just before noon. "Here are last year's bills." Tommy pointed to a library table that had been cleared off. Two stacks of invoices, each a foot high, sat in the middle.

Tommy clearly wasn't happy to be bothered, but he said, "You can sit there over the noon hour while we're out for lunch. Don't know what the hell you're looking for, but if you have any questions, holler."

"I'm not looking for anything in particular, just trying to learn what types of bills come in. Thanks for being so helpful."

Jake had brought a sheaf of copy paper with him and a long, yellow, soft lead No. 2 pencil, good for editing on newsprint, which tore easily. He flipped through the invoices. They looked like Greek to him, he thought, dismayed. After a while Jake saw some patterns. The biggest bills came from Triple A Asphalt, as he would expect. Highway maintenance and new road construction was the county's biggest and—most folks, especially farmers, would say—the most important activity. Jake decided to tally these bills, according to whether for road oil only, for oil-and-chips or for hot mix, and the mileage for each project. The total bills from Triple A for the fiscal year came to $247,000.

Jake ignored the nits-and-lice bills, small or infrequent, like law books, meals for jurors, per diem for county board members. He noted salary payments to the county judge and state's attorney for $7,000 and $6,000 respectively, almost twice what Jake earned as a printer. "Surprised they don't get more," Jake mused.

Next Jake totaled the insurance bills, all from the Cummings Insurance Co. There were about a dozen, totaling $16,500 and change, for liability and casualty coverage for the courthouse, jail, county home and highway department. Jake also saw *The Republican* invoice frequently, more so than he would have imagined. After debating whether to do so, he tallied up those bills. There was $2,200 for publishing the board's proceedings, $2,700 for ballots for the 1948 elections, and $3,000 and change for printing forms and supplies for the various county offices.

The biggest bill—Jake remembered the huge job—was for printing the individual home, farm and commercial property assessment lists for all sixteen townships in the county. Since there was no other newspaper within the county, the business legally had to go to *The Republican*. Jake smiled. Best read section in the paper, as most everyone wanted to compare his assessment with his neighbor's and try to figure out who the richest landowners were. Reassessments were done every four years, and 1948 was that year, so the bill was big, $6,000. He remembered from his days at the Pontiac paper hearing from the owner that papers were paid so much a line for these "legals." State law required they be published, and there was a minimum rate per line that the county had to pay, but Jake couldn't recall what that was. "So Jim Dunlap reaped almost $14,000 in county business in the past year. Real good, but we did a lot of work," Jake concluded.

Jake finished just as Tommy and his deputy clerks were returning from lunch. He folded his copy paper, stuffed it in his left pants pocket. "Thanks, Tommy. I'm finished. It's still mostly Greek to me, but I have a better sense of the kinds of bills the county has to pay. Glad we have such a competent county clerk and staff to handle the complexity of it all."

Tommy knew Jake was giving him bull, but he appreciated the deference. "Hope you did learn something. County board members don't have much interest in the budget, other than Si, of course."

That evening Jake recopied his sheets and sent them off to Phil Monypenny. "If you can make any sense out of this and help me develop some pointed questions for

McDermott, I'd be in your debt. And again, thanks for all the time you're putting into this."

⌛

Jim Dunlap had four season tickets for the University of Illinois home football games. He went once a season and gave the other tickets away to Harry Campbell or Dave Gelvin, who considered them a real treat. Jim invited Jake and Kay to join him for the October game with Wisconsin, a Big Ten rival. Since there were four tickets, Kay suggested Jake ask Ernie as the fourth. In return, Ernie offered to drive Jim's big Buick, as he figured they weren't going to let him pay for anything. Ernie also put his Speed Graphic 4x5 news camera in the trunk so he could take pictures of the group.

Game morning brought a picture perfect fall day—sunny, dry, shirt sleeve weather. The four had a good time on the three-hour drive to Champaign. Normally quiet, almost contemplative, Jim regaled them with stories of his teen years as a printer's devil. "The boss's son was a gullible little twerp" (which turned Jake's mind briefly to budget issues) "a couple of years younger than me. I'd send him to the gas station to get a bucket of steam or to the hardware store for a roof tightener. Can't figure out why the boss ever liked me, the way I treated little Johnny."

"And you're my father, whom I look upon as the almost—perfect man. How could you be so mean?" Everyone laughed.

They had lunch at the Inman Hotel, a favorite of Jim's. He saw two old friends, both members of the Illinois Press Association, the weekly newspaper fraternity. Kay directed Ernie to Memorial Stadium, and they parked on a practice football field west of the massive football temple. Ernie took pictures of the three of them, Kay in the middle, standing in front of the car. Kay had one hand in Jake's and her arm around Jim's waist. Ernie took several shots, having trouble getting a natural, rather than forced, smile from Jake. Kay was radiant and happy.

Kay spied a sorority sister who was fussing over two young sons, their father off to buy hot dogs and popcorn. Kay introduced everyone, and the women recalled how they had flunked cheerleader tryouts because they weren't athletic enough. The men protested at what a mistake the judges had made. Jake and Ernie heard drumbeats and turned to see a massive band marching toward the stadium, wearing navy uniforms trimmed in dark orange. The two had never been to a Big Ten football game, so Kay hurried them into the cavernous red brick edifice, streaming in along with hordes of fans, men mostly in white shirts and ties, women in long skirts, blouses, carrying sweaters or jackets in case needed. Lots of plaid that year.

During the game Jim tried to play the football expert, describing each play and the underlying strategies, all of which escaped Ernie, though Jake understood the basics of the game. Kay was more interested in explaining the history, lineage, traditions and formations of the bands. Wisconsin had brought their "Marching Badgers," and the stadium rocked with Sousa marches and competing fight songs. Badger fans waved red and white pennants, a combination that Ernie found less offensive to the eye than the orange and blue of the Illinois team.

Jake took it all in quietly, smiling, caught up in the color, music and energy in the stadium. He held Kay's hand throughout, except when they leapt to their feet to cheer a big play. Ernie stayed in his seat. Jake diplomatically asked first Jim, then Kay, questions about what was going on. The teams ended up in a tie, 13-13, and Jim wove half a dozen scenarios by which the Fighting Illini could and certainly should have won.

Jim insisted the group stop on the way back at the Pere Marquette Hotel for dinner. Thinking this might happen, Jake and Ernie had brought jackets. Ernie's was a castoff from a cousin, a bit frayed at the cuffs; but it was dark in tone, and nobody seemed to notice. Billy Hill and his seven-piece band played show tunes and dance numbers from a corner of the ballroom-style dining room. As always, Kay was ready to dance. She pulled Jake up from the table when Billy announced a Gershwin medley. They were the only ones on the good-sized dance floor. "Why did hemlines have to come down so low the past couple of years, Jake? It's impossible to dance in this long skirt. Just two years ago, skirts were above the knee."

"Women's fashions and trends mystify me about as much as football, but it's been a great day," Jake responded. The band had no vocalist, so Billy Hill played the melody lines on his soft, confident cornet. After "Embraceable You" and "Our Love Is Here to Stay," Kay led Jake back to the table.

She looked at Jim, who had half risen on her return. "May I have this dance, sir?" Jim protested but Kay wouldn't relent, so they wended their way through the tables in time for "The Man I Love" and "Someone to Watch over Me." Jim was a big, stout man, courtesy of rich meals and no exercise. He had a slouch born of long hours hunched over the Corona typewriter and the back shop make-up tables. On the dance floor, however, he stood ramrod straight, and father and daughter moved around the room gracefully.

When they returned, Kay stared at Ernie and said, "You're next." Ernie got red as a beet. Oh, how he wanted to hold Kay in his arms, if only for a moment, but his feet froze at the table. "I've never danced, Kay. Wouldn't know how, much as I'd like to." Sensing his embarrassment, Kay didn't push the idea. Ernie wished she had.

Jake drove the Buick back to Billtown. They dropped Ernie off at his cabin. At the Dunlap residence, Jake and Kay let Jim off, claiming they wanted to go "up the line" to Waunee Farm and maybe the 34 Club to see what was going on. Instead, Kay said to Jake, "Let's go over to your place." Jake pushed on the foot feed.

Jake had left the windows open at his apartment. It was cool inside. They stood, embracing, saying nothing, then, "I'm cold, Jake, let's get under the covers. I'm afraid you'll never make the suggestion." They undressed in the dark, though a sliver of moonlight struck the corner of the bed through the south window.

Jake pulled the sheet and a huge cabin-in-the-cotton quilt, which Ernie's sister Hattie made for him, over the tops of their heads. Jake lightly bumped his forehead against Kay's, and they rubbed noses. "Just like the Eskimos," whispered Kay. They embraced, their trim, firm bodies stretched taut, held firmly against one another. Kay moved herself over onto Jake. They kissed and lay still, though it was difficult. Finally, they loved. A breeze blew in the west windows.

As they lay still again, Jake wondered aloud, hesitantly, if Kay might ever be willing to become formally entangled with him. "I think I just might." Later they loved again, saying little. Jake not knowing what to say, not wanting to break the spell. He thought about becoming the parent he never had and of how he would do as a father. And whether the child—or children—would favor Kay or him, or even Montgomery Clift.

⧗

The next morning Kay went to church as always. She sang, not too well, in the choir at the First Congregational Church. Jim remained at home, not having gone to church regularly in years, though Kay dragged him kicking and screaming, he always said, on Christmas and Easter. Kay sat in the first of two rows in the small choir loft—the better to see her, a deacon once said to her quietly in the cloakroom. She fingered the satin cream-colored cowl that she and the seven women and two men of the choir wore over their maroon robes.

Jake was strong, Kay thought, during the New Testament lesson, no matter what she had said to him earlier in her anger. "And he's a good person. All the workers at the office like and respect him. And then there's that wry, boyish smile, sometimes quick, sometimes slow to crinkle into dimples—just like Montgomery Clift. And earlier, not last night, he mentioned children. I'm thirty. Two children, maybe."

Kay shook, startled from her reverie by the bombastic boom of the pipe organ leading them into some unplayable, unsingable (by this choir, anyway) anthem. "We're going to butcher this one," she thought, smiling almost menacingly at the worshippers sprinkled around the semicircular auditorium. She heard two foot clicks from the choir director. They stood in unison.

Jake had gone to the office since he missed work Saturday. He worked for five hours, first on the Linotypes, adjusting the elevator of the Model 14 ever so minutely. The long arm of the elevator lifts a line of steel mats, each representing a letter, up top to be redistributed to their respective slots in the magazine, after just having served to make a line of type. Like every part in the wondrous yet temperamental contraption, if the elevator doesn't line up perfectly, the machine jams. He also cleaned the machines thoroughly, with great respect. As he worked alone, Jake thought.

"Jim can't be taking undue advantage of the county. He's just too damned decent. This office does a hell of a lot of work for the county, more than I realized. Those assessment lists, for example. We worked our butts off to put that extra section together." He walked toward the front office to where the last three years of papers were filed. He found that paper and pulled out the two twelve-page sections, twenty-four pages of nothing but line after line of names and assessed values. "Helluva lotta work," he repeated to himself.

Jake thought of how he could prove that Jim was a straight shooter. He counted the lines in a typical column, took that number times eight for the number of columns on each page, and then times twenty-four for the number of pages and came up with 24,000 lines of type. About twenty-five cents per line, Jake figured roughly, based on the invoice amount of $6,000. The office worked overtime for weeks to put it all together shortly after Jake arrived in town, so the figure seemed defensible.

Jake knew how to confirm that this charge was reasonable. That afternoon about suppertime, Jake called his old boss, John Bailley, the editor and publisher at the Pontiac *News-Leader*. "John, I'm sorry to bother you on Sunday, but I'm on the county board in Williams County, which I'll bet astounds you. And I have a question about legal printing charges that you might help me with."

"Jake, who're you kidding. You never said more than three words to anyone in your life, except the town librarian. Nobody'd elect you to anything, even though I know you're a decent guy."

"Well, it happened, and there is a librarian involved in all this, too. But for now I just need to know what a paper like yours gets per line for running the assessment lists. That's how it's charged, isn't it?"

"Yeah, but why don't you ask Jim Dunlap? I take it you work for him. It's the only paper in that county, the lucky devil. Haven't talked with Dunlap in years."

"Well, sure I could, but I just wanted to double-check something to prove a point. So what is the charge?"

"Same for every paper, except the big dailies: minimum of twelve-and-a-half cents a line, which becomes the maximum because all the county governments complain we use our clout with lawmakers to set an artificially high rate. Actually, it is set in state statute, and we're delighted to get it, though we all complain. We get paid a good dollar for the best-read section the paper puts out. We always print five hundred extra papers that week because nonsubscribers want the issue."

Jake didn't know quite what to say. "Twelve-and-a-half cents a line, that's all?"

"Whatdaya mean, that's all? Sure it's a lot of work for you guys in the back shop, but it's gravy for us owners, all things considered. Much more than we'd get for regular ads filling up a page. And a lot more than the full-page grocery ads, which we have to discount to those regular advertisers."

Jake thought about it. What John said made sense. "Well, thanks, John; I thought it would be about what you said it was." Bewildered, Jake didn't know what to think.

He went home, still not believing that Jim had it in him to bilk the county. Jake had refigured the number of lines three times, and the resulting rate per line. His arithmetic wasn't wrong. There must be another answer. He tossed and turned most of the night.

⌛

Irene Claybaugh worked the switchboard every other Sunday till 7 P.M. She had put the call to Pontiac through for Jake. It was a quiet evening, so she listened in. Later she called Si McDermott, having appreciated the crisp five dollar bill he had slipped her when he stopped in to chat with Peyton Dexter, her boss.

"Another call from that same local party about county government budgeting, Mr. McDermott. This time some-

thing about the legal printing bills for the property assessments. Of course, I didn't understand what they talked
about."

"Was the party talking with the professor type, Irene?"

"No, I think it was a newspaperman, maybe somebody
this party used to work for. But while I can't mention this
party by name, you'd think, where he works and all, either
he'd know or he'd know who to ask."

"Well, thanks a million, Irene. This is all helpful in my
own budget work."

"Goodnight then, Mr. McDermott."

"Goodnight, Irene, and thanks again."

⌛

The next morning Si McDermott called Jim Dunlap at *The
Republican*. "Jim, I have something I need to talk to you
about. Could you drive out to my place? It's kind of important."

"Sure, Si, let me get the week started here at the office,
and I'll be out before noon."

Had there been a *Better Homes & Farms* magazine, the
McDermott Livestock Farm would have been the cover
pinup photo at some point. Not too showy, which would
have been bad taste in the farm world, but neat as a pin,
hardly a blade of grass out of place. An open, large, green
lawn sloped easily from the prairie-style white frame
home down to the oil-and-chip road. Mature oaks and
hard maples shaded the home on all sides. A huge round
barn rose four or five stories behind the house, a tourist
site for relatives who visited family in the county. Several
low-slung livestock sheds, also recently painted in standard barn red, were at each side of the barn, like peniten-
tial sentries before their Buddha.

White wood crisscross fencing enclosed small pastures
on each side of the house in front of the livestock sheds.

McDermott's two prize shorthorn bulls took up one lot, looking quite pleased with themselves. In the other, half a dozen Shetland ponies, a new dwarf breed popular at parades and shows, grazed silently. "Damned expensive hobby," Jim thought to himself, "but Si sure gets a big kick out of driving his six-hitch team of Shetlands at the State Fair."

The two men walked to the fence near the ponies. "Had word that your printer called an old boss last night to ask about charges for running county assessment lists."

"Christ, why would he do that?"

"You tell me. What did you charge us for running the assessments last time?"

"Just like we agreed. I doubled the rate for the legals and all the printing jobs. Oh, hellfire and damnation, I knew I never should have agreed to your scheme. You said nobody'd ever know in a million years."

"Now you didn't seem too hard to convince, as I remember."

"I wasn't thinking clearly. Dwight Green was going to lose the governorship, that was clear by then, and I would lose that nice monthly retainer he paid me and forty or fifty other newspaper owners to run his news releases. I need a new newspaper press badly, and they don't come cheap. And you convinced me the half of that over-billing I contributed to you would pay dividends for the whole area later, when you ran for a national association post or even for state elective office. Damn it to hell." Jim rubbed his hands together repeatedly. He lit a Camel and took a deep drag.

"And it will, Jim. Big dividends. And nobody'll ever find out a thing. Anyway, there's nothing illegal about your bills, even if they are high. The funny thing is that Jake, who sure is sweet on your daughter, wants in on the action, the greedy young bastard. I must say I admire his pluck. He's learning fast . . . too fast."

Jim's stomach churned, immediately nauseated. Jake? No!

⧗

Later Si called Jake at home and asked him to come out to the farm on Saturday morning. McDermott wanted to get matters settled down. The October day was overcast, blustery, unusually cool. Jake sported a new navy windbreaker, which he liked, and a wool English cap with the tiny bill that snaps down. He liked the Black Watch plaid but not the cap itself. Why did he let Kay talk him into it? Nevertheless, it felt comfortable this morning. He pulled it down a tug in the direction of the north breeze. He and Si leaned against the white fence, looking at the two Angus bulls, jet black coats glistening. "Those two magnificent sons-a-bitches have bred hundreds of cows, Jake. Great life, wouldn't you say?

"But to the point. You've been looking at the county bills over the last year, and you've looked at the proposed appropriation ordinance. Tell me what you think you've learned."

"Okay, so long as when I'm finished, you speculate on where you can see me going in local politics. And be honest about whether you think I have much of a future in it."

"You're on."

"Well, based on calculations and comparisons my professor friend and I have made, it sure looks to us like the amounts budgeted for road maintenance and construction are about thirty percent higher than necessary."

"You really think so? How can you be sure?"

"I can't be sure, of course. But," Jake shifted his gaze from the bulls and into Si's eyes, "we figure Triple A is charging you about forty cents a gallon for road oil, when anybody can buy it for ten cents a gallon. If so, that would amount right there to $20,000 per year—probably a lot more—in excess charges."

Si's eyes narrowed. "That's some calculatin', Jake. Not that I think you're right. What else do you figure?"

"Well, based on casualty and liability premiums charged in other counties of similar size, the professor and I estimate that the $14,000 you have plugged into the appropriation ordinance for insurance could probably be covered quite nicely for nine or ten thousand."

"Of course, it all depends upon the amount of coverage and history of claims, so you could be off base, you know."

"Sure we could, but these are the types of questions a fellow could bring up at the public hearing and which you wanted me to bring to you instead. So, is our coverage a lot higher than typical, and is our claims record so bad that the county has to pay a lot more than other counties?" Jake asked the question in a soft yet direct and challenging tone. After all, Si had told him to bring the questions to him direct.

"Well now, do you want me to dazzle you with lots of figures to prove you wrong?"

"Try me. I'm still learning all this."

McDermott let it drop. They were playing poker, trying to figure out what cards the other had in his hand. "And what else in the budget might have looked out of line? What about printing and publications, for example? We do a lot of that, as you well know."

Their eyes were still locked. Jake flinched just enough for Si to see. Jake looked back at the bulls. "I didn't have time to check that out, and anyway I'm sure that Jim Dunlap would charge a fair amount for work done."

"Of course he would. Well, seems like you've got a couple of interesting observations, both of which can be answered, of course. But I'll go back and look at the numbers again. Overall, I'd say you've really done your homework; that is, you and the professor have. Any last findings that you have before we talk about your future?"

Jake hesitated about playing this last card. Then he said, looking right through Si's eyes, "Yeah, Si, I figure you get your new Buick on trade each year from Andy Ashmore for absolutely nothing!"

That one caught McDermott off guard. "Now where in hell would you hear anything like that?"

"You asked me what I know, and I'm telling you." Jake let it drop at that.

The Buick charge stunned McDermott. Where in hell would this newcomer find that out? Ashmore said it could never be found out. He might be bluffing, trying to put two and two together. Jake sure was clever, smarter than he ever dreamed.

"Si, I respect you a lot. You're on the way up; I can tell that by watching you in Springfield and Chicago. You told me to bring my questions to you, and you'd answer them. I've given you my questions and what I think I know. So . . . ?"

McDermott pulled at a couple of pieces of long grass that had grown up next to the fence post at his left, probably the only two uncut pieces on the property. He bent them, twisted them round his right index finger, then flicked them in the direction of the bulls.

"The road bills and the insurance bills probably are a little high, and a couple of others . . . including printing." He looked over at Jake to emphasize that point. No reason not to include the possible future father-in-law to show that the circle includes a man Jake knows, likes and respects.

"Every year Ashmore and these other fellows help me with the costs of moving up in politics. You don't think Jimbo McCarthy picks up those bar tabs, do you? You don't think the County Officials Association pays for all the extra touches I add at the convention—the hospitality room, the dinner for the Senate committee? Hell no. That all comes out of my pocket.

"And," Si swept his hand around the farm, "how many days do you think I'm gone from here each year, doing township, county, state association and who-can-count all the other good works? I have two full-time hired hands, real pros, to keep this farm going and lots of part-timers as well. Hell, anymore I'm not getting anything for myself out of the farm.

"So, yes, a few of those bills are a little higher than they might be. But without the help I get from those fellows, I'd never be heading the state association, meeting with the governor, moving up the ladder. This is done all the time. Don't think I don't know that. It's the price of admission to politics for little guys. I may not act like a little guy any-more, because you can't, not and get ahead. You've got to keep up appearances.

"So the fellas and I—including Jim Dunlap—have this informal arrangement. They puff their bills up some, and they help me out. And they still come out ahead. Nothing evil about it. The county can afford it. I help the county whenever I can down in Springfield. Everybody wins a lit-tle. Nothing like Chicago. You think Jimbo McCarthy has ever done a lick of work for the city of Chicago? Hell no, but he pulls down a big full-time salary as an assistant department head, plus his state senate salary, plus his insurance business on the side. And the city provides him a big car and driver. Hell, we're pikers out here in the sticks compared to those guys."

McDermott stopped, wondering how Jake would respond.

"I kind'a thought it worked like that." Jake didn't say anything more.

"You're just guessing about that Buick, I take it?" Si was nudging Jake for information.

Jake pushed back. "It's much more than a guess, but I'm not about to tell you how I know. But I know."

"Well, that's one of the ways Ashmore helps me out," Si admitted, since he had already talked about how the fellows worked with him.

"And what about me, Si? Where can I fit in?"

"I've been thinking about that. You're smart, smarter'n I ever dreamed, and I want you on my side. How's this sound: I'll make you my informal assistant. You go with me to all the meetings you can break away for. You'll meet a helluva lot of people, you'll learn by helping me out, and I'll teach you as we go along. But appreciate that I'm still learning all the time, too. We'll pay all your expenses out of my political kitty, and I'll throw in a little spending money from time to time, which you can spend or sock away. How's that sound?"

Jake pondered the conversation a minute. "Sounds good, Si." For a moment it really did sound good. They shook on it.

🛛

That afternoon McDermott paid a call on Jim Dunlap. They sat in cushioned wicker chairs off the living room on the big wraparound porch. Kay saw them through the sheer curtains of a living room window as she walked from the back reading room toward the staircase. Kay lingered, wanting to hear what was said, because Jim had not been himself for days, gloomy, distracted, lost in his own thoughts. All she could hear, and barely at that, was, "It's all okay, Jim, nothing to worry about. I just had a good talk with Jake." Then McDermott's voice descended to a whisper and was lost.

Rather than wait in her room Saturday evening for Jake to come by to pick her up, Kay went down to the living room a few minutes early. Jim had the radio on, listening to H. V. Kaltenborn and the news. His feet were on the ottoman, *Time* magazine on his lap. He was staring straight ahead.

"Oh, Kay, you look lovely." He smiled.

"Why was Si McDermott here this afternoon? What were you talking about in such hushed voices?"

"Oh, nothing. Si, uh, wanted my opinion on how to proceed on that county farm issue that we stirred up a while back."

"Would you be surprised if I said I didn't believe you, Father? And what's been wrong with you lately? You're so down in the dumps, I can't stand it."

"You know my mood dips down every now and then. Always has." Which was true. "Can't seem to do much about it. Think I'll take a walk around town right now. That helps more than anything." And it gave him an excuse to break off the conversation. He stretched and moved toward the front door.

Kay stopped him and put her arms around him. He hugged her lightly in return, saying nothing. "You know how I hate it when you get like this. It scares me."

"I'll be fine, darling. Don't want to have you down as well. This walk will be just what the doctor ordered." And to show his resolve, Jim visibly straightened his shoulders and pushed away, down the front steps and off with vigorous, long strides. Kay tried to smile.

Kay couldn't broach the topic at the movie, nor at the 34 Club afterward. Too many big ears in the booths on either side of them. But on the drive home, "What's going on, Jake? You have to tell me. Si McDermott stopped by this afternoon and all I could hear was, 'It's all right, Jim. I just had a good talk with Jake.' Is Jim involved in this budget matter you're looking into?"

"You know Jim couldn't be involved in anything wrong," Jake said, keeping his eyes on the dark highway. "I'm just trying to figure out if Si McDermott is shaking down businesses that sell to the county. I'm not interested in anything else."

"Then why would he come see Jim and say what he did? Something's terribly wrong with Jim, something's eating at him, tearing him apart. What is it?"

"I have no idea." Jake was hating himself for ever getting into all this.

"Yes, you do. And you'd tell me if you really cared for me. If you do anything that hurts Jim, I'll never forgive you." Jake turned for a moment and could see Kay's eyes glistening. She looked straight ahead through the car windshield.

"I love Jim even more than you. He has been my father and mother and dearest friend for all these years. Jim is wonderful—so much so that I can almost see him getting involved in something wrong, if he really thought it was good for the town or for other people. You don't head up the Civic Club, the Masonic Lodge and start a new Lions Club, as Jim has, unless you're willing to do or die for your friends and your community.

"And that Si McDermott, he can be a smooth talker. Maybe he has talked businessmen, including Jim, into doing something wrong."

"I told you," Jake's voice more emphatic now, "that I don't care about anybody but Si McDermott."

"But if he has done something wrong, he'll bring everybody else down with him. You know that. You'll turn the whole town against you, Jake. Just drop it all! Forget about it. I'm sure it's no big deal, probably happens everywhere, whatever it is that you won't tell me about." Kay was spitting the words out in turmoil, worried about her distraught father.

Jake tried to sort things out. Si McDermott wasn't evil, Jake thought, but talking otherwise decent fellows like Jim Dunlap into kickback arrangements was close to it. You can't let the McDermotts of the world get away with their schemes. They'll poison the communities they say they want to help. For McDermott it's now all about playing on a bigger stage. And status and influence. And a faster life than his frigid wife and Williamstown offered.

Jake's head was spinning. "Kay, I love you more than all this great big crazy world you've opened up to me. So even if I didn't love you, I'd owe you more than I could ever repay. I'll never hurt you or your father. I just have to sort things out. Please give me a day or two, then I'll tell you everything. I promise." Jake dropped Kay off at home. She went inside without a word.

The Dunlap House

You Always Hurt the One You Love

> "You always hurt the one you love,
> the one you shouldn't hurt at all.
> You always take the sweetest rose
> and crush it till the petals fall."

Breakfast was over. Jim and Kay were still at the dining room table. Minnie had finished the dishes, except for the coffee cups. "Minnie, you get home to your Archie. Sunday's a day of rest. Jim and I are going to linger over our coffee for awhile."

After Minnie slipped out the back door, Kay turned to her father. "You simply must tell me what's going on. I now love two men, and neither will confide in me. Think of how that makes me feel."

Jim held his head in his hands, elbows on the lace tablecloth. "Oh, I guess you're right." His words came out like a moan. "You won't like your ol' man very much, I'm afraid. Maybe you'll still be able to love me somehow. I hope so."

Jim told Kay about the over billing and McDermott's political kitty. "I never should have been talked into it, I know. I rationalized, of course. The paper's doing okay right now, still in a postwar economic glow. But I see the

future, and it doesn't look all that bright. A guy named
Korvette in New York has opened up huge discount stores
that attract customers from a wide region. And with cars
now coming with automatic, no-shift transmissions, more
women will take to the highways. They're the buyers. So
in not too many years the Peoria's of the world will have
all those discount stores, and small town merchants won't
be able to compete. Main Street will dry up and with it the
advertising that keeps our paper going. And I want to
leave you with something." Jim wanted to pull those last
words back as soon as he said them. He meant them, but
why, damn himself to Hell, lay anything on Kay.

"How's all that for rationalization?"

Kay said nothing; her eyes were glistening again with
tears.

"And what's worse is that Jake—and you know how
much I think of Jake, so we have to talk him out of it
somehow, which is why I'm telling you this and why he
won't—Jake has told McDermott that he wants in on the
game. Says he doesn't make enough as a printer to marry
you."

Kay had been about to get up to hug her father around
the shoulders, until he talked about Jake. On hearing that,
she could only get up and run to her room, throwing herself on the bed, crying like a baby. Jim stayed at the table,
staring straight ahead at nothing.

⧗

It wasn't worth it, Jake decided. Nothing was worth what
could happen. "I'll tell Si McDermott I decided I really did-
n't want in on the game, I'd just stick to being a good
board member here in Williams County. I'll only ask that
McDermott trim the budget somewhat, so it isn't too far
out of line. With that, I'll keep quiet," Jake told himself.
Then he added a postscript. "I'll ask Si to work his tail off

to get a strong county farm reform bill out of the legislature, not the watered down approach he assured his executive committee about. On that issue, I'll do as much legwork in Springfield as I can, but no help from the political kitty."

With that decided, Jake felt better—not great but better. It was three o'clock Sunday afternoon. Jake headed over to tell Kay everything, except about her father's involvement.

Kay was in the back reading room on the first floor, paging aimlessly through *Raintree County*, her mind blank. Earlier she had hugged her father, told him she loved him more than anything, would always love him. A few minutes later, after an unsuccessful attempt at a short nap, Jim came by the reading room to tell Kay that he was going out to see a fellow and clear his conscience, as much as he could. "It may end up hurting us both, but I have to do it."

Before Kay could say anything, her father was out the back door and into the Buick, smoke from his Camel trailing behind him.

As expected, Jim found Si McDermott at the rough-hewn table in the family's big kitchen, drinking coffee, smoking a Lucky Strike and reading the Sunday *Chicago Tribune*. Si had convened many a meeting around the kitchen table, made of massive oak and with an old stone floor underfoot. Si's wife and daughter were away for the afternoon.

When he saw Jim, Si got up to pour a cup of coffee for Jim and refresh his own.

As soon as he got inside the door, Jim started what had been a somewhat rehearsed speech. "Si, I'm here to tell you I just can't stand this scheme any more. I'm going to own up to it publicly. I want you to know that. I owe you that much."

Si appeared to take it coolly, but his tan, leathery face took on a flushed tone. "Now don't get holier-than-thou on

me, Dunlap. You owe me a helluva lot more than that—
say ten thousand bucks or more that you've put in your
pocket over the past three-four years. And you're sure as
hell not going to tell anyone about this. Nothing we've
done on the record is illegal, and nothing will happen
unless you stand up and talk about it, which I can't let you
do. We've gone too far—and I've got too much yet to do."

"Don't tell me what I can do. I can't live with this anymore. You and I know it's wrong, no matter how we try to
justify it." Both men took determined drags from their cig-
arettes.

"Look, goddam it, Dunlap, if you ever breath a word of
this I will make sure your printer friend and likely son-in-
law gets dragged through this, too."

The men had risen to their feet, lifted by the emotions
of two old friends facing off in anger and fear.

"You can't threaten me, Si. We've known one another
too long for that."

"I mean it, Jim. I can't let you talk about this."

They were standing toe-to-toe at the corner of the
kitchen table, like two overfed stags facing off, neither
knowing what to do next. Si grabbed Jim's shirt in his
fists and started shaking him, pushing him backwards.
Jim lost his balance and went over the chair behind him,
hitting his head with great force against the stone kitchen
floor.

Si stood, frozen. Jim lifted his head groggily and
started to shake a fist at McDermott. Instead, he clutched
his chest, his florid face instantly bone china white.
Gasping, "Why you sonofabitch," Jim Dunlap collapsed.

McDermott tried to revive him, slapping his face from
side to side, but got no response.

Si got on the phone to Central. "Look, Jim Dunlap's
had a heart attack at my place. Get Doc Williamson out
here immediately, and then call Kay and tell her what's
happened."

Kay heard Jake drive up. He knocked on the screen door, then opened it but decided not to go farther. Kay didn't move at first, not knowing what she thought, let alone what she might say to Jake. Finally she went to the door. Through the black wire screen, Jake looked like a photograph in the newspaper.

"Kay, I came to tell you that I'm not pursuing my investigation any further. I'm gonna let it all drop."

"Sure you are, so you can become a part of the kickbacks and corruption. How could you?" The screened door and vestibule cast Kay's face into deep shadows, but Jake could see her eyes glisten with tears.

"Kay—"

"Jim told me this morning." Then Kay added, spitting the words out. "None of this would have ever come up if it hadn't been for you—"

"Kay, you've got it all wrong."

"Get out of here. I don't want to see you again. Jim broke my heart once today and now you."

"Kay, you're wrong." Jake stuck his foot in the door so she couldn't close it all the way.

"I gave that story to Si about wanting in on the deal so he'd explain what he was up to. And he did, but I want nothing to do with it. You have to believe me on that."

"The only thing I believe right now is that without you there wouldn't be any problems like this. Why'd you ever come to town?"

The phone rang. Kay fled inside to answer. She blanched when she heard the news.

Kay tore out the back door to her car and spun out the drive. Jake followed her, instinctively.

Jim lay on the floor on his back. Kay fell on him, crying, "Jim! Jim!" Kay was stretched across Jim, her head on his chest, sobbing, all alone now in the world. The men stood silently, heads hung limp.

After several minutes Doc Williamson gently pulled Kay up. She turned, looked through the men blankly. Jake tried to grab her arm, but she eluded his reach. Doc Williamson, who brought Kay into the world and lost her mother doing it, hugged her hard against his frail frame.

"Get Minnie White, Jake," ordered Doc Williamson. "Bring her over here to be with Kay."

Jake did as he was told. Back at McDermott's, Jake tried to console Kay, but she turned away from him. The Doc and Minnie took Kay home. Jake drove right behind them.

With Kay and Minnie upstairs, Doc Williamson and Jake talked in the living room. "I'll call the funeral home to come get Jim. Kay will take this hard, harder than even you know. Both of them have suffered from melancholia throughout much of their lives. They've had some reason to. But unlike most people, they have never been able to shake their grief fully. That's the way it is with some people. We don't know why. That's why you've been so good for Kay.

"You stay here awhile. Might be something you can do later. I'd let Kay be. Let her have her cry. Minnie can tell her you're here."

To occupy himself Jake went to hang a bulletin on the wire that stretched across the picture windows at *The Republican*.

JIM DUNLAP, 59, OF WILLIAMSTOWN,
DIED OF A HEART ATTACK
SUNDAY AFTERNOON, OCTOBER 23.

That was all the information you could get on the big sheet of newsprint and still have it seen by passing autos. Then he returned to the Dunlap home.

⧖

Kay didn't come out of her room that day. Minnie told Jake that Kay hadn't spoken a word. She just lay there, looking at the wall. Kay didn't speak the next day either, nor the following. Minnie White had been able to spoon some broth into her, and Kay would move to the bathroom with Minnie, but that was all.

Jake had tried each day to talk to Kay, even to hold her; but she simply looked straight through him, arms limp at her side, unresponsive. On the second day, Kay turned away from Jake to look out the bedroom window. Jake was scared, of course, tormented by what Kay might have thought and about what she didn't know of his decision.

Doc Williamson didn't know what to do, so he called a psychiatrist from over at the new Illinois State Research Hospital in Galesburg, which specialized in mental illness. The assistant director, Dr. Theodore Tourlentes, a young physician, came over to evaluate Kay, who remained in a trance in her room, absolutely silent.

Trained in psychiatry at the University of Chicago and at Veterans Administration hospitals, Dr. Tourlentes reviewed the situation with Doc Williamson and Jake. Kay had apparently been prone to depression. Out of the blue, once again, she had just suffered another huge loss in her life. "There may have been other losses or other factors here," Tourlentes observed, "that we don't know about. For whatever combination of reasons, Mrs. Townsend seems to have withdrawn deep into her own world where she can't be hurt anymore.

"She may snap out of this trance at any time, or she may not for years, if ever." Jake felt a sickening blow. "If she doesn't respond to gentle care and rest over the next two weeks, we can try electro-convulsive treatments. Some call them shock treatments, but we now have drugs that eliminate or certainly reduce the seizures that the treatments can induce.

"There is also insulin-coma therapy. By reducing the blood sugar, we can induce a comatose state and then startle the patient with an infusion of sugar-rich foods like orange juice. Sometimes these therapies break up mental associations and distract the patient from the disturbances that have short-circuited more normal behavior. Sometimes they don't."

⧗

There was no visitation, out of deference, it was said, to Kay's grief and inability to greet callers. Jim's funeral was held at the Congregational Church without Kay, who remained in her room in her dressing gown. Si McDermott, Andy Ashmore, Lloyd Ryan, Doc Williamson, Marshal Faw (Jim's attorney) and Harry Campbell, the longtime Linotype operator, served as pallbearers. Jake and Ernie sat together.

Jake did everything he could think of to get through to Kay. He wrote a letter every day for two weeks, each time explaining his decision to drop his pursuit of McDermott and how he had told McDermott of his interest in the kickbacks only as a deception to induce McDermott to tell all.

Minnie put each letter on Kay's lap. They lay there, unopened. Minnie set them on the dresser in a stack.

Jake talked to Kay each afternoon after work. He read to her from *Raintree County*. He read all of one of Kay's favorite chapters, "The Romantic, Ill-starred, Wonderful, Wicked Class Picnic." No response. He continued with, "Two Creatures Playing Whitely in a Riverpool." Nothing, except his own tears.

Once, in utter frustration, he took Kay by the shoulders and shook her hard. She turned her head away. Jake left, tears streaming down his face.

At *The Republican* the small staff looked to Jake for leadership. He asked Bob Pyle, the bookkeeper, and Eileen Benedict, the social editor, to share Jim's work in writing the lead stories and to edit copy from the correspondents. Jake would lay out and make up the pages. Bob was also to keep track of the job printing orders. Jake arranged with H. B. Carlock, the high school principal, for Charlie Durbin to get off at noon each school day to work nearly fulltime as a Linotype operator, which was to become his craft anyway.

As for local politics, Jake seethed to expose Si McDermott and Andy Ashmore. Jake blamed McDermott for Jim's death because he had drawn Jim into the kickback scheme; and now he blamed him for Kay's withdrawal.

Plagued by insomnia and overwork at the office, Jake became distraught and disheveled. Still, he went to the public hearing on the budget, but he wasn't thinking clearly. No public attended, just the supervisors, elected county officials and Ziggy O'Connell. And Harry Wilson, who sat alone in the back row of chairs in the courtroom.

Jake stood up and charged Si McDermott and Andy Ashmore with a kickback scheme that had bilked the county out of scores of thousands of taxpayer dollars. He charged McDermott with maintaining a political kitty funded by local businessmen who received all the county's business at inflated rates.

McDermott remained at his seat, unruffled, showing concern for Jake Trickle. "Jake, you're not yourself since Jim Dunlap died and his daughter Kay, your dear friend, became ill. Why you would take your distress out on me, I'll never know. I've given you every opportunity on this board, as my colleagues around the table appreciate.

"Of course I have a small fund that I use to help defray the costs of representing Williams County all over the state. I say help defray, because goodness knows the costs are never fully covered." Heads nodded.

"Now unless you have some evidence, Jake, why don't we see if there are other questions."

Jake, still standing, pulled the letter out of his pocket. "Here, gentlemen, is a letter from the former bookkeeper for Triple A Asphalt and Ashmore Buick." Jake read the letter, leaving Harry Wilson out of it. Supervisors looked awkwardly at one another, shifting in their chairs. McDermott noticed the uneasiness but remained cool.

When Jake finished, McDermott asked: "Well, Jake, is this accuser willing to come back and testify to those charges?"

"No, he's unable to," Jake answered lamely.

"Of course he's not able to, because as soon as he set foot in the county he'd be charged with embezzlement from Triple A Asphalt. Andy Ashmore graciously gave the little man the opportunity to leave town rather than face prosecution." More appreciative nods, the supervisors relaxing in their chairs.

"As for our roads, Williams County has some of the best roads in the state, probably in the midwest. We may pay a bit more for them, but that's the way we like them. We want the best farm-to-market roads in the state."
One of the farmers at the table said softly, "We do," like an amen.

Trying desperately to think of a convincing rejoinder, Jake started rambling about how Professor Monypenny's comparisons suggested the road costs were thirty percent higher than in other counties. He was cut off by a booming, "Excuse me, Gentlemen," from the back of the courtroom. All turned to the voice.

Harry Wilson stood up slowly to his full height of six-foot-three, took the cigar out of the corner of his mouth but stayed where he was. No one could mistake him.

"Jake's real tired. He shouldn't be here this morning. He's a good young man. The information he has put together probably wouldn't stand up in court. Even more likely, charges would never be brought forward by our illustrious state's attorney in any case." Harry glanced dismissively at Jim Emmerson, then back at McDermott.

"But each of you wonders, deep down, if there isn't something to the charges. . ."

"Now wait a minute," McDermott broke in.

"I'll have my say, McDermott. I'm a taxpayer." He went on.

"This isn't a bad little county. Lots of decent folks, many of you among them. But over time the fellows who think they run things also come to think they deserve an extra share, maybe in return for all the time they give to their work. Something like that.

"Most of the guys who come into my tavern work hard for the pleasure of having a beer after work. I hear them talk, of course. I commiserate with them. They wonder out loud how come a few people seem to pile up so much wealth while they're busting their butts just to get by. And so they just wonder—that's all they can do—if everything's on the up and up. Of course, it's your job as elected officials to see that things are on the up and up.

"I first heard the charges against Triple A in my tavern, and, yes, from that little fellow who got chased out of town for taking five hundred bucks out of the till to pay for his wife's operation. As Jake was going to say, before I broke in, the fellow said Triple A was charging you fellows forty cents a gallon for road oil that sells elsewhere for ten cents or less. I can't prove it's true or not, but he sure sounded like he knew what he was talking about. You put hundreds of thousands of gallons of that stuff on our roads every year, so it's real money we're talking about. What else may be going on? Nobody knows. Nobody asks.

"You fellows are supposed to be stewards of the public purse, just like you're supposed to be stewards of your land. You oughtta at least ask some tough questions. Instead, from all I can tell, you're go-along-to-get-along guys. You're all a disgrace. You don't want to deal with the questions that Jake is trying to bring up. Might make everybody uncomfortable. Jake Trickle may be the only honest man at the table."

Si McDermott needed to regain the offensive. "Well, this honest man, as you call him, came to me recently and said he liked politics and wanted in on any deals that might be going on. I told him we were on the up-and-up and he could go straight to hell, so now he brings these wild charges."

Jake smiled wanly, looked over at Ziggy O'Connell, who was scribbling furiously. "If you want to believe that, fellows, go ahead," Jake muttered.

Nobody said anything. Finally, Chairman Hazen said simply, "Hearing no more questions or comments, I think we should declare this public hearing adjourned."

Headed West

The Itinerant

SUPERVISOR CHARGES KICKBACK SCHEME BY WILLIAMS COUNTY CHAIRMAN

Against strong initial resistance, Ziggy O'Connell convinced his editors to run that head as the second lead on the front page of the *Peoria Star*, after the standard national lead, which almost always got the banner headline.

"Look, guys," Ziggy argued over the phone to Peoria, "it was all played out in a public meeting. I'm quoting an elected official on these charges, and he has some evidence. I'll get you equal copy quoting the board chairman and other members. But I think there's something here. And I've got this letter telegraphing Trickle's plans to try to deceive McDermott in order to pull more information out of him . . . No, I'm not part of the story. He brought the letter to me in a sealed envelope. What was I do to? Refuse it? It's a great story."

Billtown cafes and beauty parlors were abuzz the next day. Half the town sided with McDermott and Ashmore because they felt the story attacked their fine county. They couldn't help but wonder, though, if something had been going on. The other half didn't know what to believe. They didn't know Jake well, but the letter he had given the reporter seemed to protect him somehow from McDermott's charge that Jake wanted in on any deals that might have been going on.

In Harry Wilson's tavern, Harry was the hero of the day for his speech, which was quoted at length by O'Connell. "That's tell'n'em, Harry," was the satisfied refrain of the beer drinkers.

Jake really didn't care what people thought. He was heartsick about Kay. Her condition hadn't changed. Minnie White took care of her and slept many nights in the spare bedroom next to Kay's. Kay wanted nothing to do with Jake. She turned to look out the window whenever he entered her room. Jake brought Tommy Dorsey records to the house, which Minnie played frequently on the phonograph, to no effect other than to deepen Minnie's gloom. After four weeks of this, Doc Williamson arranged to take Kay to the state hospital in Galesburg to try the insulin-coma treatments. Four weeks later, they applied electrodes at her temples for the shock treatments. Nothing worked.

Marshal Faw, executor of Jim Dunlap's estate, asked the county court to appoint him guardian ad litem for Kay, so household bills could be paid and to authorize decisions like those for the treatments.

Jake went out to Ernie's cabin a couple of times a week. They talked into the evening about Kay, her condition and why. Jake had been in a daze for weeks, except at work at the paper. Ever so slowly, he was getting back on his feet, so to speak. "Ernie, you can't know how much it hurts—to miss Kay, and yet she's right there in front of me. I can't sleep. Instead I replay our dates and the canoe ride and our first trip to Champaign, endlessly, like going to the same movie hundreds of times; but it never gets old.

"I did sleep some last night. Maybe I'm sleeping more than I imagine. Who knows?"

Little Ziggy O'Connell kept on the story like a chihuahua in heat. He wasn't going to let this story die, much as Billtown wanted it to. But he needed new angles. Jake gave him Professor Monypenny's number, and the professor agreed to come up to talk. Ziggy, Monypenny, Ernie and Jake gathered late one afternoon at Harry Wilson's. The four sat at a table near the back, behind the pool tables. "McCarty, you can drink on the house in return for spellin' me while I'm consultin' with my friends." Harry tossed McCarty the bar rag after he swiped off the table.

Monypenny went over the Williams County expenditures against those of his comparison group. "These figures don't prove anything, of course, but they sure cry for answers, Mr. O'Connell."

Ziggy pushed the fedora with the press card back on his head. "I'm going to quote you on that, Professor, and I'd like to keep all these figures so I can write my story. That okay?" After a nod and "hmmmn" from Monypenny, Ziggy went on. "I want to ride this story right into Springfield. My paper is opening a new bureau in the capital. I'm one of the guys they're looking at for the slot."

After three pitchers of Griesedick Bros., a new beer Harry was trying on draft, Monypenny and O'Connell mapped out a plan of attack. On his own nickel—"the bastards at the home office won't pop for any expenses"— Ziggy would drive to Iowa and talk about road building costs with highway officials in the state capital and in Scott County, just across the river from Rock Island. "Those Iowans are purer than Caesar's wife, fellas. I'll get straight information from them." Then Ziggy would apply those costs to the work that had been done in Williams County roads the past two years and come up with a figure.

Meanwhile, Monypenny would sit down with a professor of insurance friend of his in the College of Commerce.
They would go over the coverage, costs and experience
factors for the counties in Monypenny's sample, come up
with a range of reasonable annual premiums and apply
those against the premiums charged locally by Cummings
Insurance. They agreed to meet at Harry's in two weeks.

EXPERT: WILLIAMS CO. BUDGET
LOOKS BLOATED

Ziggy got only a one-column head for his story next
day, but the paper carried much of the complicated
county-by-county budget comparisons that Monypenny
turned over to O'Connell. Folks in the cafes, even out at
the country club, were starting to wonder out loud about
county finances. A little budget padding might be
expected, but how much is too much to swallow? Folks
didn't know, but they were asking.

Ziggy and the professor got the goods on Triple A
Asphalt and Cummings Insurance. With labor costs fac-
tored out, Ashmore almost had to be charging three to
four times more than necessary for the road oil, just as the
little twerp had said. And Cummings Insurance was at
least thirty percent above the high end of reasonable,
which worked out to about $5,000 a year beyond a hefty
profit. Too much for local folks to stomach, even from
their own prominent citizens, Harry Wilson surmised at
the group's second meeting.

"This insurance guy, Mark Cummings, is a nervous
type, Ziggy," counseled Harry. "Why don't you confront
him at his office? Hint about state proceedings to jerk his
license, but you won't press matters if he explains what
was going on."

Cummings couldn't take the heat Ziggy put on him. He
blamed it all on McDermott and spelled out the fifty per-

cent kickback Si expected. Andy Ashmore was a tougher nut to crack. He never admitted any wrongdoing, but several months after O'Connell ran his facts and figures in another front page story, Ashmore sold his businesses and moved to Colorado. But much higher up in the ski country than his ex-bookkeeper lived.

Si McDermott denied Cumming's charges, said they couldn't be proved and expressed outrage at how the insurance man bilked the county, vowing it would never happen again. The milquetoast state's attorney never brought any charges.

Instead, the case was tried and adjudicated at Humphrey's Cafe, the Shackateria, Harry Wilson's, the barbershops, the Cute Cut hairdressery, bridge clubs, the country club and wherever Billtown residents gathered.

Most juries concluded that Si McDermott had pushed everybody too far in pursuit of his own ambitions. A little padding and a little kickback is okay, but this was over the line and played the citizens for chumps. Sentence: Moderate to strong aversion in public. Instead of a friendly wave and some banter, just a curt nod when passing on the street. After church, as pleasantries were exchanged on the lawn outside, conversation groups would form quickly without the McDermotts.

County board members were sentenced to serious joshing (which means ridicule in Williams County) in the barbershops and at the grocery store check-out line. "Got that budget under control this year, Joe, like you did last year?"—followed by a sharp smile from the questioner. It was particularly rough when a board member got in the barber chair, white apron wrapped around his neck. The four ancient rocking chairs surrounding the chair would rock, squeaking almost in unison. "Be careful when you're shaving him, Charlie. Old Johnny bleeds road oil, ya' know."

The following year the board demanded that all major expenditures go to competitive bid and that the finance committee be a committee of the whole board. They hired a consultant, not Professor Monypenny certainly, to analyze the budget from top to bottom and make recommendations for savings.

Mark Cummings, the insurance man: well, he wasn't worth bothering with, folks decided. He bought in, took the money and then talked. What good is a man like that? Not worth the effort to rehabilitate.

The jury at the country club sided with Si McDermott, though there was some but not universal criticism of his excesses. "This is how it's done most everywhere in Illinois," the fellows in the rathskellar concluded. "Si had to have a political kitty to play the game. We're going to be the losers for all this, the whole area, because Si McDermott is dead meat, both at home and in state politics. Too bad."

Jake Trickle also got a sentence. After all, the juries observed, he's the one who brought on all this unpleasantness. He's not one of us and can't possibly care about the community the way we do, as he showed. We could have handled this a lot differently, without all the unfavorable newspaper coverage. Dammit, that made us look like a bunch of hicks.

Still, the juries divided on Jake. The country club was almost unanimous against him. But at Harry Wilson's, Jake was the fellow who put the comfortable folks on the north side of town in their places finally, at least for a little while. Overall, the community-wide sentence: almost total shunning. No nods, no conversation, nothing, except at Wilson's, of course. Margy and Bill Humphrey also stood up for Jake when asked, as did a precious few others.

Jake didn't really expect this treatment, and it hurt. Wouldn't have when he was a loner, but it did now. So he made a decision. "Ernie, I've got to get out of here. I'm going nuts. So close to Kay, yet invisible to her. When she looks straight through me, then turns away, I die a thousand deaths. She's torturing me. Maybe that's what she wants. She must blame me for Jim's heart attack. I can't get through to her to convince her what really happened between me and McDermott. God, it's torture."

Ernie had heard all this many times, of course, but not about his leaving. Jake waited until he had affairs in order at *The Republican*. The executor and guardian was loathe to sell the business. Kay could come out of her trance at any time, though it was less and less likely as time went on, Dr. Tourlentes said. Fortunately, Bob Pyle, the paper's ambitious young bookkeeper, back from the war without a sou to his name, made a proposal to be the general manager and keep the place running about as it always had. Jake called a printer acquaintance in Pontiac, who was almost as capable as Jake, and talked him into coming over to *The Republican*.

Ernie helped Jake pack his car. Jake had bought a small trailer to carry his furniture. "I'm sure leaving with a lot more than I came with," Jake said, not sure he was pleased with the worldly baggage. "And I'm a helluva lot different person than I was when I came. I have Kay to thank for that. She pulled me out of a shell, told me she loved me. And look what it got her." He stood up straight from his packing, looked wistfully out at bare, twisted oak limbs.

Jake put a Tommy Dorsey record on the tabletop phonograph, a double birthday gift from Kay, his one and only birthday gift, ever. "I'll Never Smile Again" was about the third tune on the record. Jake sang the words tunelessly. "I'll never smile again, until I smile at you. I'll never laugh again, what good would it do . . ." His words drifted off. Jake just stood there in the big sunny room of the carriage house, tears rolling over his prominent cheek bones, down into the hollows.

Soon they had everything packed. "Where you headed, Jake?"

"West! Remember Horace Greeley." Jake forced a little smile. "Oh, I don't know, but I do know what I'm going to do, old buddy.

"I'm going to interview small town newspapers—and small towns. One ant hill may look pretty much like another, but I've observed enough of them by now to know that each little burg has its own chemistry, its own personality. I'm going to find one, maybe in Iowa or Kansas, where folks are open and friendly; not perfect, of course. And if the paper has an opening, I'll try to settle down there. Who knows, I might even run for the county board some day.

"I don't think I'm an itinerant anymore. Till I met Kay I lived my life sitting on the lip of that fishbowl, looking over all those people swimming around in their communities. Like a mermaid, Kay came up and pulled me into the bowl, and damn but I like the water. Thanks, Kay."

Jake offered Ernie a ride to his cabin, though it was hard to see where he would have squeezed in. "No, thanks. You know me and my walking." They shook hands. Ernie wanted to say more but didn't—didn't have to.

"Well, thanks to you, Ernie. I'll miss you and the cabin. Keep working on your wine. Some day it may be potable. I'll keep in touch."

He drove off, west.

Epilogue 1969
by Ernie Robson

I was expecting the letter. Jake writes every year at this time to ask about Kay Townsend.

> Dear Ernie,
> How the devil are you? It's been about a year since I last wrote. Have you made anymore of that gasoline that you try to pass off on unsuspecting passersby as rhubarb wine?
> Thought I'd write to see how Kay is doing. Has there been any change in her condition? Do you ever see her? Does she ever ask about me?
> And if you would, please check with Minnie White to see if Kay received the *Tommy Dorsey's Greatest Hits* album that I sent a couple of weeks ago.
> I can't tell you how much I miss Kay, even today.

Jake then brings me up to date. He's still in Kingman, Kansas (pop. 3,500), now owner and publisher of the *Leader-Courier*.

> The paper is barely breaking even anymore. Just like Jim Dunlap predicted, the discounters and now the malls in Wichita and Hutchinson have shriveled up Main Street here, so there's hardly anybody left to advertise.

237

Fortunately, I've developed a big job printing business. I have two Heidelberg presses, all paid off, that generate enough income for me to sound off in my newspaper whenever I want.

I'm dating a couple of attractive women but have no real interest in either. Good company for dinner and a movie, maybe a weekend in Kansas City every so often, but no emotional ties. Think I'm incapable of that. As Dick Haymes put it, "I'll never smile again, what good would it do?"

I think of Kay every day. Please have Minnie White tell Kay I love her. God how I miss her.

And I miss you, too, Ernie, especially our walks and talks along the creek bottom. When I'm really down, as I am about this time every year, and longing for that wonderful year we all had, I even miss your wine. And say Hi to Harry Wilson and Ziggy.

Your buddy,
Jake

I will write back that Kay improves little by little, with painstaking slowness. I'll tell Jake, adding my regrets, that Kay doesn't ask about him; but then he has to appreciate that the trauma she suffered years ago has undoubtedly blocked out many things she held dear.

Kay isn't the effervescent beauty who would light up a room, as she did during that magical year she and Jake had. At the same time, Kay is a handsome woman who is now out in the community and even spells me now and then at the library.

Then I will bring Jake up to date on his friends.

For example, Harry Wilson retired this past year, after almost twenty years on the Williams County Board.

After Jake left Harry threatened to run for the supervisor's post, saying he had spent too much of his life complaining about the foibles of others and not enough doing anything about them. To their credit, the township trustees instead offered Harry the same assistant supervisor role that Jake had, doubting that Harry wanted the hassle of being the town supervisor.

Harry came out of the controversy with increased respect throughout the community, from the country club to the Shackateria. His dressing down of the county board was on target but done without malice. That combination goes a long ways in a small town where too many folks spend too much energy spewing venom on the folks they disagree with.

On the county board Harry was quiet and common-sensical, and he spoke up for the little guy, providing a perspective that the comfortable farmers on the board didn't really have.

Once a year after harvest Harry hosted all the county board members and county officials and their wives (and nowadays a husband or two), for a dinner at his tavern. Aware of the sensibilities of the many teetotalers on the board, Harry had plenty of sarsaparilla and hot apple cider available for those who would politely demur on the fine cabernet and pinot noir that Harry pours that one night of the year.

Harry put linen on the tables, turned off the overhead lights and accented the magnificent back bar and room with candelabra. The candlelight reflects off the mirror and transforms a workingman's saloon into a cozy and warm restaurant, worthy of a trendy spot in Manhattan. He asks the hunters among his customers to provide him either venison or quail and pheasant for this dinner, an event that has become reason enough alone to want to run for office in Williams County.

Harry's wife passed on this past year. Harry has to be in his eighties, yet he still runs the tavern, though he has a young couple help him. I still stop in from time to time for a beer, and we pass pleasantries. The bar is unchanged and is gaining renown for its character. Harry tells me that on three different occasions, restaurant owners and developers from Chicago have come down to see the tavern, offering to buy the back bar for more money than he can calculate.

Harry tells them all, thanks but no thanks; that he likes the bar just where it is. In fact, Harry has willed the tavern to the Williams County Historical Society, with the proviso that they can lease it to be operated and keep the income but that nothing can ever be changed.

Ziggy O'Connell has been the Peoria *Journal-Star's* Springfield political reporter for almost twenty years now, and his investigative zeal has earned him the status of local legend inside the capitol. Recently he had a book published, based on his series that exposed the state auditor for having embezzled $2 million. That story probably reached the dailies out in Kansas. Anyway, the book came out last month, and Ziggy sent Harry three copies, one for each of us. Ziggy dedicates the book to the three of us and to Professor Monypenny, declaring that we stuck with our issue and saw a small town kind of justice done.

I'll enclose Jake's copy with my letter.

Professor Monypenny has just stepped down as director of the Institute of Government and Public Affairs at the University of Illinois, which he helped create in the 1950s, to return to teaching. The professor has become one of the nation's most quoted experts on state and local government. He has served on innumerable blue ribbon task forces and is counselor to governors and lawmakers, not only in Illinois, but throughout the country. He has never lost his nervous "Hmmmmn," or at least hadn't when I last saw him a few years ago, when he was in Peoria to speak at a county officials meeting. This mannerism has become his signature, and I'm told his students enjoy mimicking it when they are in the beer halls comparing notes after class.

Once again this year I can't bring myself to tell Jake that Kay and I have been married ten years now. I always loved Kay as much as Jake did. Back then I fantasized time and again about their loving, as if I were with Kay in Jake's place. Those fantasies became as real to me as the wind whipping around my cabin on a sunny warm day in May, when the air is sweet and the warblers are stopping by in the thickets on their way north. I always felt happy for Jake and Kay, yet I bled with envy when they were on their dates; and my stomach churned from the effort to bury my feelings from sight when the three of us were together.

One day I might have screwed up the courage myself to make that first date with her, as Jake did, but I doubt it. I was—am—more than ten years older than Kay, with a nose that puts DeGaulle's to shame. Anyway, she was on a pedestal—unapproachable, unreachable.

About six months after Jake left Billtown, Dr. Tourlentes called to suggest that Kay might respond if I were to read to her from her favorite books. He said her restlessness had diminished and that reading might awaken positive thoughts.

At first I went over twice a week in the late morning. I would bring a classic, like *Gone with the Wind* or *Anna Karenina*, and start reading from beginning to end for a couple of hours each session. This went on for six months. Kay seemed to look forward to my reading, which Dr. Tourlentes said was a marvelous sign, so I began to read every day. Minnie started preparing lunch for Kay and for me as well. I would read over lunch, as otherwise we would dine in silence.

After almost a year, at lunch one day Kay startled me by asking simply, "Would you read that passage again, Ernie?" My heart leapt into my throat. Minnie rushed out from the kitchen on hearing Kay's first words in more than eighteen months.

I reread the passage from Thackeray's *Vanity Fair*.

"Don't you like a spunky woman like Becky Sharp, Ernie?" Kay was looking straight ahead, into the distance, through the wall and beyond, not at me. For a moment, I was at a loss to respond.

"Yes, she has a tough row to hoe, but I think she'll make it." Wanting to add, "like you"; but I didn't dare hope so much.

That was all Minnie and I heard from Kay for several months, but I loved the reading, rather a reverie for me.

I remembered Jake saying that Kay particularly liked Edna Ferber's novels. Not great literature, but good stories about strong women. We went through *Cimarron*, with Sabra Cravat opening up Oklahoma, then *So Big*, where Selina DeJong built a family and a business from nothing.

"I wish I were strong like Sabra, Ernie."

"You are strong, Kay. You haven't given up after many tragic losses in your life."

And then silence for a week before she spoke again. After about a year, Kay began reading to me, and to Minnie when she would sit down with us.

I have never suggested reading her favorite of favorites, *Raintree County*, nor has she.

Kay has never overcome her melancholia, or depression as we say today.

I think depression rises and falls, as with anybody's moods. When Kay's mood is up, she is almost what would be normal for others—engaging, offering a hint of that radiant smile now and then—a joy to be with. But when Kay is down, she withdraws, complaining of a weight on her head and shoulders, not painful, but oh so heavy, she says. Then Kay is in her own world, not really wanting me around, other than to read or to take her on long walks along Indian Creek, which seems to help her more than anything.

Bob Pyle continues to run the newspaper for Kay, and Marshal Faw's son oversees the legal and tax matters. He and Bob report once a year to Kay and make suggestions for pay increases and equipment needs, which she always approves. Bob is smart in a business sense, and he remembered Jim Dunlap's concerns about the discount centers and now malls that sucked much of the lifeblood out of small farm-to-market towns like Billtown.

Bob convinced Marshal Faw that they needed to invest in the new offset printing processes and to put out an advertising-only shopper that would guarantee advertisers one hundred percent market coverage. This has even attracted ads and insert fliers from the discounters. So Kay is secure.

As the offset process is all about photography, Bob asked me to work about half time at the paper and teach the printers how to make the page negatives. And since there is now a darkroom at the paper, I develop my own work there, including my photographs of natural life along the Indian Creek, a number of which I've sold at craft shows and festivals.

So about a decade after Jake left, I finally screwed up the courage to ask Kay to marry me, since we were spending so much time together and since she did seem to appreciate me. We were wed in the Dunlap home and continue to live there. Life has been a joy for me. A month ago, we were to celebrate our 10th anniversary. I chanced the suggestion that we dine at Maple Shade and then go dancing at the Hub—though Kay would have to teach me how, up in the "ballroom."

Kay was silent for the longest time. I froze with concern about what I might have wrought. Finally, Kay turned to me, hesitated, then fairly blurted out, "But what in heavens name will I wear?" And we laughed.

ORDER INFORMATION

Copies of *The Itinerant: A Heartland Story* can be ordered directly from Conversation Press, Inc.

You may call 1-800-848-5224, fax (847) 441-5617 or e-mail convpress@aol.com with your order and Visa or MasterCard information.

You may also mail your check (made payable to "Conversation Press, Inc.") or your credit card information, and your order to Box 172, Winnetka, IL 60093.

A single copy of the book is $15.95 plus $3.00 for shipping and handling. Illinois residents should add $1.24 for sales tax (or enclose your sales tax exemption number).

Call 1-800-848-5224 to inquire about quantity discounts beginning at 10 copies ordered, or for shipping charges on multiple-copy orders.